YONDER MOUNTAIN

YONDER MOUNTAIN

AN OZARKS ANTHOLOGY

Edited by
Anthony Priest

The University of Arkansas Press
Fayetteville
2013

Manufactured in the United States of America

ISBN-10: 1-55728-631-0
ISBN-13: 978-1-55728-631-4

17 16 15 14 13 5 4 3 2 1

Designed by Liz Lester

♾ The paper used in this publication meets the minimum requirements of the American National Standard for Permanence of Paper for Printed Library Materials Z39.48-1984.

Library of Congress Control Number: 2013936907

Note on the cover art: Artist Bryan Culpepper comes from several generations on the Current River and spent his life preserving and teaching Ozarks culture. Through his art, interpretive programs, local historical commission, and grants through the Folk Art Society, he taught Ozark traditions to younger generations. His passion was to collect and to create images of the Ozarks as a way of preserving our heritage.

For Michael Burns—
teacher, mentor, friend

CONTENTS

INTRODUCTION

Greer Spring, which flows from the Ozark Heritage region of Missouri, is accessed by trailhead just off Highway 19 in Oregon County. Before descending 250 feet into the holler, travelers can glimpse the roughhewn, sagging ghost of Greer Spring mill—caged in the gnarled limbs of blackjack oak—guarded by the soaring climbs of shortleaf pine.

As the locals say, the trail is one mile down and two miles up, but along the way, an overstory of hickory, poplar, and pine shadow the ridgetops and stand in contrast to wildflowers: yellow lily, downy phlox, and bird's-foot violet. The real show, however, is the spring itself, which gushes 222 million gallons of water into the Eleven Point River each day.

After a day hike to Greer Spring, a traveler, awed by the force of water coursing from the cave or boiling up between the fern-lush bluffs, may contemplate the contrast between river and rock—between ephemeral and eternal.

Readers coming to this book will encounter a similar contrast between the reality and the age-old, romantic portrayal of Ozarks culture—a culture idealized for its unspoiled beauty and pastoral landscape yet one that remains steadfast in the rugged independence and make-do attitude of its inhabitants.

More than thirty years have passed since Miller Williams compiled *Ozark, Ozark: A Hillside Reader*, but time has not worn away the tenacity nor the talent of writers living in or native to the Ozarks. The writing within Williams's anthology renders not just the physical but also the metaphysical landscape that binds us together in the flow of human experience—even beyond regionalism.

Admirable features of Williams's collection include a variety of poems, stories, observations, and recollections by Ozarks writers born between 1869 and 1949. This contemporary anthology pays tribute to that format, showcasing poets, novelists, naturalists, columnists, and historians whose lives have been shaped profoundly by the landscape and culture of the Ozark Mountains.

Readers will sense a connection between voices from the past and present in this contemporary collection. Gathered here are writers born between 1929 and 1989. These six decades have produced authors whose work appeared in *Ozark, Ozark*, writers who have since risen to prominence, and those whose voices are quickly emerging. Each author is introduced with a biographical note—enabling readers to join in the history, geography, and personality of connected lives.

Having achieved recognition through publications, awards, and accolades from the literary community and beyond, the writers in *Yonder Mountain* reflect diversity and change within the Ozarks while remaining rooted in the literary legacy born out of the hills we call home.

Welcome to the Ozarks.

C. D. Albin

C. D. Albin was born on April 9, 1961, in West Plains, Missouri. He is currently professor of English at Missouri State University in West Plains, where he edits *Elder Mountain: A Journal of Ozarks Studies.* His stories, poems, and reviews have appeared in a number of publications, including *Arkansas Review, Big Muddy, Georgia Review, Harvard Review, Natural Bridge,* and *Red Rock Review.*

Four Fine Horses

I never thought I'd set foot on this property again, but here I am at the back of the crowd in my father's sale barn, watching Trent Tilson show a good Foxtrotter mare. He rides her bareback so we'll see how bridlewise she is, and her colt trails at her heels like a hound. The mare ribbons around the ring in a gliding gait bred here in the Ozarks, and Trent sits her so well I can't spot daylight between his tailbone and her spine. There's no bounce, no movement in him at all.

Off to the side Trent's father, Paul, is working hard. "You'll not see a gentler mare all day," he calls into the microphone. "You can saddle her right out of the pasture. Plus that pretty colt. Two for the price of one."

I watch Paul's eyes rake the crowd. He has a solid bid but he looks insulted, thinks the mare's worth more. "Come on now," he shouts, his microphone booming like something dropped from the sky. "Look how smooth she is. Trent's gone to sleep up there."

Trent cracks a little grin, letting us know he heard the joke. Then his face goes stony again.

To my left, an old man has been sitting cross-armed all morning, but now he gives one hand a flick, not much more than a tremor. Paul nods and his voice changes from pleading to pleased. The bid rises another ten dollars, stays there for several more minutes. Gradually the crowd and colt swing in a circle behind him. I listen to the steady drumming of hooves. Finally he drops his hand. "She's sold," he intones, and the crowd sighs.

In the center of the ring the mare slows to a walk. Trent goes loose of limb, his heels dangling below her girth. Beside me, the old man re-balances a Tindle feed cap, reaches inside his windbreaker for a tiny notepad. He scribbles something in a dull hand, then gets up and goes. The next thing he writes will be a check to my father.

I hardly knew the place this morning. It was never what you'd associate with some of those Thoroughbred operations in Kentucky—clean white fences, pastures cropped as close as fairways—but it looks pretty good for an Arkansas hill farm, which is all it was twenty years ago when Mom and I left. I spent four summers with my father after that, but one day when I was fourteen I told him I was through. He could've made me stay, we both knew that, but all he did was nod his head.

From what I could see driving in, the woods have been cleared, and there are three barns now. One of them, the sale barn, stretches across a good part of the south ridge, and where the hill levels out there's a long flat field with just a few oaks and cedars. People use that field to park, and I saw plates this morning from all over—Missouri, Oklahoma, Kansas.

I saw the sign too, the big blue one above the entrance to the sale barn that read Cecil Ryan Stables. It slowed me down for a step or two, and I didn't know why until I remembered the other sign, the hand-lettered one he supposedly nailed to the rack of his pickup the week I was born. That one read Ryan & Son: Registered Quarter Horses.

I guess I came this morning because of Trent, who's trying to pass my Comp course at the college. The kid's pretty much a lost soul with a pen in his hand, no confidence that he has anything to say or any way to say it. A couple of weeks ago I hauled him into my office and set a full cup of coffee in front of him. It was black and bad, but he took the first sip without complaining. "You're having some trouble," I said. "You think maybe you're trying too hard?"

His hand was a little unsteady, and he spilled just enough coffee to darken the dust on one of his boots. "You're the first teacher's ever accused me of that."

"No harm in being the first."

"I guess not."

I waited for him to look up from his coffee, or the floor, whatever he was staring at.

When he didn't, I flipped through my grade book. "Well, what are we going to do? You're not passing."

He nodded, and I could see the shape of his skull beneath his buzz cut. "I guess I better drop," he said.

I've been teaching six years now, two as a TA at Fayetteville, four as an adjunct at ASU. Here this kid was flunking a freshman course at Ozark Mountain Community College. It should have been an easy call to agree with him, tell him dropping was the best thing, but I decided to try. "Your boots," I said. "They Justins?"

He looked up then, shook his head. "Noconas."

"I always liked Justins."

Half a smile came on his face, like he didn't know whether to smirk or grin. Finally the grin won, but he still looked at me out of the corner of his eye. "One of those city cowboys, huh?"

I had to laugh. "No, no kind of cowboy. My dad had a horse farm though. Still does, I guess. Over in Stevis."

A light spread in his eyes, like he might be putting my last name together with my father's. We talked a little easier after that, and eventually he told me he and his dad worked most of the horse sales in north Arkansas, including every one Cecil Ryan held. Teaching is catch-as-catch-can, so I tried again. "Why don't you write about work," I said. "Something about horses."

He took a quick glimpse at the door, then brought his eyes back to mine. "I wouldn't know what to say."

I took a sip of my coffee, decided I might as well roll the dice. "Why not? Don't you know anything about horses?"

His jaw went hard as he studied me. "You know anything about teaching?"

"I guess I'm trying to find out."

Paul calls another rider into the ring now, a heavy-set man on a good-looking red mare. Paul says the man is showing her as a favor to his daughter, that he's driven all the way from Hot Springs because we know Foxtrotters here. The man slides off and jogs the mare around the ring a few times to let us see her action, then grabs the horn and swings himself back into the saddle. He's not smooth like Trent, and he has some trouble gaining his stirrups again. The mare senses him struggling and breaks stride, bolts a little to the side so that she's no longer moving in the tight circle the man wants. Frustrated, he gets rough with the bit trying to muscle her back in line, and she takes a quick little hop beneath him. A good six inches flash between his crotch and the saddle, and he comes down high in the seat. He tries to grin it off, like he and the mare do this every day for fun, but the grin is tighter than a clothesline.

Paul's been pretty quiet so far, but now he decides he ought to turn storyteller. "This man's daughter hurt her back," he says, "but he's doing what he can to help her. He needs a fair bid on this mare, and she's worth it. You'll be getting her at the good price of a daddy's love. We'll start her at $300. Let me hear you now. Let me hear."

Nobody will go near that price though. The man takes turn after turn around the ring, and each time he looks more frustrated. Finally he reins the mare back on her haunches and slides off in the middle of the ring. He reaches beneath her and loosens the girth strap, then lets the saddle drop to the ground. At first I think he's going to lead her off, but instead he hops on bareback the way Trent did and starts riding with his heels. The mare doesn't like it, and every few strides she gives a little buck.

Paul hustles into the middle of the ring now, trying to get the man's attention. "What's your low price?" he calls. "What'll you let her go for?"

The man takes a last trip around the ring, glaring at Paul the whole time. He heels the mare in close, and when he dismounts it looks for a second like there may be trouble. Instead, he shoulders his saddle and leads the mare off on a short rein. A few steps outside the ring she jerks her head hard, nearly lifting him off his feet. A ripple of laughter skips through the crowd, and Paul hurries in a new horse.

This morning when I passed beneath that blue sign I actually held my breath. I guess I half expected my father to be there at the door. Several people were pushing up behind me, so I moved on and took a seat in one of the metal folding chairs at the end of the back row. I realized then that I wanted to spot him before he saw me. That way I could decide whether to go up to him or not, whether to say anything or just walk out and drive away, no harm no foul.

I did phone him once after I took the job at Ozark Mountain, basically just to let him know. I got the answering machine and left my number. That night he called while I was in class and left his number, even though I already had it. I played the message back a couple of times, trying to match his voice with the one I remembered in my head. Finally I did, and I cleared the message.

When I was a little boy, I sometimes sat on the floor beside my father's desk and listened to him think of potential names for the new foals. At first he'd sound the names out as if they were words from a foreign tongue, his voice moving slowly through the syllables—Acie's Lad, Carter's Con, Piddling Pride—until he was sure of each name's rightness. Then he'd repeat the name four or five times, each repetition firmer and louder, until the name sounded as if he'd used it all his life.

My favorite was the one he gave to a pretty bay mare, Pappy's Cat. She had a bit of Poco Bueno blood, which meant she went back to a foundation sire, but all I cared about was the brightness of her coat when the sun hit it just right and the fact that she would nuzzle my face when the other mares wouldn't. One morning in late spring, when I was six, I left the house alone to go looking for her. The way I remember it, I made my way toward the line of trees that marked the beginning of the far pasture. By the time I got there I'd begun to wonder whether I should have come that far, but the small stand of oak thinned and opened before me, showing the deep scoop of the pond bank in the distance. Beyond the pond another line of oaks floated in a shimmer of fog that curled among the trunks and silvered the higher branches caught in the sun. I went toward them, soaking my jeans in the tall, dewy grass, even becoming a little chilled. Then, before I saw, I knew. A hoof scraped across a stone. Moments later a deep burst of breath rode the air somewhere near me, almost readying me for the sudden swelling of her head and neck as she loomed hugely out of the fog.

I stumbled backward, my concentration held by the blaze face and the long black forelock, and then the huge eyes erupting out of the forehead as fiercely as fists. Suddenly she swung her head away, curling her neck toward the leggy dark colt tripping at her hindquarters. A narrow blaze ran down his face and widened in a strange pool of whiteness about his nostrils. I moved forward, trying to touch that blaze, but she wheeled and fronted me, her hooves rasping the stony ground. Frozen, I smelled her, the salt-thick odor of horses, and then my father lifted me by the collar, holding me out and away at the end of his extended arm. With the other he waved her off before carrying me clear of the trees, his fist still balling my collar till I thought I would choke.

Halfway to the pond he set me down in the wet grass, letting me cough all I needed to before leaning his face close to mine. "Why?" he said. "Tell me why?"

I didn't know what he was asking. Dark stubble covered his face, and I remembered how the whiskers would prick my palms when I slid my hands across his jaws. I shook my head.

He looked back at the trees and pointed in their direction. "She just foaled," he said. "You've got to wait till that foal is bigger."

I probably nodded, or mumbled "yessir," anything to convince him I understood, but what has remained clearest in my memory is a moment late that night when I woke to feel his big hand spread flat on my chest. He was leaning over me, his weight coming down through his hand so that I could hear the bedsprings beneath me. "Rick," he was saying. "I'm sorry. Don't hold it against me."

Trent seems to be on a break. Another rider has shown the last few horses, and my chair is getting hard. I slip outside, where the field below the barn is dotted with vehicles, everything from truck and trailer rigs to a Honda Civic. There are plenty of spots though, because the horse market is down. I imagine most of the people here have come just to see horses, or each other.

West of the barn is a metal training ring where several people are gathered. I wander over to watch the only rider, a boy—maybe eleven or twelve—on a gray roan. The mare shows a smooth gait, clay flicking steadily from her hooves. To me she looks like a fine horse, but one of the men isn't pleased. He keeps shouting directions to the boy, trying to get him to sit straight-backed, to shorten the reins and hold them lower down, near his belt buckle. The boy looks like he's trying, but he's tentative. After a trip or two around the ring he's hunching over the pommel, both hands clutching the reins to his chest.

After a while the man draws my attention. He may be the boy's father, but he's fully gray, with leathery lines in his face and neck. His jeans hang slack about his rear, and he wears one of those wide belts with his name, Cochran, stamped into the leather. His agitation keeps building, and finally he scrambles into the ring, coming at the mare from the side. She spots him and shies, bolting so hard she nearly unseats the rider. The boy loses both reins and a stirrup, and if it weren't for the saddle horn he'd be in the dirt.

Several men scale the metal railing, and a couple drop into the ring, but it's Cochran who gets to the horse, his left hand reaching for the boy, his right seeking out the reins. Suddenly there's a surge of motion, man and boy caught in a struggle with a fractious mare. Eventually Cochran gets hold of the headstall and calms her enough that she comes to a stop, though she stands walleyed and trembling. The boy has both legs on the mare's off side, one foot wedged awkwardly in the stirrup. Cochran has to support him, holding him about the waist while the boy tries to work his way loose. "Damn it," Cochran growls. "I told you not to wear those flat-heeled boots." The boy's face blooms red, and he nearly kicks the mare in extricating himself. When Cochran sets him on the ground, he jerks away angrily. "Hey now," Cochran shouts, his voice like a pistol shot, and the boy stops in his tracks. He stands there with his head lowered, his hands fisted, while Cochran talks to the mare, slowly coaxing her toward the gate. As they get closer one of the men eases it open, and Cochran turns back, offering the reins to the boy. The kid's face is still fever-red, but he wants those reins. Taking them in both hands, he walks the mare through, matching his father's slow, careful pace.

As they pass, I hear the boy's loud breathing and realize how intently I'm listening, trying to catch anything father or son might say.

All these years I've kept a little 3x3 snapshot of the house before it burned. I think I took it from the album my mother packed away at the back of a closet in her parents' house in Fayetteville. The photo shows a corner of the barn and paddock in the foreground, with a side view of the house and white rail fence behind. Everything looks fresh and clean, almost restful, nothing like the soot and ash that my mother, angered beyond action, refused to sift through.

What I remember most about that day is not the smoke or flames coming through the barn roof, but rather the sight of my father running along the fence row, our border collie racing near his legs. I'd been playing in the yard, but everything seemed to stop as I watched him run. Suddenly his boot sole slipped on a loose stone and he went down so quickly he couldn't get his arms extended in front of him. By the time he rose—still running, his legs never stopped moving—a dull redness had bled through the sleeves of his white shirt.

My eyes were still on the redness when he ran past me toward the house. He shouted, and when I turned I saw my mother appear behind the screen door. She pushed it open and stepped halfway onto the porch. One hand still gripped the door handle, but the other rose in the air as if she were pointing to the barn and trying to hold back the flames at the same time. When she saw me in the side yard she ran, her teal shorts flashing above the white tennis shoes and the short white socks, and in the next moment I was running with her in the ditch beside the road. We were nearly a hundred yards from the house when she jerked me to a stop and thrust her face near mine. "You stay here," she shouted. "Don't set foot in that yard." I didn't follow her all the way, but I went close enough to watch her return to the yard and scream at my father's back, trying to get him to leave the wild-eyed mares in the paddock and help her wet down the roof of the house. He just waved her away, chasing the mares to the far end of the pasture while my mother sank to her knees and watched wind whip the flames onto the roof of our house. When neighbors arrived with shovels and buckets, she was weeping in the ditch next to the gate, her face streaked with smoke and mascara. The next day she moved the two of us into her parents' house in Fayetteville, and she never went back.

The training ring isn't that far from where the house burned, although the ground is rough. It won't take me long to walk, but I doubt there will be anything to see. That first summer I spent with my father, when I was eleven, he bulldozed whatever was left into the cellar and covered it over with dirt that still looked charred. There might be a few volunteer trees growing out of it now, but nothing else.

Turning back to the barn, I catch sight of Trent at the side entrance. He's helping someone check in a small string of paint ponies, but I can tell he spots me. When he finishes with the horses, I go up and give him a nod.

"Been wondering if you'd come," he says.

"I keep a naturally low profile."

He laughs. "A man can't be too careful."

"That's what I hear."

He bangs a heel on the toe of the other boot, raising dust. "So you grew up on this place?"

"Mainly summers."

Nodding, he chews a piece of straw for a while. "It's pretty. I wouldn't mind having something like it someday. It's a tough go now, though."

"Eat your Wheaties."

"No kidding. Big bowl every meal."

This time I laugh. Looking around, I ask, "How's the essay coming? You think you can find any material?"

His head doesn't drop the way it usually does. Instead, he works the straw to the corner of his mouth and hikes his shoulders a little as he leans against the door. "Well, I'm bettin' the ladies at the Writing Center are tired of me."

"Putting them to work, huh?"

"Or them me."

"That's what it takes."

He rolls his eyes a little, but I can tell he secretly agrees, like a man who's finally faced down something he dreaded. "Bring it by the office," I tell him. "We'll give it a look."

"Yeah, that sounds good." He stretches a bit, showing his wingspan, then hooks a thumb toward the barn's interior. "Better go ride some ponies," he says.

I give him a mock salute. As he leaves I step closer to the door so I can watch him work. At the holding pen a tall, round-bellied man with a clipboard pulls him aside and points out something about one of the paints. Trent nods and enters the pen. The older man glances briefly at the open door where I stand, then looks again, startled. I see he's grown a mustache now, white and neatly trimmed. I step away and close the door.

That final summer, things were pretty bad. I was about to start high school in Fayetteville, and the last place I wanted to be was on a horse farm in Stevis, Arkansas. My father had spent his share of the insurance money building his first barn, and what little was left went toward payments on a used house trailer I called the Tin Can. It had one air conditioner that blew the same weak stream no matter what the setting, and the bathroom was so small I once banged my head on the sink trying to dry my legs after a shower.

The worst part was the work. Maybe I was lazy, but it felt like the only reason he wanted me there during the summers was to bend my back. He paid for the food, let me fold out the couch at night, so any minute I wasn't eating or sleeping was free labor. I walked miles behind his baler, throwing sixty- and seventy-pound bales of fescue onto the flatbed and knowing with every toss that the hardest part was still to come, the suffocating hayloft in some farmer's barn where each bale had to be hauled and stacked by hand. Or on the days when he made extra cash driving a truck for Reeves Hardware, I had to cut sprouts and dig postholes on the back twenty, because he wanted to cross-fence it and use it as another hay field. I probably could have stood it if he'd let me work with the horses a little more than he did, but he was already starting to train and stable some of the better show horses in the area, and he didn't have time for me to learn on the job.

The blow-up came on a Sunday morning in late July. We'd hauled from six till dusk the day before, and I had a copy of *A Separate Peace* I'd been waiting to read all summer. A girl I liked in Fayetteville had let me borrow it, and I'd decided today was the day. I was about ten pages into it, stretched out on the couch and still in my underwear, when he came in from the barn.

"What are you doing?" he said.

I stared at the ceiling. "What do you think?"

"You're not up yet?"

I held the book toward his face so he could see the cover.

"You can do that later."

I looked at him then, saw that his shirt and jeans were already dusty. "Later don't come here," I said.

He stiffened, the way I'd seen him do with an uncooperative horse. "Get up, Rick."

"I'm going to read this book."

His quickness startled me, the open hand slapping the book away like a scythe blade topping a sprout. The book landed on the dirty dishes in the kitchen sink and I thought of Holly Sanders, her soft cheeks and sweet-smelling hair. I'd never hit him but I tried, and when he blocked the punch I dropped my shoulder into his chest, counting on leg strength to drive him out the door. Twice he threw me back against the couch, but the third time he grabbed hold and we wrestled our way onto the stoop, where he slung me over the flimsy railing and into the yard. I sat up, but I didn't charge him again. He stepped close and stood over me. "You can get dressed or you can come like that."

"Or I can leave," I said.

He took a funny-sounding breath, like maybe one of my punches had had a delayed effect, and I watched his shoulders slump a little as he looked out over what passed as a yard. I kept waiting for him to say something, but he never did. Finally he set his jaw, nodded, and walked off toward the barn.

At the start of every summer my mother gave me enough money for bus fare back to Fayetteville, saying, "Don't be afraid to use it." The moment he left for the barn I went back in and cleaned Holly's book as best I could. Then I changed out of my grass-stained underwear and shoved what clothes I'd brought into my duffle bag. I hiked and hitched the nine miles into town, where I sat at the bus stop for three hours before catching the ride home.

I was right about the trees. A little stand has volunteered here, mainly cedar and wild peach. The rest of what used to be the yard and paddock is fenced off into pasture, and to the west a few mares are grazing on the far ridge. I half expected this place to feel like a cemetery, but there is too little left of what had been. Maybe that makes it easier for him, if it was ever hard.

I follow the patchy remains of the drive down to the county road, and that's when I see him. His shoulders are half-turned, like he can't decide whether to come on up or go back. The sale is still going, so I'm stunned he left to follow me. The old drive is the only path through the weeds though, so I move down to where he's standing.

"Pretty big turnout," I say.

He's studying my face, the way somebody will who's never seen you without a beard, but I'm doing the same to him, noticing the blotch of brown spots at the top of his cheekbones. From the sun, I guess.

"Nobody's buying though," he says, and nods toward the homeplace. "Come back to see?"

"Something like that."

He smoothes his mustache with the back of his thumb. "So you're teaching now?"

I nod. "Trent's one of my students."

"I heard that. He's a good kid."

"Seems to be."

"He can sure sit a horse. Better than I ever could."

"I saw him. He's smooth."

"He sure is."

My father tests his lower lip with his teeth, and I'm struck by how white they still are beneath the white mustache. He seems to want to say something, and after a moment he reaches out and taps me on the chest with his open palm. "I know you hold a lot against me," he says. "No way to keep from it."

The hand is withdrawn, but I can feel its imprint, the quick, strong warmth of its weight. "We do what we can," I say.

He's still testing his lip. "I guess so," he says, and looks down, scraping the sparse gravel with his toe. After a moment he raises his head and makes a clicking sound with his tongue and cheek, like he's urging a horse into a canter. "Gotta get back," he says, though he doesn't move.

I stand here knowing I should say something, but my mind is blank. Finally he starts to turn, and I hold out my hand.

He takes it, seems grateful for it, and heads back toward the sale barn. When he's almost out of sight I notice the mares have started down off the ridge, making their way toward him as if they expect him to come to the fence and feed them sugar from his palm—four fine horses, all bays, the noon sun bright on their backs.

Walter Bargen

Walter Bargen found time along the way to be born an "army brat" at Fort Bragg, North Carolina, on July 20, 1948. He has published fourteen books of poetry. His two latest books are *Days Like This Are Necessary: New & Selected Poems* (BkMk Press-UMKC, 2009) and *Endearing Ruins / Liebenswerte Ruinen* (Liliom Verlag, Germany, 2012). He began to "seriously" explore the Ozarks around 1970, frequently camping and canoeing in the famous and not-so-famous places. In winter with the temperature below freezing, when twenty-feet-long, waist-thick icicles hung from bluffs was and is his favorite time (few ticks and no chiggers). His awards include the Chester H. Jones Foundation prize in 1997, a National Endowment for the Arts Fellowship in 1991, and the William Rockhill Nelson Award in 2005. He was appointed the first poet laureate of Missouri (2008–2009).

Photogenic

We stop for gas. I knock my sunglasses off the seat and
    pick them up before a darker vision
speeds past.
I see deep into the asphalt. Cameraless we lament,
    wish we had brought one:
the cheap never-used
35 millimeter in the sock drawer or the one in the back
    of a closet. We begin
to share pictures—

click—the flock of fifteen wild turkeys strutting over a
    greening hillside pasture—
click—the loose line
of white cows working their way around a cattail-choked pond
toward a weathered barn—
click—the condom nailed to a tree beside the river where we
    stopped for lunch—

click—the cable-suspended canoe twenty feet above the
    ground between two oaks,
its two black
plywood silhouettes, seated straight through the year,
their wooden legs cramping,
they paddle a gust of wind about to capsize them into
    currents of cold air—

click—the owl or hawk that we pass too quickly to know,
    one wing angled upright
  out of the pavement—

click—through a town named Plato, far from any city-state,
    no Socrates,
no Aristotle,
no exiled poets, more likely a chicken by a red wheelbarrow,
    but no rain
in this drought-stricken county—

click—the camera's out of film and rewinding night—click—
    there's the unused film
that's rolled under the car seat that's framed what we missed.

Wounded God

Glove, hat, ripped sleeve, hanging from the top strand of barb wire
by the pasture gate—
a dismal laundry, a hunter's brutality, a dusky feathered heap
hung there by oversight,
or under—a miscalculation of flight. A wind-driven day, light
    ironed flat
across fields,
bristling two-feet high broom-sedge underscoring the burnished
    closeting of evening.
A wide feathered face
turns slowly toward me. Hooked yellow beak half open—tired,
    defenseless.

Coonhound—a dog that follows its nose as the one and only
    direction,
already she has inhaled
acres of field and found under the last thin scars of snow,
the bodies of frozen mouse,

vole, all pulled from her eager mouth. I restrain her, turn toward
        the house.
We jog the half-mile back
to find a large cardboard box and leather gloves.
At the gate,
caught between sun's afterglow and the uprising half-moon, I can't
        see to untangle
the owl's wing.
With wire cutters and headlights, I cut on either side of its twisted
        wing.
It stares
suspended in its own museum of dying flight. Talons pried from
        the wire,
I see
that its wing feathers are shredded from flying nowhere. In the box,
wings splayed,
the bird still as road kill. I'm possessed, hoping to undo this not
        remembering,
my many flights into the undone.

At the Raptor Rehabilitation Center, I sign a form giving the owl
        into their care.
In the hallway,
the attendant's thick gloves lift the body to find its eyes wide open.
        It shakes itself awake,
stands with a sense
of unabashed decorum, as if this happens every day, one wing
        folded elegantly,
the other straight like a ragged broom
that's swept too many miles of wind. Brown tufted ears, feathers
        the colors of fall fields,
quarter-sized pupils,
hand-sized talons, it stands with a wounded defiant elegance.

The strand of barb wire still embedded in its shoulder joint. The
attendant holds out
little chance for recovery.
I propose the wing be amputated and the bird be kept for exhibi-
tion. I'm told
it's illegal
to amputate a wing beyond the first joint. It's illegal for me to keep
the bird and it's illegal
for them to keep the bird alive.
I plead though beauty guarantees nothing this night.

When death calls we pretend not to hear, refuse to listen as long as
we can. There is no one
to blame. Not even our petty selves
when finally we hear too clearly. I think of my son as I drive home.
He's passing through Amarillo, past
seven high-finned Cadillacs half-buried and forever driving deeper
into panhandle dust.
He'll continue through the dark,
he'll wind through Sandia Pass where brakes fail and cars are
swallowed by out-of-control
semi's, where lights of benighted
Albuquerque spread over the desert as he heads on to Phoenix,
hoping he will be
that broken bird rising out of the ashes of this night.

Brooks Blevins

Brooks Blevins was born November 28, 1969, in Batesville, Arkansas, and grew up forty miles away on the family farm in the rural community of Violet Hill. Descended from long lines of rural Ozarkers on both sides of his family, Blevins first took an interest in Ozark history as an undergraduate at Batesville's Lyon College. He later earned the MA and PhD in history at Auburn University. Blevins is the author of five books and coeditor of another. His first book on the Ozarks, *Hill Folks: A History of Arkansas Ozarkers and Their Image* (Chapel Hill, 2002), was a groundbreaking work in the study of his native region. His most recent book is *Ghost of the Ozarks: Murder and Memory in the Upland South* (Urbana, 2012.) The selection that follows is taken from Blevins's award-winning *Arkansas/Arkansaw: How Bear Hunters, Hillbillies, and Good Ol' Boys Defined a State* (Fayetteville, 2009.)

Jethro and Abner: An Arkansaw Counterculture

Given the perseverance of the Arkansaw/Ozark image into the 1960s and beyond, it is fitting that the era's (and perhaps twentieth-century America's) most famous comic hillbilly characters came from the Ozarks and not Appalachia. *The Beverly Hillbillies* arrived on the pop-cultural scene in 1962, at the height of the folk revival and just five years removed from the beginning of the Little Rock crisis. Created by Paul Henning, *The Beverly Hillbillies* became the nation's most-watched television program within a few weeks of its debut. Although the 1960s never seriously challenged the 1930s for the title of "heyday of the hillbilly," it wasn't for lack of effort on Henning's part. The Independence, Missouri, native almost single-handedly created a cornpone comedy empire with such long-running sitcoms as *Petticoat Junction* and *Green Acres.* But the undisputed anchor of his enterprise was the beloved and critically panned *Hillbillies,* whose eight seasons on CBS transported Americans from Camelot to the Nixon Whitehouse.[1]

Like fellow midwesterner Vance Randolph, Paul Henning had been fascinated with the backcountry people of the Ozarks since his childhood trips into southwestern Missouri. But instead of settling among them, "going native," as Randolph had done, Henning used his impressions of hill people to craft comical characters for radio and television, and ultimately as sounding boards for social commentary. Although the two approached their subjects and expressed their philosophies in very different ways, Randolph and Henning shared a romantic appreciation for what they saw as genuine people free of the corrupting influences of a modern society consumed with vacuous materialism. American audiences had seen this sort of hillbilly-flavored critique of shallow consumerism and snobbery before, from Bob Burns to the Weaver Brothers and Elviry and from *Lil' Abner* to Ma and Pa Kettle. And it wasn't difficult to recognize any of these past acts in the lineage of *The Beverly Hillbillies.*

The storyline for the show was something that Steinbeck might have concocted had he been a vaudevillian instead of a fellow traveler in the Depression years, for in Henning's universe the jalopy heading for California carried not the battered and luckless Joads but the Clampetts, a clan of naive and backward Ozarkers made filthy rich by the discovery of oil on their farm. As critics frothed to point out, each of the Clampetts represented a stock character in the rural humor stable: Granny, the straight-shooting and resourceful old woman who prefers traditional ways over the newfangled practices she finds in Beverly Hills; Elly May, the curvaceous young woman who looks like she just stepped out of an Al Capp strip but approaches life with the wide-eyed amazement and unsophistication of the nearest third-grader; and Jethro Bodine, a strapping youngster so clueless that he makes Lil' Abner look like a Rhodes Scholar by comparison. In the tradition of Jim Doggett, the Arkansas squatter (at least in his wilier incarnation), and Bob Burns's "Arkansas Traveler," Clampett patriarch Jed possesses the kind of horse sense that only a man close to nature and completely at home in his own skin can possess, the kind that gives him the edge over a more-educated and urbane but ill-intentioned adversary every time. By the end of each episode, Jed's common sense, Granny's pluck, and the Clampetts' good-hearted integrity—with an ample dose of plain dumb luck—saves the family from whatever calamity had once appeared imminent, in the process exposing the highfalutin Angelenos for the greedy, shallow frauds that they are. It was a timeless formula that had long appealed to a nation that shunned deference and primogeniture and championed egalitarianism. As director Richard Whorf, a former Shakespearean actor, observed: "The picture of the hayseed triumphant is part of our tradition."[2]

The Beverly Hillbillies was a lightning rod for critics who saw in its sophomoric plots and corny comedy the sure signs of the takeover of television by the rude masses, maybe even the evidence of the decline of western civilization. The bone of contention was never the show's stereotypical portrayal of poor southern whites, even though the sitcom's decidedly nonsouthern cast (excepting Louisiana native Donna Douglas) left it open to such criticism. Instead, critics decried the show's unsophisticated, plebian humor, its obvious efforts to appeal to the lowest common denominator of comedy. One *New York Times* critic, in a piece defending the show for its clear-eyed assessment of society, noted that detractors in his line of business had referred to *The Beverly Hillbillies* as "an esthetic regression, mindless, stupid, a striking demonstration of cultural Neanderthalism." Another found the sitcom so inane and revolting that "even the hillbillies should take umbrage."[3] But that wasn't likely to happen, for hillbillies and their fellow commoners across the country formed the core audience for *The Beverly Hillbillies* and Henning's other rural sitcoms. These were the same people who had flabbergasted northeastern sophisticates with their love of Bob Burns and had spun the turnstiles to catch the Weaver Brothers and Elviry and Ma and Pa Kettle on the big screen. Some of them couldn't discern a coon from a possum; many if not most had eaten a helping of both. But they all recognized a side of themselves in the Clampetts, something of the common man in a world operated by the privileged. They all sensed something in the Clampetts that spoke to the American dream, that respected the egalitarian traditions of a nation of democrats.

In spite of the obvious mental shortcomings of Jethro and the family's naivety, the Clampetts fall squarely into the category of romantic backwoods folk. Henning may have been more concerned with fleecing the better sort of Americans of their pretentiousness than exalting the virtues of salt-of-the-earth Ozarkers, but the product of his vision was a major contribution to the romantic side of the Arkansaw/Ozark image, and yet a contribution that, like the monologues of Bob Burns or the tale of Jim Doggett, could be misconstrued by a set of eyes fronting a less tolerant notion of the rural poor.

The tremendous popularity of *The Beverly Hillbillies* undoubtedly and ironically contributed to the reemergence of the more ambiguous Arkansaw/Ozark image in the 1960s, and even to the stereotypical buffoon unredeemed by the Clampetts' fundamental goodness and common sense. Animation studio Hanna-Barbera, building on a long tradition of cartoon hillbilly stereotyping going back to Bugs Bunny's and Woody Woodpecker's visits to the feuding Ozarks and "The Martins and the Coys" from the Walt Disney feature film *Make Mine Music*, introduced Saturday morning audiences to a steady stream of hillbilly characters, beginning in 1964 with a backcountry version of *Tom and Jerry* in *Punkin' Puss and Mushmouse.* Like *Punkin' Puss and Mushmouse*, Hanna-Barbera's *Hillbilly Bears* inhabit a mythical southern highland region free of geographical specificity but full of cultural stereotype. The studio's *Wacky Races*, which aired from 1968 to 1970, offers up a human hillbilly and, not surprisingly, identifies him with Arkansas. One of ten racing teams featured on this animated paean to *The Great Race*, Luke (whose partner was a bear named Blubber) is a lazy, floppy hat-wearing hillbilly who steers his wooden-bodied, coal-fired jalopy, the Arkansas Chuggabug, with his bare feet, all the while reclining, and often sleeping, in a rocking chair. As anyone remotely familiar with Hanna-Barbera animation can surmise, *Wacky Races* wasn't burdened with subtextual cultural commentary, so Arkansawyer Luke pretty much is what he is, a mostly worthless but equally harmless (other than the obvious navigational narcolepsy issue) hillbilly who, like many hillbillies we know, is quite resourceful and not half bad in a car race.[4]

By the time Luke and Blubber Bear debuted in September 1968, Arkansas had already gotten a taste of the oddest and most perversely entertaining symbol of the enduring Arkansaw image to grace the last half of the twentieth century. Just four months earlier Dogpatch, U.S.A. had opened for business in a little hollow just off scenic route seven in Newton County. The sprawling theme park was, of course, based on Al Capp's comic strip, by now an iconic three and a half decades old. The New Englander Capp had never located his mythical Dogpatch in a specific state or region, but his millions of daily readers likely agreed with him that the Ozarks was as fitting as anywhere, and the fact that a group of Harrison, Arkansas, investors was willing to supply Capp with a generous cut of the gate sealed the deal. By 1967, when construction began on the $2.2 million park, *Lil' Abner* and his neighbors had become part of America's pop-cultural fabric and had found their way into a variety of media and promotional products. Long before the Yokums and Scraggs found their way to the Ozarks, Sadie Hawkins Day races—derived from a Dogpatch ritual whereby young women tried to catch and marry eligible but bashful bachelors—had become annual fall events on college campuses around the nation. A popular 1956 Broadway musical starring Peter Palmer and Edie Adams as Abner and Daisy Mae (as well as future Elly May Clampett, Donna Douglas, in a small role) spawned a 1959 feature film, in which Palmer reprised his title role alongside Adams's replacement Leslie Parrish. By the mid-1960s, the pilot for a *Lil' Abner* sitcom (featuring Judy Canova among others) was in the works, and an Atlanta soft drink company had begun marketing Kickapoo Joy Juice, a carbonated take-off on a decidedly stronger beverage churned out by Hairless Joe and Lonesome Polecat in Dogpatch Cave.[5]

But Dogpatch, U.S.A. was a different kind of animal. Whereas the brightly colored costumes, faux-shabby sets, and Hollywood South accents that ranged from *Lum and Abner* to *Amos 'n Andy* lent a certain winking, bicoastal artificiality to the play and movie, the theme park offered a novel venue for Capp's hillbilly schtick. *Lil' Abner* was the most prominent representative of what might be called the New

York–L.A. version of hillbilly comedy, the brand concocted by urban outsiders and marketed to urban outsiders, the kind most likely to peddle buffoonish caricatures or, in Capp's case, to utilize one-dimensional characters as ciphers in service of social criticism. This wasn't the homegrown slapstick of the Weaver Brothers and Elviry or the store porch monologues of Bob Burns. And though similar in execution to *The Beverly Hillbillies, Lil' Abner*, infused as it was with Capp's detached cynicism, differed in spirit from Henning's romantic creation. Arkansawyers, and poor southern folk in general, have long been recognized for their self-deprecation. It is quite likely that many if not most who patronized the park or found seasonal work dressing up like the denizens of Dogpatch and parading around with corncob pipes and exaggerated drawls approached this curiosity with the usual willingness to take the stereotyping in stride. But there was still a surreal quality to the whole enterprise—a passel of mostly Arkansawyers and Ozarkers gallivanting in the remote Boston Mountains as hillbilly characters dreamed up by a cartoonist whose knowledge of the southern backcountry would not have filled a thimble.

In this sense Dogpatch, U.S.A. was a sort of postmodern experiment on the hillbilly stereotype in general and the Arkansaw image in particular. Cultural scholar Rodger Brown notes the labyrinth of irony and paradox in this "100-acre basket of cornpone and hillbilly hokum." In an effort to emulate the Branson, Missouri, area's popular Silver Dollar City theme park and to cash in on the era's folk revival-inspired appreciation for regional heritage, Dogpatch, U.S.A.'s management insisted on blending Capp's comedy with displays and performances by real Ozark craftspeople and musicians. This relayed mixed messages to patrons and rendered the crafters and musicians "'authentic' people in an 'inauthentic' stereotyped context of moonshine, overalls and feudists." Local residents were among the first to detect the irony in the West Po'k Chop Speshul, the park's miniature train that stood as the first and only railroad ever built in Newton County. Whereas the railroad had once been the premier symbol of progress and commerce and the link to a wider world, the Speshul only went around and around in a circle. Furthermore, the fact that Dogpatch, U.S.A. was built on the actual site of an abandoned and dilapidated Arkansas village called Marble Falls (originally Wilcockson) inspired more confusion between the "real" Ozarks and the region of popular imagination. "This masterful blurring of the lines between the authentic, the replica and the hegemonic lampoon is," argues Brown, tongue firmly in cheek, "Dogpatch's claim to a place on the National Register. Restored to its original condition, it could easily serve as a living classroom illustrating lessons for schoolkids in the dynamics of cultural politics and internal colonialism."[6]

In his ruminations on the Ozark holler that once had been Marble Falls before Abner and Daisy Mae came a calling, Donald Harington chronicled locals' disdain for Dogpatch, U.S.A. One Newton Countian, quoted in Harington's lone work of "nonfiction," *Let Us Build Us a City*, dismissed the theme park as a "nuisance," while another wanted someone to "tear all them ole crazy buildings down, and put some decent roofs on 'em and put 'em all on there straight instead of all *humped-up*-like . . . " The *humped-up* buildings, some adorned with statues of goats, were more accurate reflections of popcultural hillbillydom than of old-timey Ozark architecture. Many were indeed "authentic," having been hunted down in the region, taken apart, and reassembled in the park, all "obviously selected with an eye for their 'quaint' and impoverished rusticity." When authentic didn't equate to hillbilly rustic, management decreed that the old cabins "'needed to be sway-backed,'" recalled one local hired for his native craftsmanship, and called out the work crew "to smash the ridgepoles and make the roofs look slovenly."[7]

Perhaps it's fitting that our best literary account of the marriage of image and reality in the remote Arkansas Ozarks comes from the state's premier postmodernist writer. Just as visitors to Dogpatch, U.S.A. might have struggled to differentiate Ozark heritage from Arkansaw stereotype, readers of *Let Us Build Us a City* find themselves (usually unwittingly) in a world where fact and fiction overlap and flow into each other like the confluence of two meandering streams. Though it's Harington's displeasure with the theme park and its flaunting of stereotype that seasons the locals' dialogue, the novelist does seem to share the philosophy of reality underlying the work of Capp and his fellow hillbilly popularizers: the truth is a good thing, as long as it doesn't get in the way of a good story. As he admitted to an interviewer more than a dozen years after the publication of *Let Us Build Us a City*,

"All of that stuff that Harrigan supposedly found with Kim in those various towns—all of that was made up and presented as the history of these towns of Arkansas." So we really don't know if local work crews had to come back in and slouch up their craftsmanship or if locals really objected to the fun that Al Capp and a group of Harrison businessmen were having at their expense. The former sounds improbable, and, unless salt-of-the-earth Arkansawyers' devil-may-care attitudes toward the Arkansaw image had altered dramatically by the Reagan era, the latter seems unlikely. And Abner Yokum himself wouldn't be gullible enough to believe that a certain peanut-chomping former governor just happened to show up at the closed-for-the-season theme park at the very moment that the curious traveler of rural Arkansas stood in the parking lot.

There is no sense getting bent out of shape over Harington's creative nonfiction, though. He, like many an erudite observer, obviously thought that the locals should be offended by the goings-on at Dogpatch, U.S.A., even if it wasn't as easy as the book implies to find someone to articulate a disdain for hillbilly hawking. Besides, maybe the only sane way to lay siege to the perpetrators of cultural slander is through the armature of creative license. A surreal and unintentionally postmodern entity like Dogpatch, U.S.A. deserves a surreal and intentionally postmodern critique by a proud Arkansawyer. But Harington didn't have to imagine the most surreal addition to the story of Arkansas's hillbilly theme park, for the real Orval Faubus, with or without his goober peas, showed up to run the place in early 1969.

Just two years removed from the governor's mansion, Faubus was hired to run Dogpatch, U.S.A. by new owner, Little Rock millionaire Jess Odom. What a red-letter day for the Arkansaw image this was—the state's most infamous, real-life hillbilly running herd over a small army of faux hillbillies. Maybe Faubus was a sucker for irony, or maybe he just liked to picture editorial cartoonists falling all over themselves in a mad dash for their desks. Perhaps he appreciated the impact of his showdown with the Eisenhower administration on the image of Arkansas, realized just how close the state came to donning permanently the robe of reactionary racism, and sought to restore equilibrium by forging a bond between the real hillbilly and his Dogpatch doppelgänger. More likely, it was something more mundane, like the financial problems created by his recent construction of a hilltop mansion and his subsequent divorce. Whatever his motivation, Faubus's tenure at Dogpatch, U.S.A. proved brief and unsatisfying. He soon abandoned the Yokums and Scraggs and McSwines to reenter the political arena, where he would never again experience success. When pressed on the comparative significance of the old governor's stint at Dogpatch, the Faubus who appears in *Let Us Build Us a City* suggests that only "about a paragraph" of his eventual biography should be devoted to his theme park detour. Roy Reed would do him one better and sum it up in a sentence.[8] But the symbolic resonance remains inescapable. Arkansas's last hillbilly governor would ultimately outlive Dogpatch, U.S.A.; he would not outlive the Arkansaw image it promoted, however, and he would never live down his own scarred reputation.

Given the gusto with which the defenders of Arkansas's honor had carried out their missions throughout the century, it may seem surprising that the development of Dogpatch, U.S.A. wasn't greeted with an uproar befitting the memory of Bernie Babcock or Charles H. Brough. Certainly not everyone was excited that Capp's crew was coming to Arkansas. The *Arkansas Gazette* printed a letter from a North Little Rock man who claimed that Dogpatch, U.S.A. would "make Arkansas the laughing stock of the nation." When plans were first unveiled, Lou Oberste, associate director of publicity for the state Publicity and Parks Commission, expressed reservations that the theme park would revive Arkansas's "Bob Burns type image." His boss, Parks and Publicity Commission director Bob Evans, shared Oberste's concerns and feared that Dogpatch, U.S.A. would threaten the progressive image that the state had been cultivating in recent years.[9] This progressive image was perhaps best reflected by Winthrop Rockefeller, the former director of the Arkansas Industrial Development Commission who was busy settling into the governor's mansion as the state's first Republican chief executive since Reconstruction at the same time that the Dogpatch story broke.

With this story and plenty of other real news to cover, Little Rock's media ultimately gave little thought to the cultural implications of Dogpatch. Even the trepidation of Publicity and Parks Commission spokesmen was assuaged before the winter was over, thanks to a tour of the theme park site hosted by two members of the commission, one of whom, a newspaper publisher and business promoter from neighboring Searcy County, claimed that Dogpatch, U.S.A. would prove to be a good thing for the Arkansas image. By the time the park opened in May 1968, the state's official publicity machine was happily touting Dogpatch as "Arkansas's first super-duper commercial tourist attraction," though its euphemism-laced efforts to put a positive spin on the Newton County development proved (unintentionally) funnier than anything coming out of Capp's stale pen in the Vietnam era. Focusing primarily on the area's scenic beauty and natural wonders and the theme park's artisans and state-of-the-art equipment, the Publicity and Parks Commission's official press release praised "the nicely landscaped main building" and "rest rooms so swanky that they belie the pseudo pioneer impression Dogpatch is supposed to give." Lest visitors fear venturing into the rustic Ozarks or Arkansawyers sense something unsettling about the walking and talking hillbilly caricatures and the pageantry of the moonshiner-revenuer chase and shootout, the press release reminded readers that "Dogpatch U.S.A. is a lot of fun in a dignified sort of way and will undoubtedly be a credit to Arkansas both culturally and economically."[10]

The game had not changed considerably since the days of Brough and Babcock, when educated defenders argued not so much "Arkansans are not hillbillies" as "Not all Arkansans are hillbillies." This Arkansas of shoe and shirt factories, of tax breaks and industrial incentives, was more willing than ever to trade whatever dignity it might have left for a mess of pottage. Arkansans had bought into the nation's critique of their state; now the thought of sacrificing potential economic benefits was a much scarier proposition than the thought of being ridiculed. Besides, the location of Dogpatch, U.S.A. in an isolated hollow in the Ozarks might serve as a lightning rod to focus and absorb all the bolts of stereotype flung by a critical public, a sort of containment policy against the spread of the negative hillbilly image into parts of the state where it was most unwelcome. After all, if Arkansas had a Dogpatch, reasoned suburban Arkansans, it would likely show up in a place like Newton County. Let folks up in the hills degrade their heritage all they want, argued one letter writer to the *Arkansas Gazette*, "but tainting the entire state with their shame is a different matter."[11]

NOTES

1. Anthony Harkins, *Hillbilly: A Cultural History of an American Icon* (New York: Oxford University Press, 2004), 187, 188.

2. Quoted in Arnold Hano, "The G.A.P. Loves the 'Hillbillies,'" *New York Times,* 17 November 1963, SM120.

3. Ibid., SM16; "Review," *Variety,* 3 October 1962, 35, quoted in Harkins, *Hillbilly,* 190.

4. All information on Hanna-Barbera cartoons from Don Markstein, *Don Markstein's Toonopedia,* http://www.toonopedia.com/ (accessed 2 May 2007).

5. Mark Evanier, "Li'l Abner in Hollywood," POV Online, http://povonline.com/Abner2 (accessed 11 March 2009), originally published in *Li'l Abner,* v. 25. Rodger Brown, "Dogpatch, USA: The Road to Hokum," *Southern Changes* 15 (1993), 22; *Time,* 1 September 1967, 2.

6. Rodger Brown, "In Arkansas, a Dogpatch Way Past Its Prime," *Atlanta Journal-Constitution,* 11 July 1993, M6; Rodger Brown, "Dogpatch, USA," 24, 25. Though Dogpatch's mountain music and crafts may have been influenced by Silver Dollar City, it would appear that the latter and older theme park reacted to Dogpatch as well. The historian of Silver Dollar City notes: "In 1968, a permanent 'entertainment troupe' of 18 performers was hired to roam the park doing hillbilly vaudeville, hillbilly slapstick." Crystal Payton, *The Story of Silver Dollar City: A Pictorial History of Branson's Famous Ozark Mountain Theme Park* (Branson: Silver Dollar City, 1997), 70.

7. Donald Harington, *Let Us Build Us a City: Eleven Lost Towns* (New York: Harcourt Brace & Company, 1986), 109, 110, 126, 108.

8. Ibid., 130; Roy Reed, *Faubus: The Life and Times of an American Prodigal* (Fayetteville: University of Arkansas Press, 1997), 329.

9. *Arkansas Gazette,* 10 January 1967, 6A, 6 January 1967, 1B, 7 January 1967, 6A.

10. *Arkansas Gazette,* 23 February 1967, B1, 19 May 1968, G7.

11. *Arkansas Gazette,* 10 January 1967, 6A.

James Bogan

James Bogan is an emeritus professor of art history, a poet, and a filmmaker, who has taught at the Missouri University of Science & Technology in Rolla since 1969. His scholarly publications include *Sparks of Fire* (1982), an experimental anthology on William Blake, and *Burden of Dreams* (1984), a casebook on Les Blank's film. In 1986 he lectured at the Federal University of Para in Brazil as a Fulbright Fellow, where he also began his career as a documentary filmmaker with *T-Shirt Cantata.* Bogan's prose and poetry have been published widely in magazines like *River Styx*, *New Letters*, and *Walking* and several have been aired on National Public Radio's *All Things Considered*, *The Savvy Traveler*, and *Market Place. Ozark Meandering*, a book of maximal poetry and poetic prose, was letterset at Timberline Press in 1999, making it "the last hand-made book of the millennium." His current projects include another film in Brazil, a book of poetry on art, and the exploration of the Ozarks by foot, bicycle, and kayak.

River Poetics IV

RHYTHM of the river
timed into a film
of transparent images
meandering as the long

current that searches
earth for the sea

smoldering fire dawn
water releasing fog
that gathers light
slow drift
downstream
into sunrise

looming bluff seen
then seeing from there
the long reach and distant eddy
of the river's twisting course

from the bow of a canoe
a sequence of moments:

golden chains of light
dance along the river bottom
reflected up
to the arching sycamore,
the trunk blossoms
into green umbrellas overhead
one by one overshadowing

gentle the acceleration
into rapids
water rushing
and rocks
neatly eluded
into a placid stretch
to drift along the bank

attention drawn to a maze
of roots unearthed
by Spring floodwaters

track the chattering kingfisher
extending space upriver and down
hawks sail above the buzzards—
possibly an eagle soaring

linger at a blue spring
if you can find one—

enter the darkness
of a cave
and from darkness
return into
noonlight
still then
till navigating
down
a shadowed
passage
where
a vibrating
reed
rattles
a charm
spelled
in natural
time
simply stated
the feeling is of forever

a crow caws warning
instantly glints silver
flies off

green pines stand lofty and motionless
except when stirred by intermittent wind

wind ripples the water
scattering daystars of sunlight

float beneath
clouds massing
and dissolving
in their own time

trees alive
along the river valley
glow in the sundown

drifting
drifting
into
darkness

stars
fire
embers
river

sounds

Mrs. Clara Franz:
Mother Earth's Daughter

Ninety years old
and never been to Kansas City
got as far as a St. Louis suburb
once.
Still, fairly radical:
        "I ain't against pool or dancin'."
She used to walk ten miles to go dancing Saturday Nights
about the time her father sold apples for a quarter
a barrel.

She's lovely
        white mop top
        bright *old* blue eyes
        teeth in a drawer somewhere
        voice travels from the mourning dove to the crow,
                mostly crow
        four layers of flower-print dresses
        sturdy as a turnip
        didn't wear shoes in the summer until she was 73
        milked cows *every* day from the time she was 8
                til she turned 78 (Likes cows—Hates milk.)
        Still keeps chickens, says,
        "A day without work is a day without food."

Remembers what happened:
        yesterday
        last Week
        a Year and a Day ago

seventy Years ago
and everything in between—
Quick at arithmetic, too.

She's 8 when the calendar rolled over to 19-double ought.
25 when the man who will be her husband
ten years later embarks for France
to fight their mutual second cousins.
43 when the WPA builds the bridge down the road
60 when Ike gets elected for the first time
and she voted for him—been Republican ever since
Wilson lied about keeping us out of war.
76 when Otto died and that almost killed her:
"I wished I was dead. Never done that before."

Otherwise vigorous
and what her wood stove won't heat
port-wine will.

Plants her enormous garden by the phases of the moon:
"If you sow radishes by the light of the moon
all you'll git is greens.
Never fails."

Petrified of snakes, lightning and the dark:
"I wouldn't open the door to Santa Claus hisself
after the sun goes down."

She was weeding the okra one morning
when a pair of Jehovah's Witnesses
descended upon her
them in shirt and tie
her in bonnet and sweating some:

"Git on, if the Lutherans couldn't save me,
you sure as hell cain't."

Always has a can of Gold Label beer ready
and a risky joke:
"A lady goes into the music store.
She asks the clerk, 'Do you have *Hot Lips?*'
He says, 'No, but I got nine inches.'
She says, 'Is that a record?'
'No,' he says, 'but it's a damn good average.'"

Or this one told to her grandson the night she died:
"Do you know why babies are so fragile?
Because they are put together with just one screw."

Had one child of her own
cried "a barrel of tears"
when he shipped out for Korea.
Raised eleven kids,
orphans that she literally picked up off of Pine Street
"And made us work,"
says the religious one.

She listens to mathematicians
bums
English professors
minstrels
Truth or Consequences on TV
She says, "It's very educatin',"
while crocheting on her pink and white *African.*

I knocked at the door louder and longer than usual.
She finally appeared, looking like a cat shoved off a chair

I shouted (her hearing aid lives in the same drawer
as her teeth):
"What ya doing? Taking a nap?"
"What?"
"TAKING A NAP?"
"Eh—you make me sick.
I been workin'.
It's you been takin' a nap."
She was right too.

You know it's her coming down the road
engine revved
honking like a teenager
in her speeding Maverick
headed for the Big Star Market
purse full of coupons.

Always candy for kids
and for the parents:
tomatoes
and okra
and zucchini
and pumpkin
and scallions
and cabbage
and pickles
and turnips
and peppers
and radishes
and beets
and lettuce
and jelly
and flowers

When the local undertaker met her
in the potato chip aisle of the Krogerstore
he put his hand on her shoulder
to which,
Mrs. Franz,
"Ain't cold yet, Marvin."

Sara Burge

Sara Burge was born in West Plains, Missouri, and she has lived in the Missouri Ozarks most of her life. She first attended college at the Missouri State University, West Plains campus, and eventually completed her MFA in poetry at Southern Illinois University Carbondale. Her first book, *Apocalypse Ranch*, won the De Novo award and was published by C&R Press in fall 2010, and her poems have appeared in *The Virginia Quarterly Review*, *River Styx*, *Cimarron Review*, *Court Green*, *The Los Angeles Review*, and elsewhere. She teaches poetry writing at Missouri State University in Springfield.

Sacraments

My grandmother took her chickens straight
to the backyard's stained tree stump,
hatchet hanging above their squawkings a moment
before slamming through neck to wood,
their new bodies blind and bound to find
Billy's black-mutt jaws, slick and snapping.
She explained nothing
and I thought nothing of it.

Once, while holding a log steady for my grandfather,
the chainsaw chewed her right forearm

to the bone. Still
she weeded her garden, was expected to make dinner,
so she grabbed chickens with one hand,
swung them around and whipped them
like a wet towel, white feathers bursting
into springtime twilight like champagne.

Each Black Shell

Spring-cold, beer-can-strewn, littered with hillbillies
in canoes with guitars and red-bandanaed dogs—
this was the river I lived on every summer as a child.
My mother and father—drunk on Coors, not yet hating each other—
searched the slick-stoned bottom for mussels
and freed them from muck to suck them clean out of themselves.
I understood only the literal, imagined bulging arms,
legs filleted and twitching within each glistening shell.

A grown-up thing to do, find a mussel and eat it.
But then, I didn't think of love as lying on a river bed,
moss-haired and drifting. Didn't think of love at all
while skipping rocks at the cresting snouts of snapping turtles
or waiting in the shallows until the settling mire
revealed a crawfish side-shuffling from under algae stones.
Its body blended waves of light and mud
until snatched out, above the atmosphere of water.
There, it turned hideous. Tiny leviathan,
trivial as the air that stank of something dead
banked and bloated beside me.

Once a shell cracks, there's nothing but the bleeding out.
Summers began their slow nodding, and my parents' love
began to swell and slack. Our last river trip as a whole,
I didn't hear footsteps snapping underbrush,
only a voice asking why I was there.
Words spoken by a shadow eclipsing the sun,
a negative form with the outline of a shotgun.
But my father appeared, offered the man a beer
and a smile I didn't recognize, then
carried my shivering bones back to my mother.
We crossed the river's cold current, me whining
that it wasn't late yet. We still had so much time.

Michael Burns

Michael Burns helped found the Creative Writing Program at Missouri State University, where he taught for twenty-five years. A graduate of the University of Arkansas Creative Writing Program, he published two chapbooks, *When All Else Failed* and *And As for Darkness*, as well as two books of poetry, *The Secret Names* and *It Will Be All Right in the Morning*. He also edited two books of critical essays. His final book of poems, *Night of the Grizzly*, was published posthumously by Moon City Press in 2012. Born June 3, 1953, in Egypt, Arkansas, Burns retired to Louisville, Kentucky, where he passed away on October 27, 2011.

Farm Road 93

This road's so slick my pickup wants to skate
down every hill, to turn where there is no turn,
though I've loaded the back with bench-set weights
and rock from a flowerbed. A calmer man

would find a safer route where all is clear
and traffic hums, where morning plows have shut
the night-drift up, but I'm thinking it's Sunday here
—the bone and blood, the longing, mild regret—

and I might be able to get to the lake
and watch the ducks, go out myself on the ice.
I want to walk along the bridge and make
believe I'm talking to God. I need advice

on everything, not just this white on black,
and I'm almost there. I'm taking the long way back.

On the Fifth Day of the Search

—for David Tate, Neo-Nazi and accused killer

Redbud and dogwood, everywhere the flowering,
and a branch of Long Creek flowing into summer.
Here are the cardinal, the chipmunk, the whitetail,
and maybe even the black bear who has lumbered
out of his sleep. There's windsong in the treetop,

Or helicopters. Are you lying belly down
on a cool stone, resting your head on the shirt
you stole last night from a backyard clothesline?

I imagine you slithered into a crevice
where you mouth words like *hungry, bastards, cold*;
or from someplace deeper: *afraid* and *now.*

Whatever the world seemed to you in winter
in Idaho, an Ozark spring fulfills the covenant.
You move, and the mockingbird follows, and the crow.

After October Rain

—Auricularia auricular. Edible. From Latin, "ear"

Out near the fence, I found
A tree ear lying, alone
This morning
In the wet yard swing

And above it, on a log
Caught two years now
And rotting in the limbs
Of a Red Thorn

I saw dozens more still
Glowing with rain
And dew
Hung there
As if they were listening.

I've stored them now
In a zip-top bag filled
With water
In the refrigerator.

I'm going to eat them.
I can't say what they heard.

Sweet Potatoes

When I was small, my father asked me before he left
for work one day if I would like—as he had taught me—
to dig some new potatoes out from the fall garden.
I did, carefully at first, with the short shovel,
making my way down to the first red skin,
then up and over my wrists with both of my hands.
I've still got this pale scar from the cut I took
from broken glass, to my finger. I stopped the bleeding.
I laid them out in rows to show him when he came home.

I've made a spot in my back yard for tomatoes,
squash, green beans, ornamental red peppers.
And this year on a whim I decided to plant
sweet potatoes. Frost has fallen, and I'm so brave
I've gone this morning out to reap my rewards.
I spade the ground around the roots a little,
as if I were mapping some archaeological site,
but nothing shows. I take the shovel, plant my foot,
and the hell with it, I push until I hear
the cut of flesh, or something vegetable, and like it.

Oh, yes, I've found the scrawny, orange suckers
tunneling for China, like the mole, or diving
like a submarine under attack, and I go after them
with both hands again and dig for them, like runaways,
out of a rock and hard place. I swear I can feel the scar
in my finger throb. OK, you don't have to give me that,
but take time for a moment, as I must do, to imagine
my father standing here, in his work clothes and hat,
studying my crop. He laughs, but he's proud still
as I lay them down like trout, like ears of harvest corn.
I must be about as old now as he was then.

Going to See the 15th-Century Indian Head Pots at the Hampson Museum, Wilson, Arkansas

Following the path they say the glacier took
I come down out of the mountains
across Black River, back
into the land of my family, old friends.
It's not yet dawn, but a few people have left
Christmas lights burning,
and that's a song
I'd rather not sing right now.
Wood smoke drifts
over the redbrick houses, over the snow.

How can a man stake out and grid his past?
You box it in, recall
the width of the moat, the last
pretense, the height of the palisade wall.
You wash each piece, identify each layer.
Tag that. Name this.
As I get closer to Memphis,
a cold rain
falls like the words to a prayer
I'll never pray: don't let me be forgotten.

When the last great rock from the asteroid belt
came hurtling through the sky,
I believe I felt
my own heart shift. I heard the coyote cry.
A shaman said: soon I will be gone
from here to a dark place,
so I will make my face
out of the red earth

to keep me from being alone.
I touch him now. I learn what my life is worth.

Like spirits of the dead, the snow geese light
out in the flooded rows
of cotton, calling all night
across the dark, calling, for someone who knows
their secret names, those given beyond the grave.
Tomorrow I'll drive on
to another town, then on again.
I'll race a blue highway
back to a world where we believe
the dead lie down with nothing left to say.

Marcus Cafagña

Born in Ann Arbor, Michigan, Marcus Cafagña is the author of two books of poetry, *The Broken World* (University of Illinois Press, 1996), a National Poetry Series selection, and *Roman Fever* (Invisible Cities Press/IPG, 2001). His poems and critical reviews have also appeared in numerous journals and anthologies, including *Cave Region Review, Crazyhorse, Elder Mountain, The Iowa Review, Manthology, Moon City Review, Poetry, Poets of the New Century, Prairie Schooner, The Southern Review,* and *TriQuarterly.* A graduate of the Vermont College MFA program, he coordinates the creative writing program at Missouri State University and lives in Springfield with his wife and son.

Mowing

From my air-conditioned living room,
the figure of Adrian cursing the mower
reminds me of lawns I cut at his age—
he's shirtless, sweating, sunburned,
jailhouse tattoo a strand of barbed wire
cinching his neck. Over and over I hear
the engine fail, watch it spew smoke,
smell gas. I know what it is to hate

the hand that hired me with a loathing
bigger than a starter handle, a motor
that won't start no matter how I pull.
Even when it does, the blade's gone dull
from so much grass, and thistle too tough
to shorten. Just like that, I could've left
somebody's yard half-mown. My two-stroke
contraption looked a lot like his, muddy,
caked with oil. I'm embarrassed by my luck,
but I know how bugs and mice invade
a house once grass around it goes wild.
I'll have to fire him, but not today,
not with rust flaking off his car—
his wife pregnant with twins.

The Old House

It's not the old neighborhood I miss,
the streets choked with shotgun shacks,
not the dilapidated ranch we used to rent.

I can't say I miss the landlord we never met
or the possum that slept under our car.
I don't care if I ever see the man next door again,
or his German Sheppard on a chain, or the decoy
of a deer he shot arrows at when deer
were out of season.

                                        Yet there are mornings
after dropping off our little boy at school,
when I still drive by the house on Madison.

Through the windshield I spy on what chump
braves that leaky structure now, betting
whoever-he-is is sick-to-death of the mold
dotting the dining room walls, the rainwater-
bloated ceiling, sick-to-death of breathing
hard air. My wife goes by there, too.

We joke that on the day we moved out,
our cat hid behind the fridge
rather than give up eating cave crickets.
Who could forget how hot that house got
whenever the air conditioner conked?
To get the cool air flowing again,

I had to walk out the front door, around the side
of the house, up rickety steps to a utility closet
full of spiders and webs to duck at the fuse box.

But it was our first place together.
We didn't care about housekeeping,
dust covering every surface, the living room
strung with Christmas lights we couldn't bear
to disconnect.

                                        Every night was like a party
in that house, even in winter when the rusted-out
chamber of the octopus furnace cracked
and let most of the heat escape.
One repairman, dropping his wrench
with a whistle, swore it was the oldest
almost working furnace he'd ever seen.

Katie Estill

Katie Estill is the author of two novels *Evening Would Find Me* and *Dahlia's Gone*, which was named one of the top 100 books of 2007 by the *Kansas City Star*, and was a finalist for the 2008 Dashiell Hammett Prize. Her short stories have appeared in such journals as *The Missouri Review*, *The Mid-American Review*, *Ontario Review*, *Elder Mountain*, and *Surreal South*. Born in Cleveland, Ohio, she received her BA from Kenyon College and MFA degree from the University of Iowa Writers' Workshop. She makes her home in the Ozarks with her husband, Daniel Woodrell.

The Three Beauties

Lana woke up and thought she was dreaming still, for she seemed to be floating downstream, enveloped by the sound of a waterfall. Her hand sank into cold water then she understood she was sliding downhill from the mouth of her tent. Out she poured into the night, coming to rest near the edge of her stone-ringed fire pit, which was filling with water like a birdbath.

I am all right. I am quite alive, she told herself as she struggled with the zipper on her sleeping bag and cried out in helplessness and utter longing for her relatives. She thought of her family's house in the Philippines. It was made of bamboo and thatch, a platform built on stilts, so they would have slept above these waters. She longed for her sisters' voices and wished to be small again, to curl up against her mother's breast and be held and told in a soothing voice that everything will be all right. At home the rain would leak through the roof, but no more bothersome than the nightly sprinkling of cockroaches that gathered on the ceiling and walls. How was it that she had accepted the slight tap of their bodies falling on her shoulder at night as fundamentally normal as the rising of the moon in the sky, but over here, in the kitchen of the barbeque restaurant where she worked as a dishwasher, the young waitresses shrieked at the sight of a few cockroaches scuttling on the floor or crawling out of drawers, their antennae squirming about. "It is only cockroach," she'd say, to soothe their anguished faces. It was strange what people found frightening. She knew that after they closed and turned off the lights, the cockroaches would take over the night as they searched for leftovers. Like the stars, they came with darkness and disappeared with the light. Lana never told the waitresses that on her island, when she and her family woke up in the morning, they had to brush off the dry feces left by the night visitors, the droppings that gathered in the cracks of their eyelids, the seams of their lips.

But rain and wind, explosions of thunder and lightning bolts thrust down to the earth did indeed frighten her. Get to the car, she told herself. The car is dry.

Only this morning she had felt so at home in the world. She had crawled out of her tent and noticed a large spider web spanning the air between the tent ropes. The taut web was springy and resilient, glistening with dew. I am like you also, she thought, admiring the wood spider. I can unravel threads of power that will take care of me. She had waded through the morning fog, and when she walked downhill into the river valley she disappeared into the mist. This vanishing reminded her of the way she had left her small island in the Philippines. Tonight she was wretched and alone.

Then she remembered the three Nubian goats tied to a post oak. Lana flung herself from the sleeping bag and stumbled through the dark, calling, "Oh, my beauties! Are you all right?"

At the sound of her voice, their bells jingled, and the three beauties brayed in protest over what had become of this night. When Lana reached them they were bleating inconsolably. They had wound themselves up in the ropes. One had climbed up the oak's gnarled roots above the waterline. Another looked down in horror at the rushing water, while the youngest had stumbled on the tree's great roots and snagged her right front hoof.

"Oh, what is happened? My sweet one, don't panic! Stop, stop, let me see." The storm battered her head so hard she had to close her eyes as she groped down the fetlock to the hoof wedged between two roots. "Shhh. Be still, Hope." For it was Hope whose hoof was stuck, Hope who brayed in terror and alarmed the other two.

Lana grasped the hard narrow hoof and tried to distract the goat. "You have no idea what an easy life we have here. At home you might be eaten by snakes. Great lizards come out of the jungle and drag you away. We have only to manage this rain, sweet one. It's just a night of rain." She yanked the goat's hoof, and Hope yelped, but suddenly her leg was free and she kicked Lana in the elbow. A sharp, almost paralyzing pain traveled up her arm. Then one by one she led her prized goats to the shelter of her used Saturn, and the four of them spent the night in the car. With the windows rolled up, the car quickly accumulated the thick smell of wet goat hair, and later the barnyard odors of fresh droppings and the release of urine and milk on the seats, an unfortunate treatment of her most expensive possession in the world.

Whenever she felt overwhelmed she would count the blessings in her life the way the pious reach for a rosary or the way old Rotten Knees, back on the island, could always find a bottle in the middle of the night. She had been applying this splint to her pain for as long as she could recall. Her parents had sold her to an American rancher, who came to their small island to find himself a wife. So Lana left the Philippines and lived with the man in Wyoming. In return, he sent her parents a hundred dollars a month.

She was rarely allowed to leave the ranch and only if he was at her side. Lana watched TV in hopes of understanding this strange new world, and soon she became a bad wife. She continued to clean his house and tried to make him the suppers he liked. At night she dutifully opened her legs, but every day she stole some change from his pockets, or a dollar bill. She hid the money at the bottom of a flour tin, and when she had forty-nine dollars and change, she walked to the bus station in town and fled.

She traveled by bus as far as her fortunes would allow, then she followed the advice of certain television shows and stuck her thumb out to the wind, trusting that the Holy Virgin would look after her, and that was how she met Mr. Harry on the roadside in Kansas City. She'd been hoping a woman would stop and was frightened to see that the car idling on the berm had a man behind the wheel. Still, he was an older man—maybe he was safe.

He saw her wavering. "I'm a dying man," he said. "You have nothing to fear from me."

He was driving to southern Missouri, because that was where he lived. She never answered when he asked her where she wanted to get off. Harry's house had frightened her. Lana walked through the door, clutching her plastic bag of clothes to her chest, wondering if she had just placed herself under the lock and key of another man. Who would ever know? No one knew she was here.

In the foyer, he opened a closet door, and she stared into its dark entrails.

"Want to hang up your coat?"

Lana shook her head. "No. No closet," she said.

The man named Harry looked tired. His face in the artificial light appeared gaunt, unwell, and she saw from the prominent bones of his face that he had recently lost flesh. He stared at Lana for what seemed a long time, then finally said, "All right. Would you like something to eat?"

He had to tell her to slow down for she was swallowing his food so rapidly she began to choke. He did not question her. He moved slowly and deliberately, and kept a safe distance between them at all times. After supper, they watched television and the man fell asleep in the chair that reclined. At bedtime he gave her a room to sleep. He called it the guest room and said she could stay as a guest. He told her how to lock the door from the inside and stood there in the hallway and instructed her. "Turn the latch to the right."

"Which right?"

"Clockwise. As the hands of the clock move."

"Yes, it is locked now," Lana said, turning the door handle to confirm.

"Okay," he said, and as he walked away he called back to her, "Sleep tight, kiddo."

"What, Mr. Harry?"

"Oh, nothing. Just something I used to say."

Mr. Harry had been the first blessing, perhaps the greatest one, for he had wanted nothing from her but the uplifting presence of her youth, which had cheered him as he died.

At dawn, Lana woke up in the driver's seat, stiff and chilled. Faith's narrow head was resting on her lap, and the bell tinkled as the goat looked up at her. The youngest doe lay on the ledge of the rear window, forelocks draped over the seat, one leg a little raw where she'd fought with the roots of the post oak. The oldest nanny lay stretched out on the backseat and seemed entirely content with the new quarters.

Lana would never successfully remove the stench of goat from the car, and yet the acrid odors of their droppings and urine, the milk leaking from full udders, the earthy smell of their damp hair was not thoroughly unpleasant to her, for it was the smell of plenty, the smell surrounding a person who was not going to starve, but was in possession of many blessings. She sneezed with an oncoming cold and counted on her fingers the fortunes of her life. First, she was alive. No great harm had come to her on her travels, and she had survived the night's storm. Then, respectfully, she prayed for the health of her family, with whom she has not communicated in so many months. She was sorry she dropped off the face of the earth. How frightened her parents must be. Maybe she displeased her husband and he murdered her. How could they know? And now they had lost the income that her marriage had provided them. Lana felt ashamed that her family might be forced to roast the cockroaches that gathered on the walls of their house and call it the bounty of God, but she couldn't bring herself to phone and admit she was alive.

She wrapped her arms around the goat's neck, nuzzled the velvety ears. "Count the blessings," she murmured. "Count the blessings aloud." The rain was done. She rubbed the bridge of Faith's nose, then leaned over the steering wheel and surveyed the view.

"This five acres is my land. The cedar trees and the post oak. The fire circle that will dry, the rocks on top of the hill, the glade. The spring house, and the spring water that runs through the old spring house." She glanced up to the rearview mirror to the goats in back. "I have you, my beauties. You are my company, and you give me your milk, and there is so much we are making goat cheese and selling milk to the woman who cannot digest the cow. Someday we will have more goats, more milk and cheese to sell. And there is the great blessing of my friend Mr. Harry, who I should have mentioned first, because without his help I would still be standing beside the road, alone and friendless, or something bad may have happened to me. Instead I am safe. Today the sun will dry my house, my blankets and clothes, and all of last night we will put behind, and when I drive my car to the restaurant what I smell inside my own car will be the smell of plenty. I am a woman with land. It's the twenty-first century. I live in America. Someday I will live in a house."

She liked the bustle of the kitchen at the Barbecue Shack with everyone working together to cook the ribs and fry potatoes, to get the food out rapidly. A pleasure to see the smiles of customers. She was up to her elbows in suds, when Dylan, the owner, walked through the kitchen and wrinkled his nose.

"What's that stink?" he asked, putting his hands on his hips and looking around to each of his employees. "It smells like goat."

"Goat?" Lana said and shot upright with a splash. "We only have pig here. Beef, chicken and fish. No goat."

Dylan came over to her. "It's you," he said. "You smell of goat."

"Ah. Yes. Big storm last night. We were washed away, and the three beauties were so afraid."

"Who?"

"They are Nubians. Everything went downhill. We slept in the car."

"You mean the one that's out back in my parking lot?"

"Yes, certainly."

Dylan went out the kitchen door, past the trash bins where many rats lived. When Lana caught up to him, he was leaning into the driver's window, for she had left the windows open to air out the vehicle. He shook his head in disgust. "For crying out loud. Is this the way you treat a car back where you come from?"

"Oh, we had no cars. Mr. Harry showed me to drive."

"In my office," he said.

Dylan asked her to take a seat. "Lana, I'm wading through these papers from the government," he said and gestured to several piles of paper on his desk. "You're foreign, and, to put it bluntly, we gotta have proof you're not some Muslim terrorist."

"Oh, no," she said. "I am Catholic. I went to school with nuns."

"See, I've given you work, but you've given me no proof of identity. It's been two months. I don't even know if you're in this country legally. How did you get here? No one knows. All we know is you've been living out on Harry's land. But Harry's dead now."

"Mr. Harry left me five acres and three goats."

"I know, I know. With deeded access to the county road." Dylan lit a cigarette and leaned back in his chair to smoke.

"Also the car."

"Look, I don't know what to do with you. You're a good worker and you don't complain."

"No, I am never complaining," she agreed.

"But one day a government agent is gonna walk in here and shut me down 'cause you're washin' my dishes."

"But I do a good job."

"That's not the point with them. They want proof you're not an illegal immigrant."

"I live in the Ozarks. I am Ozarker."

"Right. I won't even ask if you've got a driver's license. This is information I do not want to know, because I already know the answer. You're driving that car with no license."

"Mr. Harry showed me. I drove him many months before he died."

"Look, they've got rules. The only reason you're here at all is because of Mr. Harry. Understand? Because Harry was respected in this town even though he brought home a foreign girl from one of his trips to Kansas City. Now he's dead and what are we going to do with you?"

"Do?" Lana blanched.

"You put me in a spot here, girl! You'll bring the Feds down on me. I don't even know your name."

"You know I am Lana."

"Your legal name. You got a legal name, don't you?"

"Jackson," she said at length.

"And who is Jackson?"

"I am."

"You were not born with that name. Who is Jackson?"

"He is my husband."

"Then why don't you go home to him?"

"Oh, no, please, I beg you, do not tell him!" Lana began to weep. "If he finds me he will kill me now, or keep me locked in chains."

Dylan exhaled a cloud of smoke and pressed an intercom button. "Send Neva. I got female combustion in here."

Neva was a middle-aged woman, stout and firm, who took no nonsense but gave none either. She was the head waitress, but also the kitchen manager. She trundled into the office and Dylan said, "We got a situation. Seems she's married to some dude and she don't want to go back."

"Please, please no, do not send me back."

"What's wrong, Lana?"

"He is bad man!"

"Did he hurt you, hon?"

How could she even explain? "I am so terrified. I will die if you send me back. I ask you in the name of God. You are Christian people, are you not? Do not betray me to my husband. He is not good man."

"Aw, sweetie. Do your parents know where you are?"

"You do not understand," she said.

"How long has it been since you spoke to your mother?"

"They only know they don't get the money that Mr. Jackson paid for the use of me."

"What are you saying?"

"Oh, Christ, is she saying what I think she is?"

"They sold me to him. I am not a free person."

Dylan began to swear, and Neva told him to calm down, but even she was shaken. "Look, you can't sell people in this country. Slavery got abolished a long time ago."

"My parents have other children. They need the money."

"Aw, Neva, what are we going to do?"

"Sweetie, sweetie, don't cry. Let's go call your mother and tell her you're alive. I got a phone card you can use."

The phone number was to the island café, so when old Rotten Knees answered, he had to limp over to Lana's house to tell her mother she was on the phone, which ate up ten minutes of precious time on

Neva's phone card, but finally she heard the ragged, panting voice of her mother.

"Mother!"

"Lana, is it you?"

"Yes, mother."

"You're alive? Where? Where are you?"

"I cannot say."

"What does this mean? You ran away?"

"I ran."

"What? How dare you? Listen to me. If you are my daughter, go back to your husband immediately. He is furious."

"I won't do it. He will kill me or chain me up."

"You have shamed us. We made a deal with the man."

"But in this country no one can own you. You and father made a bad deal," Lana said, and hung up.

When Lana returned to the kitchen, Neva asked her how it went.

"She told me to plant some fruit trees and make the land work, so I won't starve."

"We don't know what will happen if we give her over to the law."

Neva took one of Dylan's cigarettes and sat on the edge of his desk, her big thighs bulging from her pressed white skirt. She had quit, but allowed herself an occasional indulgence in Dylan's office. "She's legally married, she says, but he has the papers locked away. John Jackson of somewhere in Wyoming. She sure does not want to go back to wherever she came from. She's a good worker. She does no harm."

"Well, you tell the Feds to take their damn foot off my neck."

"It's always been that way, Dylan."

"How long do you think we'll get away with this?"

"Not too long, I'd say." Neva stubbed out her butt in a metal ashtray then slid from the desk. "She's a terrible driver. She's bound to get picked up or the tags will expire. I'll give Rita Benton a call over at the women's shelter. They're confidential like."

That evening when Lana returned to her land, she pulled her bedclothes from the line and worried, as she so often did, about the snakes upon the ground. Only last week, Neva had told her to plug in some big black electrical cord in the kitchen and Lana shook her head. "No, I don't touch electrical cords, not big black ones like that."

"Are they too heavy for you, dear?"

"Once in my village, I went to the house of a rich friend, who said she would teach me to sew. I went to plug in the sewing machine and the cord I held in my hand was a long black snake. I threw it to the wall and it was stunned for several seconds before it started chasing me. I have never sewn again."

"Well, gee," Neva said, bending over to pick up the cord with a grunt. "You're gonna have to get over that. They're out there on the land."

"Oh, I know they are. I take many precautions to avoid the serpents. I am praying to the Virgin for a stronger house."

"Yeah? What kind of house do you live in now?"

"It is house of cloth. A tent. But I am rich in water. There's a spring that is true and clear, and an old springhouse that is very beautiful. It is there I hang the cheese." And just as she thought of her wealth, of the redolent balls of cheese hanging from the ceiling of the springhouse, she looked down and saw a snake upon the ground. Fear made her go still, but the snake carried on as before, languidly making its path across the rocky soil. It stopped and turned its head to her. The serpent seemed to smile, then carried on with its evening walk.

Sometimes at night she walked up to the glade. On moonless nights she took a flashlight and climbed a narrow path through the night sounds of crickets and the dreamy bells of the goats trailing her up the hill. The four of them trod the path on the nights of the full moon, when she could see every blade of plant, every wild flower luminous in the night, and she looked out over the hills.

The bald knob made her feel homesick for the Philippines, but other times the place made her feel that she had found her own true home. Here on top of the glade she was closer to the sky, and Lana felt a sense of awe.

"There are three beauties," she said to the night. "They are also the names of my goats." The open collar of her threadbare shirt gaped at the neck and revealed the points of her collarbones and the swell of her small breasts. "The first beauty is faith, and I am learning that. Learning not to be afraid. Learning to trust the universe." Lana stretched on the rocky ground and made a pillow of her arms. "The second is hope. She is my youngest and very curious. Neva told me there are cougars. They were killed off a hundred years ago, but their souls have been called back, and now they have returned in body and this frightens me. So the tent is good, but I hope for stronger walls. And the third beauty is a feeling of compassion for myself and all the humans. To have a loving feeling for the others too: the trees, the waters, even the creatures I do not understand. We were so lucky to be invited into this world."

The goats had taken to following her like a pack of affectionate dogs. They preferred to graze in sight of her. They lay beside her on the grass, watching a cloud of dragonflies glinting in the full sun on the hill. One of the goats rested her chin on Lana's foot. Sometimes, they simply existed together in space and time, sharing the experience of being alive.

Lana shuddered even though the day was hot. The goat felt Lana's tremor, raised her narrow head and stared up at her. When she understood the disturbance was temporary, she lowered her hairy chin to Lana's foot, blinked sleepily, and closed her eyes. Lana was thinking of the man.

In his house she knew she couldn't go home. She would never have enough money. When he entered the ranch house the air became charged, her pulse went up, her sense of dread. He would sit down at the long table and say he was ready to be served. Lana often broke into a sweat, and this displeased the man, because his house was temperature controlled, and sweat made her look unbecoming. If some side dish was not yet done when he was ready to eat, how nervous she became, how ashamed. Her cooking was a great disappointment to the man. "How hard is it to make a decent meatloaf? Just follow the recipe. You *do* know how to read English."

"Oh, yes!" Lana seized onto this detail, trying to please him. "The nuns teach me English."

"And I heard you read out the recipe, line by line." He took her chin in his hand. "Lana, are you stupid?"

"No, John. No. I am not. I am trying. I am sorry, but I do not understand the meat. Always I have understood the fish—how to prepare the fish. I do not know the ways of meat. It is strange to me."

"Don't try to tell me you can't get red meat in the Philippines."

"Yes, but we are poor. We eat the fish from the sea. They are plentiful."

"Well, you aren't poor any more, are you? You live in a big house that's air conditioned in summer and heated through the winter. You have three indoor toilets and a whirlpool tub to soak your lovely limbs."

"My limbs?" Lana blanched, her throat constricting with fear. "What are you saying about my limbs?"

"You have all the luxuries now, but I have to get a little something in return. You're not on the island any more. You're a long, long way away. Twenty-two hours by plane from the ol' Philippines."

Tears welled up in her eyes. "Yes, yes, I know, John."

"You're in Wyoming now, and in Wyoming we don't eat the fish of the sea, we eat meat." He was patting Lana's head, feeling the silkiness of her long black hair. "I work hard and I deserve a good wife."

"Yes, John." And suddenly tears spilled down her cheeks.

"Lana, stop that. Why are you crying when I give you everything? What did I tell you about that? A cheerful demeanor. When I come in from a hard day's work a cheerful demeanor is all I ask."

But her mind was racing over the implications of his words. What punishments was he imagining? Most of all she feared he would restrain her, lock her up or put a chain around her neck.

"I am sorry, it is just that I am so lonely here."

"How can you be lonely? What are you saying? Aren't I enough company? Aren't I everything to you?"

"Oh, yes, you are everything, you are my whole world, John."

"I want a pleasant dinner. Is that too much?"

But she couldn't stop weeping. "I miss my mother and father, John. I miss my family."

"Stop that." He passed his thumb across the delicate skin beneath her eyes and wiped the tears that would not stop. "I'm your family now. I give you everything you need, and all I ask is a sunshiny face. Haven't I taught you what you need to know? Which soap to use on the floor, how to spray the rag before you dust, how to use the washing machine that makes your life so easy here. I give you everything, and you're so ungrateful to me."

He lifted her by the armpits from the table and led her from the dining room. "I think what we need is a little 'time out.' Time to think about what loneliness really is and how lucky you are, if you think about it."

He placed her in the hall closet and locked the door. For the rest of the evening she sat on the closet floor, weeping to her heart's content. Sometime later she had to pee, but she knew she dared not ruin the carpeting. Later that night he opened the door and stood towering in the threshold. "Lana, I'm ready for you now."

She stood up, blinking at the sudden light. "Yes, John."

"It's late," he said. "I've been thinking about you all evening. Have you been thinking of me?"

"Oh, yes, John." These were the words he liked: *oh, yes, John.*

"You wouldn't ever try to leave me, would you?"

"Oh no, I am happy with you. You are my husband."

"Because, when I see you crying like that I don't know if you're happy or not. I don't know what's going on in your mind. I've become very fond of you, Lana. I don't intend to lose you."

"Oh, John, I am wanting you."

Lana's tent was bleached pale by the sun. Her clothes hung from a line, bright flags gently undulating in the breeze. To shake off these thoughts of the man, she stood up from the wild grasses that prickled her thighs. All of this was hers. She could feel the air on her skin, smell the wild herbs.

How cool it would be in the springhouse now. What a thirst she had. Her feet began to move downhill. The goats watched her leave, and when she was just a dark head above the Johnson grass, their tails began to twitch. They shook off their languor, then stood and followed her.

Charles J. Farmer

Charles J. Farmer (1943–2008) was the voice of conservation in the Ozarks. For twenty years, he was the outdoors columnist for the *Springfield News-Leader.* He took on causes, such as protesting the Las Vegas–style development in Branson. Individuals and organizations contacted him for support on issues of water quality, clear cutting, dwindling aquifers, and gun control threats. He was awarded Missouri's Conservationist of the Year in 1992. He was inducted into the Missouri Writers Hall of Fame in 2001. Over the years, he and Kathleen Farmer, as a husband and wife freelance outdoor writing and photography team, wrote eleven books and countless articles for *Field & Stream*, *Outdoor Life*, and *Sports Afield* about the adventure of living and basking in the outdoors, the heart of the Ozarks. His final chapter was Alzheimer's. The next chapter is welcomed in hope of once again being in his heaven, his peace, and his church. It's called the outdoors.

from *Unspoiled Beauty*

I worked my way down the mountain through boulders and grassy terraces filled with cedars. Some of the terraces held shallow pools of water. Carpets of emerald grass, wilderness landscape of unsurpassed beauty, grew on the terraces and under the shady monuments of knobby, stunted oak trees. Beds of viola pedata, bird's-foot violet, grew profusely in these natural rock-garden beds. Wild sweet william, indian paintbrush, and black-eyed susan stood out like prom-night bouquets.

The open terraces and garden fields gave way to a splendid mix of white and red oak, hickory, sugar maple, white ash, and to a lesser extent, basswood and dogwood. The perfect forest, now untouched by the lumberman's chainsaw and free of prescribed commercial management techniques, was doing very well. Shady cool, even in mid-afternoon, this is the travel zone of wild turkeys and whitetail deer—the place of food and hiding cover. The forest zone, as I call it, is for dreaming and talking to the trees. I sat there for a few minutes admiring trunks, limbs, and leaves. Then I hiked down to the bottom and, as my map had indicated earlier, found the Shut-in Creek Trail coursing north and south.

Wilderness bottomland has a special quality to it—moist, aromatic, and junglelike, rich with grasses, flowers, ferns, mushrooms, may apples, blackberry thickets, spice bushes, sycamores, and river birches. It is in the bottoms of every designated Wilderness in the state that one of life's rarest and most precious resources can be experienced—solitude! There is full-fledged insulation from traffic noise and other man-made audio clutter, utter silence save for birdsong, the gurgle of streams, and the faint rustling of leaves in the breeze.

I trailed north at a leisurely pace and found "shut-ins," or gorges, along the stream course. Shut-in Creek, like Joe's Creek, Bell's other perennial stream, is spring fed throughout its length. The bottomland streams of other Wilderness areas are intermittent and usually dry up in the summer and fall; only Bell's are constant. Another unique feature of the bottoms are the steep talus slopes that intersect the stream course at several locations. Rocks and boulders along the stream are commonly carpeted with green and gray moss and lichens. A mix of trees, many of them river birch, grow thick near the water's edge.

I saw fresh beaver-chewed sticks scattered here and there. Elephant-shaped, rose-tinted boulders and slate blue slab rocks, similar to those found at nearby Johnson's Shut-Ins and Elephant Rocks State Parks, have created gorges, miniature waterfalls, and bathtub-size pools of cold, clear water. The actual size of the pools reminded me of those just upstream from Mina Sauk Falls in Taum Sauk

Mountain State Park, also close to Bell Mountain. Some rock pools were rounded out smooth and were just the right depth for dangling your feet or wading in, with water therapeutically ideal for tired feet that had been confined within beefy hiking boots for most of the day.

I went a step further, shedding everything. Bracing my arms behind me, I slid gingerly from the base of a smooth rock into the pool until I was sitting on the gravel bottom with water up to my neck. The water was cold but gloriously invigorating. It was for me another refreshing lesson in wilderness therapy, one of many that keep me looking at the good side of life, just me and a shut-up pool deep in the wilderness. A minute later I completely submerged, then I climbed out of the pool and let the sun dry me. I had a feeling I was not the first to bathe in Shut-in Creek, nor would I be the last. A sun-dried hiker is a happy camper. I smiled and whispered to myself, "Close to heaven . . . really close to heaven."

Gary Guinn

Gary Guinn's great-great-grandfather, a lieutenant in the Second Kentucky Mounted Rifles, moved his family to northern Arkansas after the Civil War. They have lived there ever since. Guinn was born in Siloam Springs, Arkansas, and lives there now with his wife, Mary Ann, and his lab mix, Seamus, and his Corgi mix, Peanut. He is retired from teaching writing and literature at John Brown University. His novel, *A Late Flooding Thaw*, was published by Moon Lake Publishing in 2005. His poetry and fiction have appeared in a variety of magazines, a few of which are *The Midwest Poetry Review*, *Carve*, in which his story was a finalist for the Raymond Carver Prize, *The Bryant Literary Review*, *Ghoti*, *Elder Mountain: A Journal of Ozark Studies*, and *The Arkansas Literary Review*.

Being a Doaks and All

The boy was fifteen, tall and thin, uncomfortable in town, where people stared at him, at the faded overalls that hung on him like a sack, at the worn denim shirt, the sleeves not quite long enough.

The girl walked up to him as he stood on the mercantile porch, waiting for Virgil. Her white blouse, clean and pressed, was tucked into the narrow waistband of a gray skirt. The lines of the pleats in the skirt dropped away from the curve of her hips. Her penny loafers were freshly polished.

"You're a Doaks, aren't you?" she asked. "What's your name?"

He turned away.

She walked around to face him again, looked up into his eyes, daring him not to answer. "I said what's your name?"

He looked at his feet, then glanced at the closed and silent door of the mercantile.

"You don't look mean to me," she said. "Ollie Delphia told me a body might better run up on a rattlesnake in a dry creek than meet a Doaks in close quarters." Her brown eyes were steady and unblinking. "What'd she mean by that?" Her lower lip dropped in a moist curve beneath the slight shadow of her nose and the handful of freckles sprinkled high on her cheeks. The arc of flesh beneath her eyebrows rose above the long lashes.

His thin frame leaned slightly toward the alley that ran down the side of the mercantile, as if drawn to it by invisible wires, but he stood rooted to the porch, his face flushed and his ears burning. He remembered the slumped figure of his mama the day Virgil made her drive him to town, the only time he ever remembered her leaving the farm. Job Fincher had looked out the window of the butcher shop next to the mercantile and had come out and stood on the porch and wiped his hands on his bloody apron and looked at her through the windshield and smiled the smile of a man who knows some private joke. She had stayed in the truck, gripped the steering wheel and stared at the hood. The boy wondered if he looked that way now to the girl.

"Nate Farley says you can't talk. Is that right?" The girl pushed her lips out. "Well? You can nod your head, can't you?"

The words lay heavy in the base of his throat—that his name was Mason, that she was prettier than the women pictured on the covers of the magazines in the rack in the mercantile. He swallowed. Pleasant Varner, the schoolteacher, had stood over him, her arms folded in weary silence, her tired face saying that his resistance must be a perversity of stubbornness. A boy, no matter how shy, could speak out, if only he chose to do so.

The girl waited. His feet were brown with dust, and he wished he had worn his shoes. In the stinging absence of words he looked out at the street, across the square to the hotel, where Willie May Boseman had stood the day her husband Samuel was killed when he fell from the scaffolding there as Willie May waited for him to come down and eat the lunch she had brought. Mason had stood in the open square a few yards away, watching the men work. He remembered the look on Willie May's face after Samuel fell, as she stood there without moving, holding the red bandanna, its corners tied up to make a sack for the lunch. The momentary quiet across which he looked at her. During the commotion that followed, he watched the impotent terror on her face as she stood unable to move. He wondered if he looked like that to the girl.

"It's rude not to answer when you're spoken to," she said, "but I suppose you've never been taught any better, being a Doaks and all."

The edge of the tongue-in-groove board at his feet warped up slightly, and he raked his toe across it. His eyes began to water, and he looked again at the alley.

"Mason!" Virgil Doaks's voice from the doorway behind him made him jump. "Quit standin' around like a jackass. Get in there and get that box of groceries."

Virgil Doaks, thin and bent, carrying a tight gunnysack of grain on his shoulder, brushed past. His clothes hung on him like a scarecrow tilting in rocky soil. He dropped the sack over the side of the pickup bed and started around the back of the truck, past the bare bulb of the taillight and the rusted tailgate. The boy scrambled through the door of the mercantile to get the box. When he came back out and crossed the porch, he glanced at the girl, who stood exactly where she had when Virgil came out. Her eyes had narrowed.

"I see where you get your manners," she said and tipped her head slightly toward Virgil.

As the pickup pulled away from the curb, it rattled and whined and spewed a swirl of blue-gray smoke. A thin stream of tobacco juice squirted like a silent exclamation through the truck window onto the street, and Virgil shifted the wad of tobacco to the other side of his mouth as the clutch banged against the bare metal of the floorboard and the gears ground together. On the movie marquee, "Afternoon Matinee 1:30" was spelled out in red slide-in letters. When the pickup stopped at the intersection, it groaned, and the boy watched the mercantile porch vibrate in the side-view mirror.

When they got home, he took the box of groceries to the kitchen. His mama was nowhere to be seen. He slopped the hogs and searched the barnyard for eggs, looking in all the usual places—under the tool shed, in the feed trough, behind the broken stanchion, in the glove compartment of the DeSoto behind the barn. And in the hayloft.

He lay at the far end of a mountain of bales. Beside him a gray cat suckled four kittens, their purring vibrating in the heavy air. A fat blue fly buzzed lazily around the egg basket at his feet. He thought about the mercantile porch, about the girl. She asked him his name, and he told her without taking his eyes from hers. "Mason Doaks," he said. The words came easily, like rain on the river, his voice deep and resonant. She looked down at her bare feet, unable to speak. He smiled and waved the fly away and watched flecks of dust float down the sun slanting through the gable window.

Jim Hamilton

Jim Hamilton was reared on a small dairy farm near Elkland, Missouri, where he developed early a love for his native Ozarks. He developed early, too, a love for the written word. Completing his BA in Writing at Missouri State University in 1974 gained him a position as news editor of the *Bolivar Herald-Free Press.* He returned to MSU to work on his master's and began a twenty-four-year run as editor/publisher of the *Buffalo Reflex.* Jim's newspaper columns have appeared in the *Buffalo Reflex* every week for thirty-four years and in multiple newspapers for most of the last decade. In 1994 a collection of his essays, *River of Used to Be: Reflections of an Ozarks Editor,* was published by Seven Oaks Publishing Company of Conway, Arkansas. He and his wife, Martha, share a small acreage near Buffalo with three dogs, six cats, one Texas Longhorn cow, and occasional 'coons, 'possums, and armadillos.

Father's Day

Dad's been gone seven winters, since December 1, 2005.

I miss him more with every passing year. Nearly 65 as I pen these words, with kids and grandkids, I feel I'm still a boy myself.

I thought I'd be smarter by now—more able to do all the things grown-up folks are supposed to do. I'd always have the right words to say, never get flustered, never make mistakes and always have the right answer for any question asked.

Dad died, though, before my growing up was quite done; I had a lot yet to learn. Many things he tried to teach me—mostly about cattle and such—but I wasn't paying attention the first time around.

Now that time has passed, all my second and third chances gone, and the wisdom of his 79 years have fled like the morning dew.

No, I don't grieve after these seven years. I'm not sure I ever did. Dad's time had come and gone. He was at peace with leaving, so I was, too.

It does seem, though, that I spend a lot of time remembering things I wish he'd been or done, or complaining about all he left unfinished. Mom did the same before she left me, too. She griped about the money he wasted on dogs, the farm he should have bought, the house he should have built, how he was never wrong, and all the feed and hay we hauled after he was too feeble to farm.

Bellyachin' and complaining, as if any of it would do any good, about a man already gone—it was our way, I reckon, of keeping him around.

The fact is, I never minded all the hay I had to haul in his last few years. It was as close as I could come to being a kid at home on the farm again. It took me even farther back, when I was Dad's tagalong.

The oldest of four boys, I knew Dad when he was young. Most folks—and even my younger brothers to varying degrees—only knew the portly old man in overalls with a wad of tobacco in his mouth.

They never knew the young, slender dad who took me fishing on Honey Creek where we caught big black perch, or let me go with him to the Frisco freight office some nights to pick up freight.

They weren't around when he bought me 50 chickens to raise, or when he took me froggin' in water up to my chin. They didn't follow us 'coon hunting across the Jersey bull pasture the night we barely made it to the fence, or ride with us in that 1953 Mercury that just barely touched the hilltops and tickled my belly as we sped down the highway south of Nixa.

No one but Dad was around the time I was tossed about by a Marionville twister in a blue Dodge sedan, and I was the only witness to Dad's deadly throwing arm when he chucked a rock and killed a cottonmouth in Pickerel Creek.

All the places I saw or all the things we did before I started school, before any brothers were big enough to be jealous or tag along too—only Dad and I remembered those.

And I remember them now.

Funny, how as time goes by such memories still swirl around—not just in pictures, but in sound and smell, as well. I remember hearing the patter of footsteps one dark night on the wooden planks of an old steel bridge while we fished in the James River below. We never knew what it was, but a child's imagination saw a wolf, or maybe a bear.

I can still taste Dad's old pipes I pretended to smoke after he put them down. The pungent scent of Dad's old hats pulled down over my eyes and ears.

Closing my mind's eye now, I look in the mirror at gray hair and realize that boyhood for me is, like my dad, irretrievably gone.

But looking more closely in the glass I note the tilt of my cap, and for an instant see reflected a boy again, still trying to fit under his daddy's hat.

Crossing the Old Farm

Crossing our farm on a warm November afternoon, I stopped to tie my bootlace on the stump of a red oak tree at the edge of our old hay field.

That chore accomplished, I unslung the .30-.30 Marlin from my shoulder, sat on the stump with the rifle across my lap and studied the once-familiar landscape.

An earlier generation cleared the hay field of rocks, piling them in a draw. From where I sat the big red oak tree once hovered over the rock pile and cast a wide shadow on the hay field.

I remembered the day we cut it down—maybe 20 years ago. It was one of the last times I helped Dad work up a tree. He must have realized he was getting older. It was one of the few times he asked for help felling a tree.

We could've used bigger saws. Even when cut nearly through,

the old sentinel stood soldier-straight. It took every wedge we had to throw it.

I wasn't quite sure why Dad had to cut that old tree. It was gonna fall someday, I suppose; but, it wasn't rotten at all. Guess I'd forgotten how much Dad just liked to cut down big trees. With deadfall through all our woods and in every fencerow, he'd still find a green one to drop. I think he was hooked on the fragrance of fresh oak sawdust being spit from a log.

We worked up a couple of pickup loads of wood that day. Dad finished it over the next couple of weeks, leaving washtub-size chunks of log to split. I came back later to swing a splitting maul.

Evening was slipping up on me. Shouldering my .30-.30, I tried to remember the big oak as it had been when I was a boy, a red squirrel scolding me from one of its wide-spreading limbs. I walked on through patches of buck brush and clumps of multiflora rose, retracing in my mind where I'd already been.

Stealing through our little patch of woods, I'd hoped to discover a clutch of does in the sanctuary of gnarled old oaks, skeletal dead elms, buck brush and greenbrier tangles, just as my brother had a couple of deer seasons back.

I had grown up in these woods, but they seemed unfamiliar now—different from when I was a boy. The old logging road was all but gone, overgrown with brambles and hickory sprouts, blocked by fallen limbs.

The years had reduced the big post oak squirrel tree where I once shot three big reds off a single limb to little more than a naked snag, rotting traces of its former splendor scattered in the musky leaves at my feet.

I couldn't find the persimmon tree as big around as a milk can when I was a boy. Must've fallen years ago. More likely, Dad cut it down.

No rusted barbed-wire gate closed the road where the woods met the hay field, and that expanse our seasonal haying had kept manicured like a lawn was overtaken by clumps of red cedars, rose bushes and thorny honey locust trees. It was "hay field" now only in memory and name.

Once as open as a park, just over the fence Doc Rose's woods was dense with undergrowth. No matter. I don't go there now. It's not his anymore. He left years ago.

Sassafras trees border the west fence again. We cut them all when I was a boy, peeled the bark off the fragrant wood and used 'em for fence posts.

Some brush we left, though, along that fence—enough for rabbits and quails, enough to slow windblown snow. The deepest drifts on the place were always along that fence.

Just over the north fence, in the corner by the hickory tree, was the second-best blackberry patch we had. The best one was in the middle of the woods, near where a sawmill had been run long before my time.

I meandered on, through a cedar glade, where as a boy I played Tarzan in spindly persimmon trees, to a knoll where I killed my last jackrabbit many years ago.

Suddenly, stirred to the moment by a glimpse of unexpected motion in the tall goldenrods and sage grass, I was that hunter again.

Deer.

I dropped to my knees behind a rose bush. The doe was swallowed by the rusty winter weeds and grass. I inched closer, to another clump of brush. Movement—but nothing more than swatches of dun.

My quarry knew what they were doing. I did not. Like an orange prairie dog, I poked my head higher. Nothing. Then, like spectral apparitions begat of amber light and shadow, three does bounded into the cedars, white flags waving anything but surrender.

My brother's few cows had begun to move into the meadow near where the deer had hidden. The low, fertile ground where wild strawberries grow was grazed close.

When I was a boy that meadow was overgrown with persimmon and sumac sprouts. We burned a brush pile one night about where the deer had been. We often burned brush after dark.

Dad had left standing in that meadow a solitary, young redbud tree. Spring evenings, when in bloom, it looked from the barn as if the brush pile was again afire.

This winter dusk it glowed again, as warm as the sun on my back as I shouldered my rifle and headed back to the house.

Donald Harington

Donald Harington was born in Little Rock, Arkansas, on December 22, 1935. Before his death in 2009, he authored fourteen novels, among them *The Architecture of the Arkansas Ozarks, The Choiring of the Trees, Lightning Bug, With,* and his final *Enduring. Let Us Build Us a City,* an exploration of small towns in Arkansas, is nonfiction. His fiction is largely set in the imagined town of Stay More, Arkansas, its denizens fondly known as Stay Morons. A Distinguished Professor of Art History at the University of Arkansas, living in Fayetteville with his wife, Kim, Harington was the recipient of literary prizes including the Porter Prize, the Heasley Prize, and the Robert Penn Warren Award. In 1999, he was inducted into the Arkansas Writers' Hall of Fame and in 2006 was presented the Oxford American award for Lifetime Achievement in Literature. Having lost his hearing at age twelve, Harington is praised for his reproduction of vanishing Ozark folk language; he spent his boyhood Ozark summers in Drakes Creek, the village a model for his beloved Stay More.

Telling Time

One time there was a man in our town who could tell stories. Lion Judah Stapleton was his name, but everyone called him simply Lion Jude, or I thought they did, taking the nickname to refer not to his lionheart nor to the emblematic lion of Judah (Genesis 49:9) but to one of his stories involving a mountain lion. Years later, I had gone away to college and was lying in bed one night, just lying there free-associating, as one does when one can't sleep, when the memory of Lion Jude came abruptly back to me, and I suddenly realized my error: his nickname had not been Lion but Lyin' because he told such stories.

But I decided to go on remembering him as Lion Jude. Not that I wasn't willing to accept the truth that all of his stories had been lies, but because, as one does when one learns one's mistake, I preferred clinging to the original spelling and even to endowing the memory of Jude with leonine qualities to go with it: he did, after all, possess a rather long, shaggy mane of hair, was muscular in the right places, and, when lounging, as he nearly always was, he lounged with a catlike languor.

He was the only loafer on Ingledew's store porch who didn't whittle. Some said it was because he couldn't whittle and talk at the same time, but whittling didn't stop the other men from talking, not even Fent Bullen, who alone among the whittlers was actually carving something artistic. The other men just endlessly sliced their barlows across sticks of cedar, basswood or white oak, systematically covering their ankles with worthless shavings in the course of the day, but Fent Bullen employed a variety of fancy knives, some with spey blades and spear blades, to carve wooden chains, intricately linked, some links with a ball-in-cage or a slip joint, illusionistic, complicated, pleasant to the eye and fantastic to the finger. Nobody anywhere could compete with Fent in the carving of wood . . . but my story is about Lion Jude, not Fent. Nobody anywhere could compete with Lion Jude in the telling of stories. Or so we thought.

In fact—and this is a little story I sometimes tell on myself, in self-deprecation, because I was the only son of Stay More ever to attend college—until I was about nine or ten years old, and had saved enough from my little earnings picking tomatoes to buy myself a barlow and join the other whittlers on the store porch, I had the impression that a "store" is a place where "stories" are told! Oh, of course I knew that the store sold things, and practically my earliest memory is giving Miss Lola Ingledew two pennies and receiving in return a large peppermint stick, but not long after that I went out onto the store's porch and sat on the edge of it and listened to Lion Jude tell the one about the babes in the woods, which like to have scared me to death. It was a Saturday afternoon.

Years later, whenever I went to a movie on a Saturday afternoon, I remembered my first story at the store . . . and sometimes reflected, after a bad movie, that stories are much better than movies. Even today, when watching an occasional rented movie on my VCR, I prefer to play it on a Saturday afternoon. I guess I was seventeen or so, and as grown up as I'd ever get, when I heard the first truly bawdy tale from Lion Jude, the one about Cora and the Coke bottle, and realized it was a Thursday, not a Saturday, and discovered, much belatedly, that Lion Jude told his clean, wholesome, "fitten" stories, albeit however terrifying, on Saturday afternoons when younger people or children might be present, and on Thursday's the store porch was reserved only for grown men, and not even Miss Lola Ingledew herself was welcome to go out onto her own store porch.

Didn't Lion Jude ever exhaust his repertoire? Oh certainly the regulars on the store porch had heard each one of Lion Jude's many, many stories more than once, but still, whenever one of them would say, "Tell us that 'un, Jude, about that there preacher's wife and the Injun," Jude would rehash a familiar tale in such a way that his audience would roar with laughter as if they'd never heard it many times before.

With a youth's misperception of anyone over thirty as "old," I thought that Lion Jude was an old man, and thus well traveled and experienced with a long life from which he drew his tales. Actually, as someone once told me, Lion Jude had never traveled farther away from Stay More than the county seat, Jasper, a day's hike. He had a small, rocky farm somewhere on the yon side of Ingledew Mountain, and a wife and children we never saw. But he was one of us: he had Stapleton kinfolks all over creation. When I researched his background for a college project, I learned that he was the grandson of the legendary Long Jack Stapleton, a Stay More minister famous for his ability to tell Bible stories so well that his audience could actually see and hear them. Lion Jude wasn't *that* good, but he was proof that storytelling skill is hereditary.

He was poor, and it was known that Miss Lola Ingledew, the storekeeper, usually fed him, at least his noon dinner, and an occasional snack of Vienna sausages and crackers. And then, when Miss Latha Bourne bought out Bob Cluley's little mercantile store at the other end of Stay More's short main street, and even succeeded in taking the post office away from Miss Lola's store, it was rumored that Miss Lola began to give Lion Jude a "salary," in the form of Day's Work chewing tobacco and occasionally a new pair of denim overalls or even a pair of shoes from the dusty and unfrequented clothing department behind the balcony on the second floor, in order to "keep" him at her store. It wasn't known whether she had expressly forbidden him ever to sit on the porch of Miss Latha's store, but whatever, he never went there, not even to check his mailbox. Probably he never got any mail.

Thus for a long time the Ingledew store porch remained the primary gathering place for the men of Stay More, and the theater for stories. In winter, they'd just go inside the store and sit around the stove, saving the best chair, the captain's chair, for Lion Jude. As far as I know, or can remember, Miss Latha's store didn't even have one of those big potbellied stoves with a smokestack ramming itself through the roof, or a pickle barrel with a checkerboard mounted on it for the men who wanted to play games instead of, or in addition to, listening to Lion Jude's entertainments.

Now it just so happens that there was a fellow, sitting inconspicuously behind Miss Lola's stove, in winter, or at the least-traveled end of the porch in summer, places I myself preferred and was thus sitting alongside him without knowing it, a fellow by the name of Henry Tongue. He was just one of the regulars, although there were two things irregular about him, or perhaps three, if you consider that there weren't any other Tongues in Newton County: one thing was that he hardly ever spoke (which, at least for a few years until the jest grew stale, was the source of comments from the others and possibly the cat had got Tongue's tongue), and the second thing, doubtless a result of the first, was that nothing was known about him, nothing at least worth remarking upon. It was not known what he did for a living; if like nearly every other man he had a farm, nobody knew where the farm was located or how large it was. He was neither rich nor poor. He was neither young nor old, thin nor stout, tall nor short. He was neither handsome nor ugly. His whittled shavings were the same size as everybody else's. If he had any identifying quality other than his taciturnity, it was his fondness for corn liquor; whenever the stoneware demijohn jug was circulated among the men on the store porch, he seemed to bob his Adam's apple a time or two more than the other swallowers. He probably did some further imbibing on his own, wherever he went, whenever he left the store, because he seemed to be in a kind of perpetual haze of intoxication, not sodden nor even obfuscated but just piffled, tipsy, mizzled.

Nearly everybody called him Harry, not Henry, and I, just as I'd misunderstood "Lyin' Jude" to be "Lion Jude," misunderstood this as a teasing nickname, "Hairy," referring to the usual condition of his tongue, which was coated. Strangely enough, although Tongue's tongue was coated, he didn't have strong breath or bad breath, not that I can remember, but perhaps we just didn't notice it because he rarely opened his mouth.

And when he finally did begin opening his mouth, in a big way, it was not at Miss Lola's store. It was at Miss Latha's. This was after she'd finally married her childhood sweetheart, Every Dill, and thus was no longer Miss Latha Bourne but Mrs. Every Dill, or simply Miz Latha, as everyone had to begin to call her. One Thursday afternoon, while Lion Jude was trying to add some new spice to a retelling of the one about the city girl's first encounter with a cow's teats, we noticed that Harry was missing. But one of us, by squinting his eyes and shading them against the sun, pointed across the quarter of a mile separating the two general stores, and observed, "Yonder he sits." Sure enough, Harry was sitting on a sail keg (the most common store porch furniture) on the wooden porch which ran the full length of Miz Latha's storefront. He was not only sitting there, he was also talking, and accompanying his words with gestures of his hands. He was not only talking, but he also had an audience of half a dozen folks, including Miz Latha herself. We waited, speechless; even Lion Jude was paused at the point where the city girl notices the cow has *four* of them. "Sonny," Frank Murrison said to me, "why don't ye mosey over thar and see what he's up to?"

So I went. I hung around Miz Latha's store only long enough to eavesdrop and be able to return to Miss Lola's store and report to the men there. "He's a-tellin some kind of a story."

"I God!" Lion Jude swore. "You don't mean to tell me!"

"Ain't he got a nerve, though?" Fent Bullen said, but before long Fent, as well as Frank, Luther Chism, and myself, had all abandoned Miss Lola's store porch in order to, we told ourselves, measure the audacity of the upstart Mr. Henry Tongue.

We had to report back that indeed the upstart was narrating stories, and rather eloquently in view of his years as a silent listener. Lion Jude was a mild man, never betraying any excitement except when he was feigning it in the acting out of some character's temper in one of his stories. But this situation, the fact that Harry had begun telling stories on Miz Latha's porch, made Lion Jude roar like a lion. Lion Jude angrily declared his suspicion that Harry had been sitting around silently all these years just to "gather up" Jude's stock of stories, and now, having stolen Jude's material, was capitalizing on it. Probably Mrs. Latha Dill was paying him, maybe even cash money, maybe even . . . Lion Jude observed that Miz Latha, despite being such a sweet, lovely, proper, reserved lady, married now to the town's only auto mechanic, had been the subject of rumors for a long, long time before Every Dill came back into town and made an honest woman out of her. Nobody knew where she had been for the seven years she was missing from Stay More. Some folks had even suggested she might have lived in a large city supporting herself by prostitution. True or not, it was commonly known that before she disappeared she had been confined for nearly three years at the state mental hospital, and many respectable citizens of Stay More still had reason to doubt her sanity. And it was commonly known now that the pretty little redhead, Sonora, who Latha had claimed for years was her niece, was actually her illegitimate daughter. Lion Jude wasn't going to come right out and accuse Miz Latha of seducing Harry, but it stood to reason, he said, that old Harry must be getting *something* out of it.

We were constrained to have a report back to Lion Jude that Harry was not actually stealing his material, that is, the stories he was telling were not stories he had heard from Lion Jude. All of Lion Jude's stories were tales as tall as the mountains surrounding Stay More, fabulations, fairy tales without fairies. His characters were nobody anybody had ever known. His events and episodes, whether ribald or chaste, were not only fictitious but farfetched; they entertained us by permitting us to experience vicariously things which could never possibly happen to us. They further delighted us by having happy endings.

Harry's stories, it was soon noticed, were taken from "reality," whatever that is. He may have been the only Tongue in Newton County, but somehow he seemed to know the entire history of Newton and its neighboring counties, and especially of Stay More. Harry could tell legends of the Ingledew founders of Stay More, Jacob and Noah, that not even the living Ingledews themselves had ever heard, and he could take incidents that had just happened, or just been reported, and convert them into dramatic and often humorous narratives. When I was at the university, I took a course in folklore from Professor Mary Parler, and learned that such stories are called memorates: narratives of actual events, possibly events which the narrator himself has witnessed or experienced. I cannot find memorate in my unabridged dictionary, although I can find marchen, which is what Professor Parler said that Lyin' Jude's type of story is called. She was a quirky professor but an honest one. In fact, since part of the course assignment was to write a research term paper ideally based upon some aspect of one's own hometown, I wrote for Professor Parler a paper called "Telling Time" about the rivalry that developed between Stay More's two storytellers, Lyin' Jude Stapleton with his marchen and Harry Tongue with his memorates. (I might have earned a higher grade for the paper if I had not had the effrontery to include a footnote in which I observed parenthetically that my instructor's name, Parler, was the French past participle of "talk," which is what both Tongue's name and talent suggested. In her notes of criticism on my paper, Professor Parler did not comment on that; she did call my attention to the existence, in England, of a folklorist by the name of Ruth L. Tongue, who had written *Somerset Folk Lore, Further Somerset Folklore, The Chime Child,* or *Somerset Singers,* and a fine book which I now possess, *Forgotten Folktales of the English Counties.* Miss Parler wryly speculated that my Henry Tongue might be a distant kinsman, at least by marriage, of this Ruth Lyndall Tongue.)

But as far as Tongue's "payment" was concerned, Harry was not known to be receiving from Miz Latha even the "salary" that Lion Jude was getting from Miss Lola, that is, Harry was taking his noon dinner elsewhere before showing up at Miz Latha's in the afternoon, and if she was treating him to free snacks, soda pop, candy, or tobacco, nobody ever caught her at it. Since Tongue was pretty well lubricated when he told his stories, it was commonly believed that Miz Latha was keeping him well supplied with some of Luther Chism's best moonshine, Chism's Dew as it was known, but nobody ever saw her passing him a jug.

Why, then, did he betray Miss Lola Ingledew by taking business away from her store? For indeed, not very long after Harry had begun to regale the porch-sitters at Miz Latha's with his memorates, Miz Latha's business noticeably improved, and Miss Lola's noticeably declined. One by one, Lion Jude's congregation deserted him. In desperation, he himself, one memorable July afternoon, suddenly interrupted his account of the rich man's daughter and the beggar, short of the climax, and, thwarting his listeners (although they knew how it turned out), stood up, hitched up his overalls, spat a larger than customary globule of half-masticated Day's Work, and ambled slowly up the dusty road toward Miz Latha's store.

The large crowd listening to Harry tell the story of the visit of Jesse James and his gang to the Stay More gristmill of Isaac Ingledew turned their heads away from the speaker to observe, almost sheepishly, the approach of the former unchallenged master of storytelling. Harry himself suspended the great James gang on their horses as they attempted to ride up the mill porch, and let his stilled tongue lie stunned in his mouth.

Lion Jude spoke to Miz Latha, handing her a nickel. "Need me one a them sody pops." It was one of the things Miz Latha's store carried that Miss Lola's did not, since Miss Lola had never bothered with the expense of subscribing to the delivery of block ice for a soda pop cooler. Miz Latha took him into the store and let him pick his choice, a Grapette, from her cooler.

All of this was just a diversion, so that nobody would pay much attention when Lion Jude slipped back out onto the porch and tried to hide himself in the shade of the doorway, where he leaned up against the wall and drank his Grapette and listened while Harry went on with his story.

Now there was another essential difference between Jude's stories and Harry's stories apart from the one being fabulous and the other actual: it was a matter of style; Jude was a taker-outer and Harry was a putter-inner. Any story by Jude always began simply, "One time . . ." never mind the fact it might have been the thirtieth time he was telling it. I always appreciated the ambiguity of the two words or their allusion, not just to the long-ago, faraway, never-never time of the story but also to the fact that whatever plot he was narrating, whatever episode or imagined event, happened only *once*, it was unique, it would never, ever anywhere happen again.

A story by Harry, on the other hand, might begin with a variety of introductory phrases. He eschewed the customary "Once upon a time" as being not only trite but condescending to his audience. If the story he told was prompted by someone's mention of the person involved or the family involved, he might begin with, "That puts me in mind of . . ." or "Speakin of ole So-and-so . . ." but more likely something like, "Did ye know that many year ago it come to pass that . . . ?" or "Let me tell y'uns about the time that . . ."

If for instance (hypothetically, of course) each of these storytellers were given the charge to tell a story about himself, Lion Jude would have begun, "One time there was a feller who had a name for spinnin right wondrous yarns . . ." whereas Harry would have started out, "Now it happened that there was dwellin in Stay More a certain ole boy who wasn't good for nothing, but come the shank of evenin around the porch of Miz Latha's store he shore could charm the peepers down outen the trees with the masterest histories . . . ."

Lion Jude listened carefully to Harry's resumption of one of these master histories, about the James gang, and then the one about the nearly incredible Battle of Whiteley's Mill, during the Civil War, in which Newton County soldiers on opposite sides fought each other for two hours with rifle and cannon without one single battle death occurring. I watched Lion Jude out of the corner of my eye, but could not quite imagine what he was thinking. His eyes were fixed into a squint of concentration to go with the furrow of his brow. I believed he was taking a lot of mental notes, especially about Harry's methods and style, if not his subject. Surely he was studying Harry's delivery, so much in contrast to his own: Harry's inflections, his gestures, the changing tempos of his speech, even the postures of his body were so different from Jude's. Harry's were more elaborate, more conspicuous, more a part of the story itself. Lion Jude remained there until the shank of the evening had become the thigh and everybody went home for supper.

But was Lion Jude inspired by his rival to switch to the telling of memorates? No, he was not, nor was he motivated to emulate Harry's more convoluted and embellished style, nor to mimic any aspect of his delivery. To the contrary on all three accounts, he began to tell, to his diminished audience at Miss Lola's store, stories of increasing make-believe, implausibility, and unnaturalness. His delivery, already inflectionless and nongestural, became almost invisible. And his style became more spare and terse, even to the point of what modern literary critics have called minimalism. For example, one of his favorite risqué anecdotes, involving a man and a woman in a hotel room playing a drunken game of rushing naked at each other from opposite sides of the room to meet in congress in the middle, had required perhaps five minutes to tell in his original version of it, but was now reduced to less than sixty seconds of clipped short words foreshadowing the punch line, "Everybody's upstairs a-watchin the doctor try to git some woman off a doorknob." It was hard to believe that any of the incidents in Lion Jude's stories were actually capable of happening.

Strangely enough, but fortunately as far as I was concerned, Lion Jude began to win back some of his lost audience. Since I personally preferred him, I was one of the first to return to Miss Lola's store, and thereafter I "rooted" silently for Lion Jude to win the contest between the two storytellers. In my paper for Professor Parler, I attempted to analyze the reasons why Lion Jude eventually won the contest, and while Professor Parler challenged my arguments with many red-penciled notes in the margins, I think I was correct in observing some essential differences between the two, not simply that Lion Jude was always sober while Harry was drunk (which would seem paradoxically to contradict the basic nature of their stories, Harry's being soberly factual and real, Lion Jude's being intoxicatedly farfetched and fantastic), but more importantly that so many of Harry's stories had tragic endings while Lion Jude's had happy endings.

If a story had to end, people felt, perhaps knowing that Stay More itself was ending, it ought to end with a smile on its face. A story ought to end, if not with some revelation that leaves you feeling good (and I am saving a revelation for the end of *this* story), at least with some hope for oneself. Lion Jude's stories were optimistic; Harry's were pessimistic. That's what it boils down to.

Whether or not Lion Jude "won" the contest, the restoration of Lion Jude's congregation was actually more exciting than the actual numbers of listeners might have indicated, because Stay More was dying, and the people disappearing from either Miss Lola's porch or Miz Latha's porch were not doing so in favor of the rival storyteller but because they were leaving to go to California or to some larger town in Arkansas, Jasper or Harrison or Little Rock, or simply to die. Whatever, they were not staying more.

Miss Lola was wrong to blame Harry for the decline and death of the old Ingledew Store. Her store closed and was boarded up not because of the competition from Miz Latha's store but because of the competition from all the fancy stores in California and from something new in Jasper called a "supermarket." Miz Latha's own store would not last much longer before it too was shut down.

In fact, if we consider the victor to be the last one left in the field, Harry was already gone before Lion Jude told his last story to the crew of workmen whose job was to nail up boards over the doors and windows of Miss Lola's store. My research for Professor Parler's project was not successful in tracking down Tongue's ultimate whereabouts. He was known to have lived in Jasper for a while after leaving Stay More, and to have told a lot of stories there. He later moved to Harrison, the largest town in that part of the Ozarks, and there is a photograph of him holding forth to a large crowd of whittlers and loafers on the steps of the Boone County courthouse. There is an item from the *Arkansas Democrat* which names him as the second-prize winner in a state storytelling contest, and gives his residence as Little Rock. Where he went from there nobody seems to know, although one informant related that he had moved to a larger city, Memphis or New Orleans.

Now it seems to me that Tongue lost the Stay More competition for one simple reason (and Miss Parler's red handwriting at the end of my paper says, "Perhaps you are right."): although he told memorates, although everything in his stories supposedly had actually happened, although his stories were so "real" that like life itself they did not end pleasantly, he could not avoid converting all of his "ordinary" people into heroes and heroines, and thus making them extraordinary, and thus making us, hapless listeners, feel inferior to them.

To really love a story, we have to lie to ourselves, and the biggest lie we tell is a telling of time: that the *one* time of the story is our time, is *now*, for the life of the story, for the life of our listening to it, being in it. Harry Tongue took people and events and elevated them to some pantheon where we could only admire them but never be them. And all his people died and all his events ceased happening, and his time was *told*, and old, and gone.

Not so long ago, I drove back to Stay More for the first time in many years. My parents no longer live there; I have no relatives living there. The town was abandoned except for some bum living alone in the old Ingledew place that had briefly been a hotel. I didn't speak with him. Miz Latha was still living on the outskirts of town, and I visited her a little and mentioned the paper I had written for the folklore class. She smiled and told me that Jude Stapleton was still alive. She occasionally spotted him, along the banks of Banty Creek, or in her orchard meadow. Since he was always talking, she assumed that he was just talking to himself, as old people sometimes do ("As I often do," she confessed). She never spoke with him; she hadn't spoken with him since he'd bought that bottle of Grapette from her so many years ago. But she discovered that he usually had some kind of audience, in the form of birds, or an occasional rabbit or squirrel, or even insects. "You've heard of 'tellin the bees'?" Miz Latha asked me, and when I nodded, she said, "Well, he's tellin his stories to the bugs."

I searched for him that day, but couldn't find him. I knew he was there, I know he is still there yet. Harry Tongue made Stay More into a mythical place that belongs in books on shelves; Lion Jude Stapleton keeps the time of Stay More and tells the time to stay more, and be *one* time.

William Harrison

William Harrison, a Texan, is the author of nine novels, three collections of short stories, two major screenplays, and a book of essays. He was the cofounder of the program in creative writing at the University of Arkansas and still lives in Fayetteville.

Tickets to Nowhere

After he was laid off the oil rig Vernon drove out of Midland, Texas, heading home to Arkansas, but the transmission in his old Ford went out, so he sold the car for junk in Weatherford. He decided to get to the Dallas–Fort Worth airport, buy himself a ticket with his last money, fly home penniless again, and admit that his life was a beer drinking disaster. On the bus to the airport he felt like crying, especially when he passed a string of barbecue joints with their neon beer signs already ablaze.

Late that afternoon he stood in the departure lounge of a commuter airline with a ticket in his hand and forty-six cents in his jeans. He faced a dozen uniformed airline employees behind tall counters. Beyond the counters were assorted gates where small jets were scheduled for such places as Lawton, Harlingen, Wichita Falls, Fayetteville, Muskogee, and Texarkana. He dreaded flying back to Fayetteville, then hitching a ride north to his daddy's farm and another round of family lectures. Vernon was creeping up on forty years of age and looked like grit and sludge: jeans stained with oil, dirty fingernails, thinning hair, and a sweater that had been stuffed down in his toolbox too often.

Addled and tired, needing a beer, he stood on one leg then the other waiting, when he heard an announcement regarding his flight. The plane had been overbooked, so the airline was offering a $200 travel voucher and $20 airport mean ticket to anyone willing to give up his seat and take a later flight.

Vernon hurried to the appropriate counter and addressed a pretty Latin attendant, a girl with a bit of hair on her upper lip.

"That meal voucher," he began, drawling out his words more loudly than he had to. "Is it good for beer or just food?"

Ten minutes later he sat in a bar decorated with Dallas Cowboy photos and football gear. He emptied a schooner of Shiner Bock and nibbled at a shrimp cocktail. Another beer was on order from the bartender who wore a neck brace, a guy who seemed like one of the nicest persons Vernon had ever met. In fact, all the occupants of the bar seemed nice and respectable; upscale folks in suits and dresses, folks with important places to go, bankers and such. In a far corner beneath the overblown photo of a quarterback sat the only unhappy customer, a young woman with her head down, crying, without so much as a glass of water in front of her.

Vernon studied the travel voucher laid out before him.

He wondered if such a prize could be converted into actual cash money and thought, hell, I could damn near buy another used car with this amount. With such speculations, daydreams overtook him. He could drive to Mexico and work with Pemex. Find himself a nice little border cantina. Send a letter to his Baptist daddy with a hundred-dollar bill folded inside it, a partial payback.

At the appointed hour he strolled back down the concourse to the commuter gates only to learn that his next flight was now overbooked, too, and he could receive yet another $200 voucher, two more $20 meal certificates, and a free night's lodging in the swank Airport Sheraton.

Grinning and satisfied with prospects—and with a tiny buzz on—he gathered up his vouchers and certificates and returned to the Cowboy bar to celebrate.

By this time a deep twilight had settled on the airport. The planes beyond the concourse window looked wildly beautiful shinning with reflected lights. Vernon felt that as if by magic he had been transported into another social class, a cut above the cigarette butts and whanging country music of Midland's honky-tonks and the smelly oil towns of west Texas.

He wished he had a sports jacket.

The Cowboy bar was packed with a new crowd except for that sad girl who occupied the corner table. Her face was now turned to the wall, though she didn't seem to be crying. Swathed in black and wearing a ratty black turban—sort of Oriental gothic—she looked hungry, thirsty, stood up, and stranded.

He strolled over and offered her his extra $20 meal ticket.

"It's good for booze too," he assured her.

"Do I look like I need charity?"

"No, not a'tall, but what'll you have?" he persisted. "I got money for drinks and dinner on these vouchers and, well, tell you the truth, I'm celebrating. My luck turned good."

"Then I'll have a glass of red vermouth with ice," she said, and her voice was formal and uppity, sort of British, yet not.

Vernon had two more beers with her and they split a bag of potato chips. She said her name was Marbella and, yes, she was stranded, stuck in the airport for almost two days with a worthless credit card that her poet boyfriend had maxed out.

"So he's, what, a professional poet?" Vernon asked, looking into the mascara smear of her eyes.

"Nobody's a professional poet," Marbella informed him, waving a potato chip. "I mean, Wallace Stevens worked at an insurance company and T. S. Eliot was an editor at Faber and Faber. Poets have other jobs. And they're sometimes fakes and neurotics, but at their best they create images tossed up against the crush of destiny."

"That's for sure," Vernon replied, trying to be agreeable.

"For years I tried to cultivate the literary language myself," she admitted. "But now I'm older and considerably more hip and I want to get rid of it. If I ever finish my dissertation, I probably won't even teach. Because I'll crave a greater reality. I mean, a doctorate can just mire one down in the second-hand life. But one wants a reality that truly confirms itself. What's that on your jeans?"

"Right here? Grease."

"Exactly what I'm talking about. Hard reality. You're wearing it. Zero at the bone. The dirt of the real world. Did you say you have another meal voucher? Suddenly, I'm starving. And if I'm going to sleep in those god awful airport chairs tonight I need to eat."

"You don't have to sleep here in the airport," Vernon told her. "You can share a room with me at the hotel. I've got a room voucher, too."

"No sex," she said, agreeing.

"Whatever," he answered, and for a moment they gave each other a look of worldly insouciance—her look considerably more successful than his—then went off to the Big Tex Buffet Corral.

After a full meal they rode the tram to the hotel.

As they presented themselves at the registration desk, Marbella stood aside while Vernon signed in, and he was grateful because she looked a bit like a vampire, or, at best, the soloist in a rock group. On request, he showed the desk clerk his Arkansas driver's license with a photo that made him look like a convict, and the clerk sniffed at it, stamped the room voucher, and pushed a plastic key card across the marble desktop.

The room was far better than anything Vernon had ever occupied: plush golden carpets, overstuffed chairs, a 35-inch TV set, a king-sized bed, and a tiled bath with a single white terrycloth robe that Marbella quickly confiscated.

Later, draped in that robe and sitting cross-legged in the middle of the bed, drying her hair, she watched Vernon pacing the room and talking about his new idea. Her shiny brown hair looked much better than that ratty turban, and her knees, tanned and pretty, poked out of the robe.

"I know this airline and it overbooks every day and passes out them vouchers," he said, pacing. "Two years ago when I was pretty flush and headin' home for Thanksgiving they was doin' it. Anyhow, if we could figure out how to turn the vouchers into cash money we could make ourselves a fine livin' right here in the goddamned terminal. It'd be indoor work and air-conditioned. I know it'd be a hell of a lot better'n being a roustabout."

"Go on," Marbella encouraged him.

"See, we study the flights that are constantly overbooked. We sign up, never go anyplace, and collect vouchers. All we gotta do is get bumped off flights. We eat on food vouchers. They got places in this airport complex that don't even serve barbecue. Also, we figure the late flights and stay in these fancy hotels."

"You're including me in this?"

"Why, sure, between us we can make plenty if we unload them vouchers."

Inside those dark pools of mascara Marbella's eyes were wide and alert with possibilities. Meanwhile, Vernon, having no idea of the full effect of his money-making scheme, paced the room, stopped at the little mini-bar, removed another Shiner beer, and popped another cap. He touched the cold bottle to his temple so that he could think more clearly and continued to pace.

"Somebody will buy them damned vouchers," he went on. "I've seen newspaper ads. In the classified. Outfits that pay for airline vouchers and certificates."

"By god, you're an entrepreneur," Marbella said with a sigh.

"We could get rich. Take ourselves a real little holiday now and then. I'd like to see the Caribbean, wouldn't you?"

"You're a tycoon all right," she told him. "Come over here."

Vernon sat down on the bedside, taking a quick glance into the open robe. A stray thought hit him: he had assumed that the middle of this king-sized bed would be banked up with a wall of pillows but maybe it wouldn't. As he considered this, Marbella walked across the bed on her knees and began massaging his neck and shoulders.

"My dissertation is on forms of deconstruction, but not exactly," she began, working on his tight muscles. "It's more like the relationship between catastrophe theory and creativity. Not that I'm all that personally confident about psychoanalysis and literature. Far from it, God, Vernon just relax. Anyway, my therapist warned me that I could become obsessed with this idea, but, see, psychic energy can actually become systematic. So what exactly do you like to read?"

"The sports pages," Vernon sighed, giving in to her touch.

"Naturally. Game theory, sure, I should've known. Actually, that might be helpful in defining the catastrophe of creative origins. Let's see, help me, I'm looking for the right metaphor here, but what I want to say, actually, is how destruction is a primitive form of possession."

"Like offense and defense," Vernon offered, thinking of football.

"Exactly! That's wonderful, yes! Oh, God, Vernon, you have such a deep basic instinct for life! Here kiss me."

Their kiss, long and wet, resulted in the robe falling away, their bodies entwined, and her breathless confession.

"Vernon, Sweet, my name's not really Marbella," she told him as they ended the kiss. "It's actually Bobbie Rae Smith."

"Well, sure, okay," he managed, nuzzling close.

"Marbella is a Spanish island," she informed him.

"Hell," he replied, "don't worry about it."

By evening of the following day they had collected six travel vouchers, an equal number of meal certificates, and hotel accommodations for two. No longer encased in her conspicuous mascara, turban, and gothic black, Bobbie Rae wore her current disguise: reading glasses, a beret, and a long Picasso scarf. Although Vernon felt euphoric and slightly tipsy from all his beer breaks, he still worried about how to convert their treasures into real cash.

As they sat in the Wrangler Bar pondering this, each of them preoccupied with just how much in love the other might be, a large black man slid into a chair at their table. They assumed he was just another traveler in the crowded room, so lowered their voices and continued their business.

"I wish we could keep a hotel room all day, so I could change into my different clothes," Bobbie Rae complained. "Coin lockers and the ladies room are a hassle."

"We got a few kinks in our workday," Vernon agreed.

"How true," added the black man, leaning back and grinning. "Like that wad of vouchers stuffed down in her handbag."

"I beg your pardon," said Bobbie Rae in her most arch and formal accent.

"I've enjoyed watchin' you two," the black man went on, grinning.

In the breathless pause that followed he opened his wallet and showed them a shiny badge: Airport Security. Both Bobbie Rae and Vernon now raised their eyes to the blue name tag pinned on the man's lapel, a tag that bore a single name: McCreedy. From that they lifted their gaze toward his seemingly malevolent smile.

"Now just lookee here," Vernon told him, braving it out. "We just like to travel places. No harm in that. Or in collectin' ourselves some vouchers."

"If you plan to travel," McCreedy answered, grinning, "you might decide which direction you aim to go. So far today you've bought tickets to Muskogee, Brownsville, Memphis, and El Paso. As I see it, that's north, south, east and west."

"We're saving up for a trip to Budapest," Bobbie Rae put in, her voice achieving a truly regal accent.

"Now don't get smart. You haven't done anything illegal and I don't aim to arrest you."

"Then it's no business of yours," Vernon added, sensing a small advantage.

"No, at the moment it ain't. But if you intend to unload them vouchers I can always offer my humble services."

"We don't need no partner," Vernon said, although he was now sure that they already had one.

"You can peddle the vouchers to a couple of agencies here in Dallas, but they'll take fifty percent or more of face value," McCreedy confided. "I can get us a much better deal. My take will be fifty bucks per voucher and a daily meal certificate."

"You are a crooked cop," Bobbie Rae said slowly, failing to keep the admiration out of her voice.

"Trust no other kind," McCreedy replied.

As it turned out, McCreedy had three kids, a wife with a bad back, and a night job standing guard over nine acres of discarded automobile tires. He explained that he had to get rid of that extra night work.

"My nerves are all frayed and I'm listless all day here at the airport," he said, leveling with them. "I'm crazy with too much coffee and my sleep patterns are shot. Also, it's humiliating protecting a goddamned mound of worn-out tires that nobody would ever steal."

"You poor thing," Bobbie Rae told him, and Vernon couldn't tell if a little sarcasm leaked into her tone or not.

Over a second round of coffee, beer, and red vermouth they struck a deal on the vouchers.

The scheme had flaws—a few times they didn't get bumped as expected, so ended up with paid tickets—but they kept at it for ten days. McCreedy's wife donated clothes, so that Bobbie Rae could keep up her disguises and Vernon became attached to a cubbyhole bar called Sagebrush Junction that served frozen pints of his favorite Shiner Bock.

They worked steady and made fair money, although Bobbie Rae had a few criticisms. "You trying to get a master's degree in beer drinking?" she asked. When she turned sassy like that, Vernon actually adored her. Sometimes she went off into the concept zone, talking absolute nonsense, but her angelic and wildly serious expressions on such occasions also won his heart. Although the deceits and gambles of the day were exciting, he now lived for the nights. He found himself crash landing into love: a real flame out, a tailspin.

After a few more hard days in the commuter lounge, though, Bobbie Rae became even more petulant. One night she even criticized his lovemaking techniques.

"Vernon, it is the end of the twentieth century, you know, and the female clit—like all major continents—has been discovered."

"Yes'm," he said, and went about his duties.

In calmer moments he decided that Bobbie Rae's attitude, after all, was just what he needed. He could count on her, he figured, to take care of checkbooks, bills, business matters that he didn't have a knack for. Like having a pet bulldog: a confrontive soul mate who'd face down the phone company, the tax man, and maybe even his hard-nosed daddy.

One night, sprawled out beside her in the fever of afterglow, he said, "Bobbie Rae, I want you to meet my family up in Arkansas."

"No way," she answered sleepily. "I'm not good with families."

Afterward, he gazed at the ceiling wondering why he'd said such a goofy thing. Did he want to marry her? Was he overcommitted? Or did he just want to turn Bobbie Rae loose on his daddy? With that last thought he grinned, closed his eyes, and soon fell asleep.

The next morning, McCreedy paid them several hundred dollars, but issued them a warning.

"Somebody might be onto us," he told them. "Might be good if you two knocked off for a few days."

"C'mon, we need to keep at it," Vernon complained. "What makes you suspicious?"

"This guy at the airline says they might stop giving out vouchers because they're worried about abuse. He didn't mention anybody in particular, but I'm frettin' over why he said this to me."

Vernon suggested to Bobbie Rae that they might fly down to Laredo and cross over into Mexico for a couple of days, but she just sniffed at the idea. "We just saw our first money," she argued. "We don't need some shoddy low-rent holiday." Her voice did that thing again: shoddy sounded as if it had been dropped by a duchess.

For another day, then, they tried to figure out the overbooked flights, succeeded in getting bumped, and collected. During the lulls Vernon sat on a stool at Sagebrush Junction talking to a salesman about an old idea of his: Popsicles flavored with gin, beer, bourbon, or rum. It was his favorite beer joint topic of conversation and he was explaining his marketing ideas when he happened to glance out at the concourse to see Bobbie Rae talking to a long-haired guy who had an acoustic guitar strapped to his backside. Somehow Vernon immediately knew: the poet was back.

Vernon took a deep breath, gathered himself, and casually strolled out to introduce himself. When he extended his hand the guy just kept talking to Bobbie Rae, ignoring him, and he was a snotty type, clearly, who had taught Bobbie Rae all her phony accents.

Vernon persisted, interrupting once more.

"Yeah, just a minute," the poet told him, and continued his long explanation and apology, asserting that he had looked everywhere for Bobbie Rae and that the credit card was actually good, so that it annoyed Vernon that she would stand there listening to all this.

"You know that's a by god lie," Vernon told the poet, hoping that the guy might throw a punch.

"Marbella, just go over to that newsstand," said the poet. "Go over there and charge something on the card. You'll see that I'm telling the truth."

"He's bluffin'," Vernon persisted.

"Do you mind?" the poet asked in a voice that sounded faintly French.

"Vernon, please, just let us alone for a minute," she asked.

Disgusted with both of them and mad at himself for caring, Vernon turned and stalked back to the bar, where the drunken salesman seemed eager to discuss Popsicles flavored with booze. Vernon's hands shook with anger and he hated his drawl: a hick voice with a twang like everyone else's on the rigs. With elocution lessons, he felt, he could've been district supervisor of something.

In their hotel scarcely an hour later Vernon saw all the bad signs: Bobbie Rae had returned to gothic black, wouldn't talk about the poet, and wouldn't go out to dinner.

"C'mon, Bobbie Rae, I was thinkin' about that fancy restaurant over at the Marriott. White tablecloths and wine. How about it?"

"Will you please call me Marbella?" she replied, not looking at him. "I've been trying to get away from Bobbie Rae all my life."

"Okay then, Marbella, are you going back to that poet or what?"

"I don't know."

"Well, see, I'm pretty much in love with you, whatever your name is. And there, I've said it out loud."

"Pretty much? Is that quite a lot by your definition?"

"It's a whole hell of a lot for any roustabout and for me especially," he said, and he broke into laughter at his own clever down-home wit.

"Then that forces me to tell you, Vernon, that roustabouts are the sort of men I've been avoiding all of my life, too! Also, bricklayers, dry wallers, mechanics, city workers, truck drivers, and janitors!"

He hated that they argued, but came back with, "See here, then, musicians are the worst! And that ain't no fancy poet! He's just another deadbeat guitar pickin' asshole sonavabitch as anyone can plainly see!"

"He's a fine folk singer," she put in defensively, and seemed on the verge of tears.

"Besides, a roustabout saved your pretty butt just a short time ago! Or don't you recall that you was sleepin' out on the concourse with not a single meal certificate to your name?"

By this time she was packing. Disappointment overwhelmed him, yet he blamed himself; once again his confession of love arrived as the object of his affection banged out the door. And he felt the finality of it like a sudden and unexpected slap. Say nothing, he warned himself; stay cool and keep your self-respect.

Yet he asked, "You got someplace to go?"

"I'll manage."

"Then that means you won't be here at the commuter airline counters tomorrow?"

"You bet I won't," she said sharply.

He watched her toss clothing into her bag, including some of McCreedy's wife's things. He wanted to bite down on his lip and keep his silence, but it all hurt too much.

"No kiss, then, and no fare thee wells?"

"Vernon, I just don't feel like any of that."

"Bein' mad at me is something you've had to invent," he said evenly, as if he were analyzing the catastrophe from a great distance. "Because I ain't done nothin' wrong, Bobbie Rae, and you can't say otherwise. You've just worked up this mad so's you can leave."

She was crying now, but scooping her heavy bag and struggling to the door.

"I'll look for you in the airport in case you get stuck here again," he called after her, but his pathetic words of bitter good will were spoken to the closed door.

Andrea Hollander

Andrea Hollander was born in Berlin, Germany, the child of American parents stationed overseas after World War II, and raised in the United States. In 1977 she moved to Mountain View, Arkansas, where she and her husband built their own house, raised their son, Brooke, started a natural foods store, and ran a bed-and-breakfast. (They divorced in 2011.) In 1991 Hollander became the Writer-in-Residence at Lyon College, and in 1993 she won the Nicholas Roerich Prize for her first poetry collection, *House Without a Dreamer.* Other honors include the D. H. Lawrence Fellowship, the *Runes* Award, a Pushcart Prize for memoir, two fellowships from the National Endowment for the Arts, and two from the Arkansas Arts Council. Her other books are *The Other Life*, *Woman in the Painting*, and *Landscape with Female Figure: New & Selected Poems, 1982–2012.*

Finches or Sparrows

First the wheezing wind, and then I saw them,
hundreds it seemed, yellow and brown
and yellow-brown. I wondered how they knew
to fly in such parallel lines and so fast and
together simultaneously from the shaking hickory
the wind had disturbed, straight out from the tree

so fast I couldn't tell which they were, finches
or sparrows. Then the wind hesitated
for a moment the way in that final bed
my mother seemed to, her chest still, breath
suddenly gone for a moment, but actually
held in—savored, I thought later—
the way her body had tried to hold me
a little longer, the cord that had kept me
alive now wrapped around my throat,
pulling me back the way all those years later
I wanted to pull her back. And now, outside,
the wind wheezing again like her breath
escaping from her chest. There was nothing
I could do to make her keep it, those birds—
finches, sparrows—moving so fast
I could not tell which. Then the wheezing
stopped, the wild, invisible gods released them,
and I saw I had been mistaken: All at once
they dropped, fluttering to the ground,
nothing but leaves, yellow and brown.

Large Boulder Above Honey River

If you look closely: a tiny crack
in the stone that to an ant must seem
a chasm. Closer, you see a procession
of scurrying insects smaller than ants.

Think of winters there. Think
of their intricate dwellings,

their roads impossible to detect,
tunnels thin as hairs

weaving into their deep cities
of blackness where the roots
of this old sycamore help
to open the earth. The river

isn't really a river but a creek
my grown son named as a boy.
The name stuck. Ever since the ice storm,
I don't come much. Too many

toppled trees, the difficult climb
down from the cliff. Thick
tangles of briar. Snakes.
But today I've come anyway.

In part for memory, in part
to listen again,
to experience something
humans didn't make or say.

A hawk hovers for a moment
on the other side, then rises
and circles away. A single branch
of the sycamore shivers above me,

likely a squirrel I cannot see.
Then for a moment, nothing—
no movement, no sound. This far
from the house, no news to read about,

no radio to turn off. No terrorists. No wars.

November

When a young, tailored woman walks into the old
general store on Peabody, the old men forever
gathered by the potbelly stop jabbering

long enough to take her in. And even though
they go on with their mouths
full of autumn talk (deer stands and guns,

the finished cattle guard), with their eyes
they take a quick shot of her, each man
pressing it away, the way all year he keeps

the odor of morning up in the stand,
the taste of outdoor coffee,
the first trace of sunlight shivering

onto the mottled Ozark ground, even the slight
snapping sound behind him in the tree
when a squirrel lifts to a higher limb.

Then—just picture it—a buck, perfect
in the clearing, but staring up at the stand
and into the man's eyes as if he were

someone it knew, his rifle at rest
against his cooler, the rest of the story
embellished now among his friends,

like the story he'll tell himself in bed tonight
about the way the woman looked
at him, nodded her head, the subtle way

he understood what she wanted.

Ice Storm

Along our narrow road the row of giant oaks,
parade of sassafras that turned so richly red last fall,
the slender hickory, redbud, dogwood—
all have bent their heads nearly to the ground.
And half our poles have snapped in half, collapsed
across fence rails, crushed bushes,
bringing with them electrical and phone wire,
now stretched and split, some of it
tangled in the branches of fallen trees
or caught in briar and lying dangerously alive
across the roadway and footpath.

But when the sun comes out to survey
the destruction, moving in close enough
to inspect the broken forest we call home
and thereby warms everything in sight—
crystal sheaths around each branch
of each tree, each glazed shrub,
each stalk of spent weed, the forgotten
leash beside the plastic trash can,

we'll watch from our kitchen window
as ice begins to crack, loosen, unsheathe itself,
slip from limbs, shatter to the ground
sounding like a series of small explosions
as it collapses beneath hunched trunks
and bent branches into shining piles
of tiny silver splinters brilliant as diamonds
that cover the forest floor.

And as the afternoon weans, the thinned ice
will recede, thaw, melt. We've seen it all

before. Water will drip from branches
and roof edge, stream beneath the crust
still masking the footpath.
It will pool, settle, seep,

until the whole forest
that all day drooped as if forsaken
in the ruined December light
nevertheless begins its resurrection.

Art Homer

Art Homer was born in Ellington, Missouri. His memoir, *The Drownt Boy: An Ozark Tale* (University of Missouri Press, 1994) details his early life in the region, and a return as an adult for a canoe trip on the Current River. Published as a finalist in the Associated Writing Programs Creative Nonfiction Award series, the book was the basis for his receipt of a National Endowment for the Arts Fellowship. Recent work in *Elder Mountain: A Journal of Ozarks Studies*, and his five books of poetry, most recently *Blind Uncle Night* (WordTech Communications, 2012), and elsewhere draws deeply upon his Ozark heritage. He has taught at the University of Nebraska at Omaha for thirty years.

A Discussion in the Woods

Ralph & Sarah

"I'm glad we did it, though," says Uncle Ralph, looking tired at the memory of the work. "You've got to have a good strong fence." Ralph is 72.

I'm staying with my Aunt Sarah Lois and Uncle Ralph while I chase around Shannon and Reynolds Counties, visiting old family home sites, graveyards, and looking for a controversial band of wild horses.

Sarah, Ralph and Ralph's late brother invoked a little-known Missouri law allowing interested citizens to create a trust fund and turn it over to the county to pay for upkeep of the graveyard where his family is buried. Clearing brush, installing a small pavilion so services can be held on site, and fencing the area has fallen to Ralph and whomsoever he can hire or get to volunteer. The local hills are rocky, cherty peneplain, given to frost heave and erosion. Ralph has just finished telling me how they set lengths of telephone pole for corner posts.

"Why such a strong fence?" I ask.

"People are dying to get in."

Sarah feigns disgust, laughs.

Older than the oldest punch line, these hills are a good place to look for history and minerals. Thirty or more years ago ASARCO and Doe Run mining companies found 90% of the U.S. lead reserves here, the Viburnum Trend—a 12-mile-wide strip of lead mines running 60 miles north and south—creating a boom in the local economy, and concern about the environmental costs to the groundwater underlying the Jacks Fork and Current Scenic Riverway.

Early the previous morning, on my way to visit Floyd Sutterfield, a family friend, I crossed Logan Creek in whose waters I was baptized forty-five years ago as the congregation stood on the bank and prayed. The creek seemed to be running clear close to one of ASARCO's largest operations.

Floyd & Marge

Floyd's house is set at the junction of Adair and Logan Creeks, on part of the family farm he bought back after retiring from a career in real estate.

He and Marge restored the saltbox house and the grounds. Past Floyd's new 4-wheel-drive pickup and a late model Coupe De Ville sits an old military 4-wheel drive—3/4 ton suspension at least—that he uses for rough work as he builds fences for other landowners.

Inside, ". . . we tore out all of the back part. This is all new. The original home is up front, and there was an old shed kitchen on here. And your dad has eaten right here in this home many times. He used to come here with Mr. Homer. Mr. Alfred Homer worked a lot for my dad. And we used to come right here and eat and so you've come full circle with where your family's been today. . . ."

"Yes," I say. "Yes I have."

Floyd has moved on to the kitchen. "We have a meat block here, Art, that belonged to old Uncle Newt Anderson from up here by the Stall Hollow. We bought that at his dispersal sale, and that's over 100 years old."

Single or childless adults middle aged or older are "uncle" or "aunt."

The house has exposed beams of native wood, and the original yellow pine siding, which Floyd and Marge removed by hand, reversed plank by plank, and reattached.

Marge worries that I'm dragging Floyd off into the rugged country where the wild horses hide. "With all the rain we've had, though, those creeks are all up over there . . ." but Floyd says no, "not where we're going, Honey."

Before we leave, we pause outside at what Floyd calls the "Neighborhood Wall" composed of hearthstones, foundation stones, well-top covers, and doorsteps from the cabins that once dwelt in the Logan Creek Valley, brought here in the old truck.

"And this was old Uncle Dan Hill's hearthstone in front of his fireplace. That's cracked right there, but that's one big stone. Here was a well-cover, half of it—wish I could've found the other half—from a dug well. Someone chiseled that out." Floyd points out the ribbed sandstone, formed by ripples in an ancient sea.

As we pull out onto the road heading south, Floyd points to a pasture rising up the hill across the road. "Your grandfather. . . . You see that yellow truck up on the hill?"

I nod.

"One year he was hauling a load of fodder for my dad out of the field up to the barn. Fodder is real slick, the stalks are, and when he got up to just about where that yellow truck is that whole load slid off the wagon. And it threw that poor old man about thirty, forty feet right out into the field. It skinned him up pretty bad, but he got up and reloaded it and took it on up to the barn."

He was Floyd's present age, maybe younger.

Between his land and his son's, Floyd points out an emerald green mound with small yellow flowers amidst the paler green of the sown field.

"I dug many an Indian artifact out of that when I was a kid."

"What's in a mound like that, a burial?"

"Well some were. Others they just lived on to get up off a swamp area."

Adair creek has been within feet of Floyd's door within the past week.

"This is a valley where your family knew everyone—like we do now," says Floyd.

New, tight fences cross the bottomland. "Since we've been down here, Art, the last 10 or 11 years I rebuilt all these fences. They were all a shambles and I've built them all new. I've enjoyed it."

At the end of a long drive a house sits amongst trees and next to Joe Beck Spring, named for Floyd's great-grandfather and now part of the two-acre property of "Bob Goggins, who would have been a neighbor to your folks . . . a good neighbor and does leatherwork in this old home that used to be my great-grandfather's home—beautiful spring."

And it is, flowing up from a low spot with a springhouse and off into a nice brook which is obviously steady year-round.

"When we were kids, now—your dad and your Aunt Sarah Lois and we all spent many an hour there on Sundays. That was quite a favorite gathering place for youngsters."

Thinking of the ground water, I mention that the ASARCO lead refining plant in Omaha has closed, and wonder about local attitudes toward the mining companies.

"There's some mixed feelings, Art. For the most part people appreciate them for the payroll they bring into the community. There's been some controversy over the stream damage, and I had a meeting with them just last week over air pollution. They have about 150 acres of dry lime bed up there that, in windy season, made it unbearable. We have these problems that we work with them on. I'd say for the most part they're appreciated."

Sweetwater Valley

We're pulling up a gravel road to a gravel parking lot with several late model cars in it, an entry booth, a fence, several metal structures. "This right here, Art, is one of their most active mines. They say if

8% of all the ore they take out of the ground is lead or zinc or copper it's profitable. Two years ago they struck a 33% vein of ore."

"This is the flotation mill right here," of a steel building that seems to have a round tank incorporated into it. "They float it out just like flour."

"So they crush it then?"

"Yes. It comes out as huge stones. That's the crusher plant over there. It's floated over in a smaller form into this building where it's further refined down to a dust, and they send the lead this way and the sludge—crushed up limestone—that way. They've dammed the Adair Valley. They have about three or four hundred acres under water up there now."

"See those vapors?" He points to a mineshaft with the large wheels of an elevator turning slowly and a cloud rising from it. "That's going down 1600 feet."

My U.S. Geological Survey maps mark the highest ridges here at about twelve hundred feet. Floyd, who has taken several tours of the mines, reports that they do go below sea level, stay at a constant 57 or 58 degrees, and house machine shops, canteens, and miles of railroad line.

The mine road crosses a ridge into the Sweetwater Valley. Floyd points to a bit of masonry which is the front doorstep of the Sweetwater School where "50 to 60 kids went to school every year," one of 59 country schools in Reynolds County until the late 50s, shortly after my last year there in second grade at nearby Corridon-Reynolds school.

"What've we got up here?" I interrupt. At a wet, flooded section of road two hounds are running around a large pool and one turns so quickly it slips on the muddy edge and falls, but is soon up and after the other one, a large muddy patch marring its calico haunch.

"Dogs running a deer," says Floyd, pointing at the heart-shaped tracks smeared around the pool. "The deer got in the water to throw them off. They'll lose five minutes."

At the creek bottom, a side-track leads up to the cemetery. A wash of rubble crosses the road above the gravel ford that is the only way to cross the stream. Floyd crossed here days before, and I know Ralph and Sarah Lois have been here recently, all people in their seventies, still crossing fords to get to the cemetery on Decoration Day as it is still called in these parts.

Floyd drops into four-wheel drive, glad, he tells me, not to have to get out and lock the front hubs, or as his father would have done, lead a team of mules across. But if necessary, I know, he'd be able to do it, just as my grandfather could blacksmith well into his seventies.

"Good thing I didn't bring the Cadillac," says Floyd as gravel rasps along the undercarriage. "Marge would never forgive us."

"Young fellow from St. Louis came down here and bought the old Tripp home place right here on the bank. I thought he was building a barn but it turned out to be a house. No other family lives in this valley."

I wonder aloud if they have access from a county road on the other side.

"No, this is it. This is Hominy Creek; this valley comes off of Sweetwater."

"Nice hideaway." I'm envious.

We soon come to the Sweetwater Cemetery where my Uncle Ralph's brother was recently buried. I didn't know him, but Floyd still speaks of him in present tense.

"He's older than Ralph."

In Loving Memory

". . . and this is where he wanted to be," says Floyd speaking of Ralph's brother, also named Floyd. "When I was a little kid, Art, these little valleys had two-room houses in about every little side hollow. A lot of people lived here. Then World War II came along and there was a mass exodus out of this country for the city. Now they're coming back."

I am not sure if he is speaking of those who are in the grave yard, those like himself and Marge and Sarah and Ralph who come back to retire, those like me who come back for family history, or the newcomers.

We've pulled up to a fenced clearing in the forest. Trees and saplings are cleared back from the fence. Inside, grass grows sparse as the hair on a man's arm in the cherty soil.

I read aloud the bronze plaque Ralph's brother willed the cemetery:

> In memory of great grandma, Margaret Cox Conway, great grandpa Major Conway, grandma Elizabeth Alzaida Cox-Tripp, grandfather Alfred Nichols (Bud) Tripp
>
> —Loving grandson 1996.

The two brothers raised the funds to replace all the stones in this cemetery. The homemade markers having been illegible for many years, their mother had marked in all the names on a plat of the cemetery. Ralph painted markers every few years to keep track of the graves.

Floyd says, "If he's looking for piece & quiet. . . ."

Names & Numbers

Floyd wants to show me Polk Cemetery, the graves of a woman and many of the children born to her in her 37 years of childbearing, most born dead or a few days old at birth. "A Radford," Floyd tells me. "And in later years she said, 'I know the names of every one of those babies, and I'm going to put stones in there for their graves.' And she did. And she left a trust fund, for flowers to be bought after her death and just the other day, Albert Radford and his wife brought flowers for every one of those graves."

Which story brings us back to the ford above Blair's Creek, "unquestionably the most rugged, godforsaken land in Missouri," according to Floyd and my contour maps, "and that's where the horses are at—rattlesnake country. . . . There's lots of horses, harmless really. They don't bother anything."

"How long since this was free range?"

"They closed free range in the 60s, over 30 years now," says Floyd, eyeing the crossing and downshifting. "Now there's a Tripp—buried up there in the cemetery—a man shot him." As we return across the ford, Floyd tells how three men "got into a discussion out in the woods."

"He and another fellow were making liquor—and drinking it—and Bob Ferguson was riding a horse, cruising for timber. He came upon Oether and his friend. Oether picked a fuss with Bob and started to chop Bob off his horse with his ax, and Bob had to shoot him three times to kill him. He's buried up here in Polk Cemetery."

At the church next to Polk Cemetery, I sit under the shade of an eastern red cedar and wait for my head to stop spinning with names. The wooden church and the cedar are each 100 years old. The retaining wall around it is another neighborhood wall of Floyd's design, built of the hearthstones and doorsteps of more former neighbors.

"Walter Arl & I built that," Floyd says in passing, and it is time to move on. "Now this old lady—I'm gonna show you a date—she's born in 1867, died in 1948." The stone reads Edith Radford. "She married my grandfather's first cousin: Uncle Buddy."

I'm counting on my fingers: 67, 48 . . . she was 81 when she died.

"Now Radfords and Homers were good friends; they visited back and forth all the time. This Edith was one of their daughters who lived to be an old person and she's the one who bought all these stones right here. Let's go down here and I'll show you."

We approach the area he wants to show me, and he points to an old stone. "This baby was born in 1885. Now remember her birth date of 1867; she'd have been about eighteen years old. Then she had twins, Mark & Mary, both born August 8. Mark died at birth, and she lived a couple of months. "One two three. . . . This is not one of the children, and this. . . . Then she had two more children in 1900. Now this is 15 years later. Again, the boy died at birth and the girl lived a little time."

Pearl Ethel.

"Then in 1903, she had this baby, lived a couple months. Notice the little flowers from the trust fund that lady left. Then she had two children they didn't even name. We're getting to thirty years."

Further along, "This is her grandchild here, that was her daughter's."

I'm still counting. She's forty-eight and burying a grandchild.

"This was her last baby—1922. Twenty-two and fifteen; that's thirty-seven years." Fifty-five when she bore her last child.

I'm still trying to remember the dates on the grandchild's stone when we come upon recent stones.

"This woman right here—Edith, that your parents knew—was

a sister to all these kids here, and this woman here," he points to the second stone, "was a sister. That Doyle," a grandchild buried between the aunts and uncles he could never have known, "was her baby."

We are at the end of the row of stones and walk uphill toward the gate, the church, and the cedar as Floyd finishes the younger Edith's story. "She lived to be about 30 and she died trying to deliver a 17-pound baby. She'd had one or two children. That was in the days when doctors didn't give much care at all in childbirth . . ."—the days of my parents' and Floyd's youth, nearly unchanged when my mother bore two sons here.

"But isn't this a beautiful view of this valley?" Floyd seems buoyed by our outing, though he is fighting a cold.

A man is filling a grave near the side of the cemetery, where one of the local landowners has willed an acre or so for expansion.

"One of the Arl girls lost her husband here a few days ago."

The clayey dirt and gravel the man shovels into the ground is red. We come upon the large black headstone of Floyd's father.

"He told me 'If you're here and I'm not, don't ever get me a red granite stone. I don't like red granite.' So, we sent to Georgia and got this black granite. And I think he'd have been pleased. The stone weighs 7000 pounds with the base. My mother and dad were both born in this same little valley down here two or three miles from here. We buried him in 1984."

Floyd points out the new work on the church—some stones added to the foundation to square up the corners. "This would have been the kind of job Alfred Homer would have been great at. He had a knack for that sort of thing."

Inside the church, the sepia tones and grays of older photos give way to color snapshots from recent Decoration Days and many funerals. Floyd and other local residents have collected the photos and the names of the generations of members of the Polk Church & Sunday school, among them, B. F. Sutterfield, and one Marcus Radford, one of the surviving children of Edith. Earlier in the century, there was a trend in naming women after states—Iowa Tripp or Arizona Anderson. Men, as elsewhere at that period, are named for historical figures—Benjamin Franklin, William Pierce.

Crossfire

On the way to the area of my family's former ridge land farm, we pass abandoned farms, closed stores, small frame houses with asphalt siding and cars in the yard. Soon, we are on Corridon's Main Street, a gravel road with brush and trees where a bustling community once prospered alongside a logging company rail line.

The ruins of two public buildings still stand—the small general store, once redolent with harness leather and oiled floor, and the Corridon-Reynolds Church, supported by saplings grown through the walls. The church would certainly have collapsed by now were the bell not long gone from the steeple—stolen for the metal.

Inside the church, a large, cobbled-together table stands in lieu of pulpit, gathering light on its surface. The pot-bellied stove is gone, as is the pail of well water with dipper that sat on a table in the foyer, sweating in the heat of summer. The single room is dark now, half of the windows boarded over, the rest blocked by trees, diffuse light from thin overcast leaking through holes in the roof. The pews are gone, the fans in the hands of women, the women in their print dresses and hats—gone.

From one window behind the pulpit, I can see Floyd across from me, peering around a tree trunk into the gloom.

"There's an old piano in there," he says.

Pushing myself up on a sill soft with dry rot, I can see the black, full-sized upright with raised trim, very likely the piano my mother once played, reluctantly, caught in the crossfire between the music written in the hymnal, and the local ear for gospel.

Did He Own a Milk Cow?

On the way down the county road that follows the track of the old rail line, Floyd tells me the name of the family that now owns the site of my grandparents' house—long since lost to fire: Maclaren? Maness? Mann? They have built a new house there, and forest has replaced the lawn. We pull in, greeted by kids and dogs, by Mr. M, a sandy-haired, bearded man, and several of his friends. A dune buggy with a sturdy roll cage is pulled up on one side of the turn-around.

The men seem to have been working on it, though they don't seem to have any particular focus at the moment. They have walked over to the truck and look expectantly at us as we get out.

Floyd introduces himself and is explaining that his friend wants to look around at what used to be the house that his granddad built with his own hands when the landowner speaks suddenly.

"I don't know you," he says, looking at Floyd.

These guys look like they could be some rough boys if they put their minds to it. The implication seems clear to me: if he doesn't know Floyd, he sure as *hell* doesn't know me. I'm thinking of Floyd's "discussion in the woods."

The roughest-looking, most rawboned of the group—a dark-haired man in his early twenties who would be handsome were his jaw line symmetrical—speaks up.

"I know him," he says. "My family's known him as long as I can remember."

"You one of the Radfords?" says Floyd, squinting.

It turns out that he is, though he has not seen Floyd since he was "about the size of this fellow here," says Floyd, pointing to one of the kids, who cuts a caper in the leaf duff of the yard at the notice.

"I guess it couldn't hurt any to look around," says Mr. M gruffly, as if to remind everyone that this old home week is happening on his property, after all.

There is little to see. The house, as I know from previous trips down this road, burned down at least twenty years ago. The foundation and parts of the chimney stood fifteen years ago. All that remains is a ten-foot section of foundation, a stone wall, much of which was originally out of sight behind the back door steps of the original building, for the mortar held none of the decorative pointing that graced the visible sections of stonework.

Mr. M's interest in masonry and ancient history is slight. He says his father built the new house. We cross the road to where my grandparents' fields and barn once lay, now the home and business of a sawyer, his mill running off the PTO of a large Farmall. No barn remains. The owner takes a break, idling his daughter and son-in-law *qua* mill hands, to shake my hand and answer some questions about the land, site of my grandparents' first house on the property, the house that was there when they bought it, and that they lived in until my grandfather could build "the big house" across the road.

"A real old couple was down here to see the old house site. She said she'd lived there as a girl. It ain't nothing there but I told 'em to go ahead. When I got a chance, I come back to talk to them, but they was already gone. Guess they'd seen enough."

On the way out, Floyd points out the handiwork of the mill owner's house, many additions, some made of trailers, and an arrangement of stovepipes that defies logic—as Floyd dryly remarks, "a handy man with a welder."

A mile and a half down the road is the cabin site where I lived as a child. The log cabin my father built, I understand, is long gone. As we park at the big metal stock gate, double wrapped with chain and padlocked, Floyd suddenly remembers. "I sold this place. It was years later, but I had no idea this was the place your folks lived. It always seemed like a perfect hideaway, back here in the woods."

My parents received six hundred dollars for it.

It's about a half-mile walk through the forest that has reclaimed the two grazing pastures and the orchard of our former neighbors, the Vales. The new owners remain unknown to the neighbors, evidently summer people who seldom use the place. When we reach the cabin site, little is changed. A 40-foot trailer and a solidly built playhouse on stilts have replaced the cabin. Where our chicken coup sat is a large shed, inside which, we can see by peeking through the padlocked double doors, is a riding mower and a fifteen-year-old Japanese pickup. Something churns up the oak leaves littering the ground and I bend to pick up a box turtle with curiously asymmetrical cleft in its carapace.

The brush has been cleared from beneath the power lines since the last time I checked the property from the road. In the draw that separates the yard and the road a quarter mile away, there was once a pond. The USGS maps, updated by aerial photography in 1987, still show it. A spider web plasters my mouth and I splutter as I walk along the draw looking for the pond, remembering the cool shade, the moss and rafts of frog eggs.

"Oh, I was a little bit off," I say as I see the rock and gravel containment dam.

Floyd has been standing in a clear spot under the power lines. "Is there a pond up there?"

"Used to be—it's just filled in." This dry bowl shape in the gravel looks as if it could never have held water.

"Your dad may have built that."

"I think he did."

"He have any stock?"

"No, he didn't have anything." The words and laugh that follows them are bitter, and untrue. It surprises me, but not Floyd.

"Did he have a cow?" Floyd asks calmly.

"A milk cow," I remember then, and chickens, and a pig to fatten. . . . "There had been a cabin here before us," I say, but neither one of us knows who might have lived here before my grandparents and parents. There have been so many migrations.

In the yard, we find a peach-leaf willow, the old cabin step, and four young walnut trees. The blue trailer has one broken window.

We walk out. The road is not overgrown, so it must have regular use. "I must have been forty years old when it came to my mind: *I want to come back,*" Floyd says suddenly. "When I left the farm in 1942, well, times were rough—just like I'm sure it was for your parents right down here—and I had the same thing; we all did. But after I'd been around the world and raised my family, I said to Marge, 'I'd like to buy that old house from Dad and Mom and some acres. . . .'"

We walk in silence for a while.

"What's this?" I ask, pointing to a bush with leaves shiny as holly, but rounded, one of several I've seen along the roadside.

"I don't really know, Art. I've been wondering that myself. Something of the plum family, I'd say. I've been wondering if somebody planted them. Anyway these are the prettiest woods in the county."

When we get back to the graveled tram road, we drive south a few hundred yards to the long-abandoned home of Gene and Thelma Vale. "Look at this," says Floyd, pointing to a concrete catch basin located where runoff from the roof would collect in it. "A cistern, just about the worst way in the world to get your water, though a lot of folks did it that way."

The Vales had a well on the property across the road, from which both they and we got our drinking water. The cisterns at their house and ours were used for wash water.

Floyd points out that the chimney barely clears the roof, not nearly enough rise to create a decent draft, and following his pointing finger I can see where rocks seem to have been dumped in a pile and slathered with mortar to stabilize a corner of the foundation. "Should have asked your grandfather to have lent a hand with this. He'd have made a better job of it than this. I can tell you that."

Corridon-Reynolds Cemetery

After lunch in Bunker, we circumnavigate the Viburnum Trend, stopping at the Corridon-Reynolds Cemetery, just past the two-room school—now a home—where I attended second grade.

I always have trouble finding my grandparents' graves, and am stumping through the pale, sparse grass growing from the red and pink gravel when Floyd finds them. When he calls to me, he must raise his voice to be heard over a murder of crows. Besides Grandfather, Grandmother, and her mother who lived with them before her death, Floyd has found the Mays, a family I remember, and other neighbors.

As we get back in the truck to leave, I notice that pews from the church that now leans against saplings have been arranged in the pavilion. My mind is full of names, the Aikens boy, Ammon Ray Hubert—Obie D 1904–1930.

All the gravestones here are red.

Jane Hoogestraat

Jane Hoogestraat was born in South Dakota, earned her BA from Baylor and her PhD from the University of Chicago, and arrived in the Missouri Ozarks in the fall of 1989. Since that time, she has taught at Missouri State in Springfield, specializing in 20th century poetry, literary theory, and creative writing—poetry. Her first chapbook, *Winnowing Out Our Souls* (2007), was published by Foothills Press; her second chapbook, *Harvesting All Night* (2009), won the Finishing Line Press Open Competition. She has also published in such journals as *Elder Mountain, Fourth River, Image, Midwestern Gothic, Potomac Review, and Southern Review.*

Listening to Fauré

This morning the darkest green, the coldest spring
fell away before a sunlit clearing where a cardinal
and a jay teased a squirrel. Later an overcast sky held
until we were inside, purple irises withstood the storm.
When in the night you turn to cross another year,
think of this music, how it will not cease
returning the same lines, richer year by year
like those late green thunderstorms we've watched nights
from the living room. We keep our candles lit
long after midnight, after the sirens,
in the region of what little peace there is.

By June when the first fireflies are out, a neighbor
will light four corner candles for guests to play croquet
far into night. Others will watch from a porch swing.
Another visiting poet has written to say *you live*
in very paradise there, where the evening light
falls less eerily than the fireflies after they have flared,
too suddenly green, gone. Enough evenings like that,
we won't curse the cold spring storms that leave this town
too green, or think instead of all that we were spared.

Bela Fleck and the Flecktones Play the Ozarks

Yes, the banjo can hit the ironic,
scale the world's notes, which we would have known

had we tried earlier to learn the real music of the place
where we live, tried a little. Can a banjo, also, carry

the craggy resources of a place, a violent area,
where outside the garrison town, there was no law,

a bitter place that simmers in its stories,
needs its banjo, fiddle, if you will, to call the riffs,

the dances, to name the stories . . . to lighten and to lift,
to keep the score, to remember what it cannot heal?

Phillip Howerton

Phillip Howerton, a sixth-generation Ozarker, was born in Webster County, Missouri, in 1962. He is associate professor of English at Missouri State University in West Plains, and his photographs, reviews, poems, and essays have appeared in various journals and reference books, such as *The Hurricane Review*, *South Carolina Review*, *The Journal of Kentucky Studies*, *Red Rock Review*, *Big Muddy*, *Arkansas Review*, *Elder Mountain*, *Writers of the American Renaissance*, and *History through Literature.*

The Family, Circa 1919

The people who live in the Ozark country of Missouri and Arkansas were, until very recently, the most deliberately unprogressive people in the United States.

—Vance Randolph (*Ozarks Superstitions*, 1947)

In this photograph the old folks
and assorted cousins stand aligned
in front of their two-story balloon-
frame house with its tattered porch
and time-blasted wooden shingles.
The men sport stereotypical slouch hats
and the women wear aprons and sternness.
At one end of the line, Great-

Grandmother, probably called away from her
cookstove for the nonsense of this photograph,
folds her arms to hide the glove
pot holder on her left hand.
At the other end of the line, squarely
facing the camera as though peacefully
surrendering to the firing squad
he is storied to have served
in as a Confederate soldier,
stands Great-great-grandfather,
bow legged, long armed, and widowed
in overalls and a white beard.
Near the center, is Great-uncle Estel
just home from World War I, in a dark,
pin-striped suit and military straightness,
his stare focused upon the hill farm beyond
the camera, having seen enough of the world
and its testing fields of progress.

Old Homestead on Federal Land

They have been gone forty years—
forced out by eminent domain—
but their absence pulls
weathered boards from the barn
and clapboards from the house,
wrenches gates off hinges,
pushes foundation stones out of plumb,
and occasionally drops a window
glass or tears wall paper.
A path leads to the front lawn,
the broad, shaded porch invites,
and both front doors are always open,
but we should never believe
that we are still welcome.

Dave Malone

Dave Malone's great-great-great-grandfather Cyrus Newberry was one of the first settlers of European descent in Howell County, Missouri. His family purchased land near Moody in the 1840s. Born in Rolla, Missouri, in 1968, he fondly calls West Plains home. Whenever he travels away from Mountain View, Trask, or West Plains, he still feels very connected to this place, this landscape, and the people. Much of his creative work reflects his interest in Ozark culture. Malone is the author of four volumes of poetry, most recently *Seasons in Love* (Trask Road Press, 2012). His poems have appeared in online and print journals including *The Cape Rock*, *Cave Region Review*, *Crosstimbers*, *Elder Mountain: A Journal of Ozarks Studies*, and *Kentucky English Bulletin*. In April 2012, one of his poems aired on the "Muses and Metaphor" series from NPR's *Tell Me More*. Malone publishes a monthly e-newsletter, *If I Had a Nickel*, whose title derives from the sentiment of his former rascally Ozark grandfather. For more, visit davemalone.net or twitter.com/dzmalone.

Hawksbill Crag

We rise
four miles
into Ozark bluff
by gravel road,
our truck
hugs the slant
of timber line
thin as a pencil streak.

At Hawksbill Crag,
we tramp
thousands of feet
above shaggy pine
and the thumb of Jehovah.
While I clutch walking stick,
you slide to the edge
of the bluff face
and act as if you
fall
to
your
death.

My heart
once thin as ivy
bulges,
shrieks
like a hawk
until you slip off the boulder
back into the buttonholes
of the pines.

Blackberry Cobbler

The night you wore your white blouse
into the barn where cloggers yanked up dust
to their knees, all the corn farmers pulled at pressed shirts
behind bib overalls to breathe, overcome by a similar
feeling they knew in their muscled backs
when pressed against church pews
their granddaddies made before the only real War.

Pies perched on shiny red-checkered tables
and stretched out like barb wire
plucky with red blackberries
that had been set on waiting
for June heat before turning belly up.
On the far end, by that woman horse Delilah,
you plopped the blackberry cobbler
your Granny Rowlett showed you how to make
the summer you visited the Ozarks,
the one afternoon she kept you out of the canoe
and hot box with the boys from the crossroads.

It's this blackberry dance, the high red note,
the gold crust, all against your white blouse
and tan hands—this is the refrain
that stopped the cloggers
and silenced their jingle taps
and turned the square-dancers into
elliptical waltzers. It's this music
that cost me two Andrew Jacksons
as I held the bills high in the barn
over the sad hound-dog eyes
of Shooter McKenzie who hoped
he had a dating chance.

Anthony Priest

Anthony Priest was raised on an Ozarks farm near Ebenezer, Missouri. He earned a Bachelor of Arts in Writing from Missouri State University in Springfield and a Master of Fine Arts in Poetry from Washington University in St. Louis. Currently, he is associate professor and chair of the English department at Missouri State University in West Plains.

Aux Arcs

When the first French explorers swept down
into the heart of these Ozark hills,
found the bois d'arc—the Osage orange—
and followed the course of Little Sac
trading bows and bear skin for tools,

who could have imagined this? Fair Grounds,
Crystal Cave, Route 66 spilling
light and an endless stream of billboards:
Queen City Diner, Hillbilly Doc's,
Fantastic Caverns cave you ride through.

Standing on a bridge above the drowned
Sac valley, I like to think the still

shapes of trees are Osage come to mourn.
Dark waters move. Below where I walk,
old gods of the rain lie wrapped in pools.

Settling Velocity

Particles of sediment and light
sink in the weight of laminar flow.
Below the surface, no wind, no waves,
black oak groves are abrading their bark,
buckling low into beds of moss.

Down here, there is silence. Down here, night
knows no other name. Beyond where cold
seeps deeper than darkness, under the base
and graded slope of the lake's great arc,
dendritic streams are making their drop.

Silt motes swirl, begin to slow. In time
they will stop, sift their debris below
the bedrock ledge, the pilaster-framed
bridge where blind fish scoop the muddy dark,
spitting out clay and the lake-bed's rot.

Roy Reed

Roy Reed was born in Hot Springs, Arkansas. He spent most of his working years as a newspaper reporter after graduating from the University of Missouri School of Journalism. He worked a year at the Joplin, Missouri, *Globe*, and eight years at the *Arkansas Gazette* before joining the *New York Times* in 1965. He spent the next fourteen years for the *Times* as a correspondent in Atlanta, Washington, New Orleans, and London. He returned home to Arkansas in 1978 to teach journalism at the University of Arkansas. For three decades, his home has been in the hamlet of Hogeye in the heart of the western Ozarks. Much of his freelance writing during those years has dealt with life at Hogeye. Among his books are *Looking for Hogeye* and *Faubus: The Life and Times of an American Prodigal*. His latest, a memoir, is *Beware of Limbo Dancers: A Correspondent's Adventures with the New York Times*, published by the University of Arkansas Press.

from *Faubus: The Life and Times of an American Prodigal*

Snow was falling on the darkened hills. Neighbors tiptoed through the cabin, whispering. The old midwife muttered about his size, barely two and a half pounds. The doctor declared—out of the mother's hearing, we assume—"This baby will never live 'til morning." But they got him breathing, then cleaned and wrapped him and sat down to wait.

It enrages common sense to suggest that anyone there might have thought, much less uttered aloud, that this wretched infant not only would survive but would someday become known throughout the world, would be remembered among other things as probably the last public figure in America to have been born in a log cabin. These were not Kennedys. There was no fortune waiting to finance the ambitions of genius. And genius itself was not much in evidence. Of all the children, who eventually would number almost as many as their contemporaries the Kennedys, only this one would go much beyond the ordinary. No burning siblings would be watching from the wings.

On that first night, January 7, 1910, it is probable that the only one in the cabin who believed in the baby's chances with any shred of conviction was the seventeen-year-old girl. Her motherly longing and belief must have been absorbed by the child, and in a few days he had grown large enough that the girl could no longer display him like a kitten cupped in one palm. In later years, she would tell people that her newborn son could have fit into a quart jar with the lid on.

So how could he not have been afraid, not just at the beginning but on down? The claw of fear was in him as he tested the wildness of first the rocky hillside yard and then, slowly, the extending forest of Stanley Mountain and Ritchie Branch, and then the outer world that seemed enormous to a frail, quiet boy: Greasy Creek winding down to the White River, the town of Combs, the railroad disappearing into the mystery.

Much later he would come to think of nature as his friend. But in the beginning, nature was his monster. It was nature's deep spring of sweet water that he fell into when he was just old enough to say a few words, reaching to retrieve his only toy, a tin cup—and somehow did not drown but clambered out in time to meet his frantic mother racing down the path.

It was nature that killed his two playmates when he was seven, one felled by diphtheria and the other by a sawn tree. He learned early that if you move slowly, the woods will crush you, and that if you attract the wrong germ, you will slowly suffocate.

For years, he feared that he would choke to death. He had the croup one night when he was a year old. His father snatched him from his bed, ran out into the cold air, and plunged a finger into his throat to clear his trachea and make him breathe again. Many years later, as an old man, he would walk a visitor through the Combs cemetery and point out the shortened grave depressions all over the yard, the tombstone inscriptions saying, "Infant of. . . ." One plot had four short graves in a row bearing cousins of his, each tombstone labeled, "Infant of Mr. and Mrs. John E. Faubus."

Flux swept the community when Orval was a boy and killed two children in a neighboring family, a three-year-old girl and her seventeen-month-old brother. They died thirty minutes apart. "I never will forget. I went to the funeral, and you could hear men crying half a mile away as they came walking up through the field there to the cemetery where they were buried."

Death was everywhere. Farm animals died. Dogs were executed for killing sheep. Hawks were shot for killing chickens. Crippled chicks were not pampered; they were killed. His mother handed him an unfortunate chick one day and told him to get rid of it. "It was a cold day. And I cupped it in my hands, and it began to cheep, you know, like it had found a friend. And I had to take it out there and kill it."

Old people did not die in hospital rooms. They died where they stopped breathing. His grandmother Joslin died of a heart attack while she was holding Orval's baby sister Bonnie. The boy watched as his father caught the falling infant. The family's friend Will Hunt died working in a field.

> The ants were crawling over his face and in and out of his mouth. Those things make an impression on a rather timid youngster like I was. There were a lot of hardships and things that the modernists today say would cause trauma. Hell, we never heard the word then. We got over it all right without all the counseling that you have to do now.

Then there was the fear within the boy's own dreams. For he was burdened with great pride. He saw the scorn of the neighbors when his father preached his radical opinions. The boy would do almost anything to avoid scorn or looking like a fool.

I once heard a story of a drunken stag party at a hunting camp at which he, by then the occupant of the state's highest office, by then a man of chilling gravity, deliberately made himself ridiculous by riding a donkey backward through the crowd. I do not believe that it happened, not unless, against all odds, he was so drunk that he managed for a brief hour to escape the terrible confines of his mind and become ordinary.

Even as a boy, he knew that he was not ordinary. Pride and self-knowledge set him on an early course for what was in the beginning merely escape from that place and circumstance. He could not claw his way out through brute strength, as some had done. He remained frail almost until manhood. But he also knew his advantages. He had a good mind and an extraordinary memory, so that he was able to store all that he read and heard.

He could read before he entered first grade at the Greenwood School. He had a gift for language, and he learned that language bestows power.

Through it all, the dread and fear remained. And of all the fears the boy acquired and cultivated, one was more persevering than all the others. He would eventually conquer his fear of nature's monstrosities, of illness and accident, of war, finally even of death itself. But there was one apparition that he never outran. The dreadful shadow that haunted him all his life was the fear of failure—the fear, in its everyday, ordinary form, of looking like a fool.

Orval Eugene Faubus was born in a rented log cabin on the slope of Stanley Mountain a few hundred yards above Ritchie Branch in Madison County, Arkansas. Ritchie Branch waters the Gulf of Mexico by way of Greasy Creek and the White River. The White flows impertinently north through the Arkansas Ozarks into southern Missouri, then back south across hills and delta into the Arkansas River and thence into the Mississippi and on into the world.

Where the parents got the name Orval is uncertain. There is no uncertainty about the middle name. Sam Faubus's hero was Eugene V. Debs, the Socialist leader and labor organizer who, in less than ten years, would be in federal prison for his beliefs. Sam and nine other men of the Combs community chartered their own chapter of the Socialist party in May when the baby Orval was four months old. John Samuel Faubus was twenty-two years old when he became a father and a Socialist.

The farming community of Greasy Creek, a mile and a half north of Combs, was no more prosperous than any other rural habitat of the Ozarks. The residents scraped by and felt lucky to do so. Food came from the soil, cultivated by both parents and all the children old enough to handle a hoe, and from the meat of animals, wild and domesticated. Money came from selling one's spare labor in the woods—cutting and hauling logs, barrel staves, and railroad ties. Quiet cash could be picked up in the distilling and sale of whiskey. Women and children often had a little egg money.

Combs throve. The dirt streets were always busy with wagons drawn by horses or mules. When Orval was a boy, the town had three hotels, two physicians, two blacksmith and barber shops, and enough general stores to provide a brisk competition. The Black Mountain and Eastern Railroad built tracks through the town to transport the crossties and other wood products to the manufacturing centers. There was a sawmill and its lumber yard next to the railroad. As a boy, Orval dreaded going to Combs because the steam engines frightened him.

> Think about that vast isolated region where the loudest sound you ever heard was the sound of the chopping axe and the voice. And then that big hissing steam locomotive would scare the mules to death. You had to get out and get them by the bits and hold them. So I was always afraid we'd come to the railroad the time the train was coming through, and I was always scared the mules would run away.

Nearly every family kept a milk cow, even in town. Cattle, sheep, and horses ran loose on the streets, as they do today in many of the cities and towns of Asia and Africa. One Halloween, some boys of Combs built a high pen of crossties around one man's cow. It might have been the same bunch who disassembled a farmer's wagon and put it back together on top of Barron's Store.

The dappled and improbable history of the South that has engaged scholars for generations is mainly that of the plantation country. Black and white whirled together there, tolerating and rubbing each other raw, joined like carelessly attached Siamese twins in something more than a dance and something less, usually, than mortal combat. For better and often for worse, they stole each other's manners, speech, style, music, and tastes. These became the southerners of popular romance fiction.

Up on the rim of the South beyond the fertile cotton land, an entirely different history teased itself out. The upland southerners were, except for the steadily displaced Cherokees and the other indigenous tribes, predominantly Anglo-Saxons and Celts from the British Isles. Many were Scotch-Irish, a convenient label for those Scots who had paused in Ireland for two centuries without ever becoming Irish and had then paused again, just briefly, on the Atlantic seaboard of North America before pushing into the wilderness, taking the frontier with them, living always on what Frederick Jackson Turner called the meeting place between savagery and civilization. The upland southerners evolved into something quite different from the lowlanders. These were Orval Faubus's people.

By the late sixteenth and early seventeenth centuries, the Scotch-Irish had shoved up the Shenandoah Valley of Virginia and into the piedmont of North Carolina. They crossed the Alleghenies into Kentucky and Tennessee during the time of the American Revolution. From there, they drifted south and west along the ridges and valleys, settling the higher altitudes of Georgia and Alabama, and finally—just before reaching what would become the barrier border of the Indian Territory—Arkansas.

Thousands of Scotch-Irish arrived in the Ozark Mountains of Arkansas during the middle of the nineteenth century. They huddled in the hardwood hills, isolated except for the adjacent Germans and French of the Missouri Ozarks and the Cherokees who, prodded by the Europeans, had drifted west and settled uneasily in the same Arkansas hills and hollows.

The French and Spanish had moved into the lowlands of eastern Arkansas late in the seventeenth century. The Ozark highlands were virtually innocent of Europeans until early in the nineteenth century. Fayetteville had become just a village by 1828. It was connected to the more populous eastern precincts by a single path known as the Carrollton Road. By 1829, much of eastern and central Arkansas was served by postal routes; west of Batesville, the Ozarks were untouched by this hint of civilization. Settlers followed the numerous rivers in other parts of the state. Ozark streams were as unnavigable as the wooded slopes were impenetrable. Only those Europeans who were foolhardy or desperate or hardheaded or visionary saw any reason to venture in.

There were some advantages. While the soil of the slopes was thin, that of the creek bottoms and the northwestern prairie was reasonably fertile. Wheat and corn did well there. Madison County, where the Faubuses settled, was among the top-ten corn-producing counties of Arkansas by 1860. But for cotton—that is to say, for real money—settlers chose the malarial delta, and brought slaves. Migrants into the lowlands tended to come from the lowlands of Mississippi, Alabama, Georgia, and South Carolina. The stubborn Scots sought the infertile highlands, as if enslaved by a genetic disposition against wealth.

There was another difference. The uplanders were never quite southern in the demonic sense of the word. Lacking large numbers of slaves, or indeed any neighbors who did not look like themselves except for a few Indians, their race prejudice was not the same as that of the lowlanders. On the one hand, they were largely free of the virulent fear and hatred of black people that lowlanders were capable of. On the other, they lacked the sympathy for blacks that the lowlanders were also capable of. Bereft of proximity, the uplanders had no deep feelings toward black people other than a strong and atavistic distaste for strangers.

The Faubuses were not among the first settlers in the Ozarks. Those first arrived in some numbers during the 1830s. Orval's ancestors the Thornberrys and Salyers were settled in Madison County before the Civil War—some perhaps as early as 1840—after the savage edge of the frontier had been dulled a little. They were known, in fact, as prosperous farmers. One of the Salyers became a leading merchant of the town of St. Paul after the Civil War.

The first American Faubus known to the family was one William. He spelled it Faubous. The name has had many spellings. It is believed to be derived from the Scottish Forbes. In America it has been Forbis, Forbush, Furbush, Forbus, Fawbush, Faubush, Faubous, and Faubus.

Members of the family remember being addressed as Fawbush as recently as 1954.

William was a Scot who migrated to New York about 1750, without benefit of hiatus in Ireland. He fought under George Washington in the French and Indian Wars and perhaps later in the Revolution. A military size roll of 1758 or 1759 describes him as a planter living in Virginia. It says he was 5 feet 7 1/2 inches tall, of fair complexion and red hair, and lusty (stout, robust) with good limbs. He would have been about twenty-five years old.

Orval's family records show no direct connection with William Faubous. However, Orval's great-great-great-grandfather John Faubus was born August 25, 1759, in Frederick County, in the hills of western Virginia, about the time and place that the immigrant William would have produced children.

The Faubuses were hill people from the beginning. Before the Revolution, John's family moved on down the Appalachians to Burke County, North Carolina. Family lore has it that young John fought the British in the Revolution, and that he was wounded in one eye by a bayonet at the Battle of Eutaw Springs. About 1786, he moved his family to Washington County, Tennessee, still clinging to the hills.

Further family lore says that Orval's great-great-grandfather Thomas Faubus enlisted in the War of 1812 and fought under Andrew Jackson at the Battle of New Orleans. Afterward, Thomas pursued the traditional family occupation of farming and added a new venture, distilling whiskey. Thomas's son, Ellis, Orval's great-grandfather, was born in 1827 in eastern Tennessee. The family moved again when the boy was sixteen, this time to Laurel County, Kentucky, less than fifty miles northwest of the Cumberland Gap. If the Faubuses ever owned slaves during any of their hill-country migrations, it would have been in meager numbers.

In 1868, when he was forty-one years old, Ellis made the longest family move since William's voyage from Scotland to New York. Gathering up his family, including a babe-in-arms, Ellis migrated six hundred miles from eastern Kentucky to northwestern Arkansas. The family legend is that they made most of the trip by boat and disembarked on the Arkansas River at the town of Ozark, thence overland to Madison County. By 1889, Goodspeed's *History of Northwest*

Arkansas reported that he had left his original homestead, nine miles away, and was "now the owner of 200 acres of excellent land, it being in the White River Valley." It was there in the White River valley of Madison County that a core of the Faubus clan would remain, in various numbers, on through the twentieth century.

There are indications that the new country in Arkansas was not uniformly generous, even with the "excellent land." Ellis wrote to a nephew in Kentucky in July 1892. It appears that the nephew had been left in charge of selling some Kentucky land in which Ellis had an interest. "If there is any thing for me," he wrote, "I will Expect it as soon as possible to make all things rite." In the same letter, Ellis reported that crops in the White River valley were favorable in spite of a "terrible wet and backward spring" that had delayed planting. Then he added a dark note: "Times is hard in this country."

Hard times or not, the Faubuses reproduced in abundance. William Henry, the baby when Ellis brought the family from Kentucky, grew up and married Malinda Sparks. The Faubuses probably considered it a good marriage for young Henry. Malinda's mother was from the prosperous Salyer family, which owned much of the town of St. Paul. A distant relative in the Sparks family became governor of Alabama. The Sparkses also provided the northern sentiment when the Civil War was remembered; Malinda's father, Eli, had been a Union soldier.

Henry and Malinda produced seven children. The oldest, John Samuel, was born October 24, 1887, on Mill Creek a little south of Combs. Sam Faubus was destined to enter history as the father of a famous man. If history had been more logical, a little less given to luck and caprice, it might well have come about that the first Faubus to be governor of a state would have been not Orval but his father.

Jan Peterson Roddy

Jan Peterson Roddy was born in 1957 in Kirkwood, Missouri. She has roots in the Ozarks dating back to before the Civil War, where her family homesteaded forty acres along the Gasconade River. Her childhood was split between St. Louis, where her mother had moved from the farm to find work, and the old home places that they would return to whenever possible. She came back to attend College of the Ozarks. More interested in studying the world than books, she dropped out after a time and held waitress, barn-painting, and factory jobs across northwestern Arkansas, before buying a wooded holler in Izard County. She returned to school eventually, earning an MFA in Art from the University of Illinois. For the last twenty-five years she has taught at Southern Illinois University, living in a cabin perched on the eastern-most edge of the Ozark Uplift in the Shawnee National Forest.

Geography I

The relentless forces that carved valleys, cracked stone and twisted old cedar trees remain in their very substance. Melt water in stream trickles, torrential rivers, and crashing falls. Winds from the belly of the earth and the far reaches of the sky. What we drink from deep wells and percolating springs is the same ancient water that rained down on hot, infant rock and again on the old one's garden plots. It lives in our flesh, blood, spit and returns again in the end. Bald knobs we climb and dirt we work are the remnants of the glacier that paused right before it was about to slide over the Ozark Plateau, deciding it had pushed enough land flat. Minerals hid in fossils lie next to carrot roots, potatoes planted in the dark of the moon, and migrate into our bones.

Called Down

I have gone down to the altar during the call. I have spoken in tongues. I have felt the sweet surrender, falling willingly backward into murmuring streams. Baptized in what they call Tablerock Lake, for now, while men's dams stand and where the White River waits for a while on its way to Arkansas.

I skinny-dipped in those same waters with girl- and boyfriends on clandestine escapes, out after hours from the bible college where we were counted in our beds each night. Homemade moonshine burning hot in my throat, drunk straight from plastic gallon milk jugs—a not-quite ancient rite that joined us to ancestor hillbillies and steaming back-wood stills.

Tender faced, willowy boys led me to hidden rope bridges and underground rivers whose whispering siren's moan lured us into a skin-felt faith in our own yearnings. We were called down into splits in Ozark bedrock, fissures that open and close into caves that wind endlessly, secretly, under Missouri.

Caves

Families eke out livings from tours led past souvenir rock displays and homemade artifact cases on through underground caverns that their grandfathers strung with electric wire and bare bulbs. Native bones that thought they'd found their final rest in the earth's belly advertised on gaudy, painted billboards. Jesse James hid out, slept here. I believe it, hearing echoes of the drops of sweat and desperation splattering on the worn glassy floor.

Wild caves hide high in bluffs, behind river bottom cane or beneath newly opened sinkholes in forest floors. Find them by the odor of damp, ancient stone and the deep, dark they exhale. Adventurous girls foray lamp-less past the smoke stains of old fires. Boisterous boys dare each other down the rope into Devil's Well who's slick bowl walls and bottomless lake have tried to swallow a few.

Sweet corn mash steam from bootleggers' stills lingers yet against the low rock ceiling between stalactites. Curved imprints of slumbering bears molded in the clay of a dry chamber. The hearts of blind cavefish throb through quartz clear skin as they circle silently in black pools that plunge into lost rivers.

Bodies of young lovers wash up in the next county, having been trapped in back caverns by rising water leaking through gravel soil, past roots and chert from thunderstorms above they never heard.

With an unnatural lust for the abysmal, divers sink silently into pitch-black underground river tunnels, wandering further and deeper through cold as the grave water filled chambers. Some heave their last breaths beneath a ceiling of mile-thick rock searching for a sign of the sky.

Border State

Their moans mingle still with the mist and thick sweet smell of honeysuckle on damp mornings in creek bottom clearings where camp was made. They drift between tangles of grapevines that writhed like serpents in feverish waking dreams. Pale, veined gooseberries in thorny brambles recalled the glassy eyes of worm-eaten Yankee boys they had passed on the roads. The water is so willful this season that it seeps right out of a sand ridge 15 feet above the river. Oozing like the blood from soldiers' dying bodies, slaves' beaten bodies, women who were defending their homes' bodies.

With the border a state wide we found enemies in brothers, cousins, neighbors and strangers. Missouri grew turbid and sour like river water that backs up a slough without a way out. Great-great-grandma rode to town with her youngest on horseback to sell pies to Union troops traveling south, before her husband and sons fought the same men a few miles further down the trail—Secesh.

Longhaired Bushwackers stormed the woods in showy hand-sewn

blouses and jackets whipping in the wind, young Jesse James among them. Jayhawkers, Militia, Union, Confederate, Regular, Irregular. Bands of men ran loose across the state. One bunch or another dangled a woman by a rope over her own hearth fire to burn, or say where her coins were buried. She had nothing to tell.

Re-enactors rehearse history perennially on old battlefields and town parks at the edge of swollen creeks, conjuring a selective remembrance of heroes and sacrifice as spring floods wash up remnants of back-woods meth labs tangled in a mud-stained rebel flag, a child's once-yellow dress and worn wooden-handled hoe.

Silas

I went in search of the soul and grave of Great-great-grandfather Silas, who fought and lost, trying to take Missouri south of the Mason-Dixon line. The trail of sparse notes written on scraps of old papers led to the small U.S. military cemetery in Fayetteville, Arkansas. Wandering through well-kept grave markers amongst the orderly rows and tidy landscape I found neither material nor spiritual evidence.

Eating a fried chocolate pie back in the truck, with the door open, trying to court any breeze that might have risen to have mercy on that blistering July day, a notation on the map jumped at me—"Confederate Cemetery."

Narrow roads snaked back up and around steep hills a few miles away. Crumbling, hand-piled stone walls and wrought-iron gates had settled forever into the lay of the land. Towering trees filtered mid-day light into an eternal soft twilight while wild vines took gentle ownership of long lost men. On the north side of a single center spire that lifted a statue of Johnny Rebel high towards heaven, I found the carving. It faced down the shadowy hollow toward 144 rough, unmarked stones. "Pea Ridge, Missouri Division." He was there somewhere, I felt him.

Driving a few more miles to stand on the battleground where all that blood had seeped into the dirt, I hoped his would recognize itself in me and reveal whatever it was I was truly looking to find.

Collie Holler

I met fate a week ago Sunday, who proceeded to introduce me to Miss Mary. We shared coffee and the surprising knowledge of a way back place that few would know of. As knowing sometimes does, it opened a gaping cavern beneath our feet that we would have to climb out of, or be swallowed by. She grew up in Collie Holler. I had heard of it all my life, its dark-skinned inhabitants being peculiar enough to my people in that place and time, to give rise to passing comment whenever we drove Highway T on the way to Waynesville.

Her mama had to warn her every step, "Don't go no further than the yard, child," when she was out the door to hang up boiled white sheets. Long, coal-colored arms wrestling the steaming cottons onto the line. Her daddy's protection left her lonesome. He'd go into town alone, and only when the meal had run out. My mind conjured the details of the dangers her dignity would not allow the telling of to a near stranger.

Greens and cornbread, pinto beans, ignorance, bigotry and rumors of violence. We were tied up tight in a mutual history. Fists held up against the fear of inherited sin holding one end of the rope, resurrected anger in old raw hands, the other. A tug of war of mere mortals, who, like Jacob, must wrestle with the spirits to death, or until they agree to bless them.

Pattiann Rogers

Pattiann Rogers was born in Joplin, Missouri. She received a BA in English literature in 1960 from the University of Missouri-Columbia and an MA in Creative Writing from the University of Houston in 1980. Her first book, *The Expectations of Light,* was published by Princeton University Press in 1981. She has published eleven books of poetry, two prose books, and a book in collaboration with the artist Joellyn Duesberry. Her most recent books are *The Grand Array, Writings on Nature, Science, and Spirit* (Trinity University Press, 2010) and *Wayfare* (Penguin, 2008). Her next book, *Holy Heathan Rhapsody,* will appear from Penguin in fall 2013. Rogers is the recipient of two NEA grants, a Guggenheim Fellowship, a Literary Award in Poetry from the Lannan Foundation, and five Pushcart Prizes, among other awards. Her work has appeared twice in *Best American Poetry,* and four times in *Best Spiritual Writing.* She has taught as a visiting professor at the University of Montana, University of Texas, Mercer University, and Washington University. She was an associate professor at the University of Arkansas from 1993 to 1997. She is the mother of two sons and has three grandsons. She lives with her husband, a retired geophysicist, in Colorado.

Fury and Grace

Shoal Creek, near Joplin, Missouri, where I grew up, is, for me, the archetype of all creeks. We went to see Shoal Creek often when I was young, like visiting a highly interesting acquaintance who lived a strange but purposeful life. The creek was always there, more or less in its same place, doing its mud-and-fish, worn-rock-and-ruffled-rapids, racing act.

I could wade through the clear waters where it widened near a small dam, bend down, and look from my world through a silver, reflective boundary into a world that was forced to remain within that boundary—tiny black snails like spots on the stones, fat tadpoles that seemed just heads with wispy tails, crawdads propelling backwards to hide beneath muddy leaves and muck, olive-green minnows so narrow and rock-colored that they were almost invisible until they flicked and moved as one body from sun to shadow.

And when I looked up again into the world of air and sky, it seemed I had been existing in another life, among alien creatures whom I nevertheless knew and regarded with respect.

I occasionally swam in Shoal Creek, learning of it in another way, standing waist-deep in its murky water, pushing against its force on my body, or sitting in its shallow rapids making it rear up, ruffle and surge against my back. Who was it? It came and went constantly yet was always present.

McClellan Park was situated on a steep hill, a high cliff above Shoal Creek, a cliff covered with rocky bluffs and caves typical of the area. A picnic at McClellan Park always involved a precarious hike down the hill, everyone slipping on rocks and gravel, skidding and grabbing bushes and trees to keep from falling. I held onto my dad. At the bottom we would walk for a while beside the creek, which ran close to the hill, pressing against the rise of land. My dad skipped rocks over the surface of the water, big leaps and then smaller. My brother and I tried.

A favorite story of my dad's was the time my brother, six years old, started running down the hill and couldn't stop, shouting and yelling. My dad, running after him barely grabbed him by one arm, swinging him out over the creek just before he would have plunged into its deep, rushing waters.

Once we went in the rain to see Shoal Creek mad and powerful, high over its banks, its white froth climbing and fighting against the thick poplars marking its old boundaries. It rolled and thrashed over its single-lane bridge. We were consigned to viewing the flooding from one side, many cars lined up before the impassable crossing. People in raincoats and boots stood around outside their cars watching in amazement, proclaiming in low voices, with reverence and respect, as if Shoal Creek were justified in this show of frightening rebellion.

But I love Shoal Creek most, I think, because I first learned about the bodies of boys while parked beside it at the end of dirt fishing lanes, the sound of its life continually cresting and flowing, swelling and rhythmic in the background among the whispers and laughters and joys of those nights. The affirmation and promise of moving water has been present with me since, in everything I've ever experienced of sexual love.

The being and cadence of Shoal Creek is part of who I am, defining both fury and grace, influencing the pace of my passions, shaping the undercurrent of my sleep, resonant always in the waking motion and music of my language and my thought.

The Background Beyond the Background

On an autumn afternoon, perhaps selecting
apples from a crate or examining pickled beets
and onions in a jar, or watching two honeybees
at one red clover, we stand unaware
before a background of behest and sanctity.

Or floating down a river through elm
and cottonwood shadows, past sandbar
willows and lines of turtles on sunning logs,
over underwater thickets, bottom beds
of leaf roughage and mud, we are, all the while,
made finely distinct upon a more distant
background of singularity.

Anywhere we turn, this background
stays, a domain for mortal and immortal,
for crystal grids, for shifting furls of smoke,
for structure and fallibility, for each nexus
of sword and cross.

Atop a barn roof, a glossy green-tailed
rooster with auburn feathers lifts his wings
against a backdrop of dawn. Is it the passing
moment of occupied event or the passing fact
of barnyard morning that creates the impression
of presence before this silk of elusive
light behind light?

Like a clear horizon at the edge of a wide
field, the background beyond the background
of sky reveals most explicitly the figures
of those that come before it—elephant
or ostrich or seed-heavy grasses, saint,
sow, runt or sire, summer lightning,
blowing ice. It achieves us all.

Far, far beyond those far mountains of stone
and cavern against which I am outlined now
there is another background—translucent,
    stolid, eloquent, still.

Marideth Sisco

Marideth Sisco performed as the singer and was roots music consultant for the Oscar-nominated film *Winter's Bone* and is the lead singer in the Blackberry Winter Band. A retired journalist and specialist in Ozarks folklore, she is host of a radio show, "These Ozarks Hills" on KSMU-FM public radio in Springfield, Missouri.

Sisco explains how she was introduced to the world of entertainment: "I began my singing career at age 3, standing on an ice cream freezer at an auction, when my great uncle Tom Ferguson stood me up there during a break in the sale and told me to sing for the crowd. I've never stopped."

She's never stopped talking about the Missouri Ozarks where she was born and raised, either. A consummate storyteller, especially when it comes to sharing tales of the unique Ozarks culture that is fast passing away, Sisco is much in demand as a public speaker from formal presentations at the Ozarks Studies Symposium to local and regional clubs and gatherings.

Butterfield: An Introduction

There are many things to say about the Ozarks, from its natural beauty to its history, to its unique culture. And many of them have been said. People are likely to believe, when they come here, that they're looking at a perfect example of small-town America.

But it's not really. What they are looking at is actually a remnant of the American frontier. We who grew up in the television age equate frontier either with Kentucky, via Davy Crockett, or the old West, via the horse opera. But this portion here in the Ozarks held on to its character as the westward flow of immigrants passed it by, chiefly because nobody wanted it. It was too rocky, too full of ticks and chiggers. Too hard. So only the toughest, meanest, most doggedly determined sought it out. Some actually relished the difficulties. Others had nowhere else to go. So today, you don' t have to go far off the beaten path to find that (1) the frontier hasn't been gone all that long, and (2) it left some fairly notable traces behind.

Some of my best evidence of this comes from my own memory, because the fact is, I'm getting old, and I remember back quite a few years. But I must also caution that memories, the older they get, tend to transform themselves, so that we tend to remember just the good parts—however we may define them. I, too, remember mostly the good parts, and cannot in good conscience swear to their reliability. I remember what I remember, and have forgotten a good deal more. So I will tell not how it was, but how I remember it. I'm sure some of it will be recognizable to the folks in these small remnant towns, certainly to the old folks. For the stories they will tell, although they may differ in the particulars, are remarkably similar in some respects. They tell of a life that ignores, for the most part, world events and passing fads and fashions. They may talk of the Great Depression, for instance, in terms of what was the same, rather than what was different.

There was no money, they say. Just like always.

They don't talk much about going hungry, because they remember it too well, when there was no work to be had, and the only time they had meat was if Papa shot a squirrel. Then they'd have squirrel and gravy and biscuits. Or just biscuits. Or just gravy.

I can't count the times I've gone to my aunt's house and removed the two back rows of canned goods from her cabinets. I started doing that after something exploded back in there one day. She hoarded food. She didn't feel safe unless there was plenty to feed her, and her family, and whoever might knock at the door. After living in those times, her cupboards were never going to be bare again, by God.

She would often speak of her childhood friend, Josie, with whom she played dress-up in the little apartment over the store owned by

Josie's husband. They were both 14. The girls, not the husband. He was quite a bit older. He had come to Butterfield when he retired from his career as a circus clown. He chose Butterfield while passing through on a train, because he noticed that the station agent and he were kin of a sort. They were both dwarves. So he stopped, stayed and bought a little store that sold notions and dry goods. Then he decided that since he was settling down, he needed a wife. He inquired of the neighborhood as to where one might be found. Then he went out to Josie's parents' house, where there were way too many children and not nearly enough to feed them, and he offered them a 20-lb. sack of bread flour, in return for Josie. They, and Josie, accepted. I don't know what Josie thought of it at first, but she came to be very satisfied, because she wasn't hungry anymore. And she and her friends could spend hours upstairs playing dress-up, with her husband's former props and costumes.

They weren't the town's oddest residents. They weren't even near the top of the list. There was the little girl named Birdie, who stopped growing at about age four or five, but who lived to be a very old child. I played with her when I was six. She was 43 at the time.

Then, of course, there were the Wilsons, the dwarf train agent and his regular-sized wife, his regular-sized brother, and their three daughters, one large and two small. They had a very ordinary life for such extraordinary looking people. Except for the brother. He worked as a clerk there at the train depot, but eventually he left town, at his brother's suggestion. It seems he developed the habit in summer of attending the ticket window without his pants on. The young men of the town thought it was hilarious, but after a while, women would make their husbands, or any passing male, buy their tickets for them. They wouldn't go to the station, or anywhere near him, even with his pants on. So it just didn't work out for him. He was bad for business. He looked the most normal of the bunch, but then, I guess it's true that looks often deceive.

Butterfield wasn't much of a town when I lived there. The official population of the town was 125. But it was said they got that figure by including all the dogs. In describing it after I moved away, I told people the whole town fit between two Burma Shave signs. Not true. It was three, I think.

There was a post office, a feed store, two small grocery stores, and the town's centerpiece, Goldie's Café, run by Goldie Henley. Her husband, John, ran the barbershop that occupied half of the storefront. That made the front part of Goldie's kind of narrow. So when you walked in, there was just room to walk by the candy case and the ice cream freezer on the left, then make a little jog, because the coke cooler was next on the right. Then the room opened up enough for three or four tables, arranged around a potbellied wood and coal stove. A long counter stretched across the back of the room, with high stools, like in a saloon. Goldie fixed one main meal, and would make you a hamburger if the entrée didn't suit you. It was usually pot roast, or fried chicken, or meatloaf. And she made wonderful pies—all on a little four-burner kerosene stove with an oven. There were two loafer's benches outside, and the little partitioned-off room in the front that held the barbershop had a door at front and rear, so you could sit out front waiting for your haircut, move to the barber's chair when it was your turn, and exit into the café for lunch, or coffee and pie.

When I was a kid, one of my favorite things was to weasel out a dime from somebody, go to Goldies and sit at the counter and buy an RC float. Pop was a nickel, and so was a scoop of ice cream. You could hang out there in that dark little room with open windows and listen to the old men tell their stories. I probably heard some stories as many as a dozen times.

One of my favorites was when Uncle Hugh Nickel and his cousin Peggy, and why they called him that I don't know, but they'd get started telling of their adventures in the First World War, when they shipped out and went to France. They never talked about the fighting. Just the time they'd spent on leave in Paris, when they walked down the Chance Elysee and were greeted and thanked by the grateful French, and how they would pretend they could speak French, and when people greeted them, they would wave, and say, Barn Door, Manure. Just thinking about it would set them off into fits of giggles again.

Boy, it's a good thing we got them back to the farm.

Bonnie Stepenoff

Bonnie Stepenoff was born on July 18, 1949, in the hills of northeastern Pennsylvania. After graduating from the Ohio State University in 1971, she studied history at the University of Missouri in Columbia. In the 1980s she worked for Missouri State Parks, and one of her tasks was to document buildings and structures made by the Civilian Conservation Corps (CCC) during the Great Depression. From 1993 until 2011, she taught history and historic preservation at Southeast Missouri State University in Cape Girardeau. During a sabbatical in 2002, she spent the fall semester in the Ozark National Scenic Riverways writing a report on the old state park constructed by the CCC at Big Spring in Carter County. While there, she kept the journal that became *Big Spring Autumn* (Truman State University Press, 2008). She has published several other books as well as poetry and essays in many journals. She and her husband, Jerry, have two daughters and a grandson.

from *Big Spring Autumn*

August 21, 2002

I have been working in the Cultural Resources Building, in the back room, reading the archival files on the development of Big Spring State Park in the 1930s. Donald A. Blake, the chief architect, wanted the sleeping cabins, nestled in a secluded area on a hillside, to look like dwellings in fourteenth-century England. I wondered why he would want a twentieth-century tourist park in the Missouri Ozarks to resemble a medieval village. But it does make sense as the expression of a longing for Sherwood Forest, a time before lumbering and tie-hacking and charcoal factories deforested the Ozarks, a time when people lived primitively, but snugly, in the woods, and the woods had wolves in them, and wildness was something that did not require a highway to reach, and people built houses with their backs and their muscles and their hands. It also made sense, because most of the people who settled in the Ozarks traced their family histories to England, Ireland, Scotland, and Wales, and tended to speak English in a flowery, old-fashioned way that sounded more like Shakespeare than prime-time television. So it made sense. And the buildings that Blake designed are still beautiful with their heavy native timbers and the hand-hewn stones, the way they cling to the landscape like the roots of old trees.

August 22, 2002

In the 1930s, a New Deal bureaucrat wrote:

> The Ozark country, which has been noted for its frontier log cabins, has stepped forward into a new and lovelier construction of cabins, since it has been opened by national highways that reveal its hidden beauties. The Ozark uplift, which exposes the oldest geological formations of the Earth's crust, contains some of the most beautiful and unique building rock that can be found anywhere in America. These rocks are of different shades, and are exceptionally suited for building construction.

There are many different kinds of rock buildings in the Ozarks, mostly built in the 1920s, '30s, and '40s. There are cobblestone houses, faced with small rough round stones, white limestone houses with cut-stone faces in regular courses, slab-rock houses with sandstone veneer, and giraffe-rock houses covered in irregularly shaped flat stones joined with raised and colored mortar. There are "red-granite" houses made of hard pink rocks, cut in squares of varying sizes and joined with raised mortar. Whoever built these houses had a love for the soil and the material underneath it, the hard, surprisingly beautiful substances that mountains are made of.

Over the years, a lot of people have studied these Ozark rock houses. Stonemasons practiced their craft in Missouri in the nineteenth century, but in the twentieth century a new kind of rock architecture developed in the hills of southern Missouri and northern Arkansas. It is hard to say whether the CCC craftsmen influenced local builders or whether it was the other way around. Local masons drifted in and out of the CCC camps, where they instructed unskilled recruits in the techniques of making stone walls out of the sandstone and limestone that underlay the Ozarks.

The Ozark rock houses of the 1930s and 1940s were small houses of wood frame construction with decorative walls of natural stone. Local builders dug the rock for these houses from just below the surface of the hills. Traditional masons dressed the stone into regular rectangular shapes and laid them up horizontally. Ozark masons took stones of varying shapes and sizes and fitted them together vertically like pieces of a puzzle or the markings on the coat of a giraffe. Some people call this "giraffe-rock" architecture.

To accent the color and shape of the stones, builders used "raised" mortar (formed around metal tubing) that they painted in bright red or green. Most of the builders remained anonymous, but some left a signature in stones arranged in particular shapes—the shapes of animals or daisies. Some builders prided themselves on finding and using peculiarly shaped rocks that resembled animal snouts or sea shells or rocks containing fossils. The makers of these houses wanted more than just shelter. They wanted to tell us something. They were artists.

By the 1950s, people were buying factory-built mobile homes instead of building these little stone houses, which began disappearing from the landscape. When the last of these houses has crumbled back into the earth, there may not be anyone left who remembers or cares, but the human race will have lost something—something important—and people will be different because it is gone.

These are houses that stand for something. I suppose all houses do. But these houses came from a place where most of us have never been—from a culture of self-expression and self-sufficiency that has mostly been lost.

Be careful where you sleep at night; be careful what doors you close behind you. The structure that shelters you can shape you—and also reveal the secrets of your heart.

August 23, 2002

Sometimes when I see a metal barn on a hillside, I cringe. It almost makes me flinch, as if someone stopped me on the road and flashed a knife in my face. That is overly dramatic, I know. After all, what is so horrible about metal buildings? No building is natural, I realize that. But wood and stone buildings rest a lot more gently on the ground. Eventually, when they crumble, they will return to the soil and become part of it again. Trees will grow out of them. When metal buildings fall, they lie there in heaps, perhaps for generations, generating nothing but rust. Take a walk in a junkyard sometime. See what grows there.

Actually, now that I think about it, the Cultural Resources Building is a metal building, set back in the woods behind an old farmhouse called the Cotton House that the NPS has renovated to house seasonal workers. In the early twentieth century, it belonged to a wealthy doctor (Dr. Cotton), who owned a tract of land near the spring. People believe he donated the land to the state park, but he didn't. He sold it and actually drove a pretty hard bargain. In the 1990s, the NPS constructed the metal building on the property to house archives and artifacts relating to the riverways. There are johnboats in the storage area along with map cases containing blueprints of the CCC buildings, old photographs, and all manner of bureaucratic files. I work at a desk in the same room with Doc Price. When I need to take a break, I walk out of the building and down a dirt road into a field full of wildflowers, brush, and chickadees. Deer often browse there, and a groundhog noses around the cars parked in the lot. Some kind of animal keeps getting under the hood of Angie Miller's car and chewing various cables and belts. No one ever sees it in the act. At lunchtime, we sit at the picnic table on a concrete slab outside the building and speculate about what kind of critter might do such a thing. The groundhog is way too fat. It has to be something skinny like a ferret or a weasel or a rat. Angie keeps taking the car in for service. But no one can come up with a solution to the problem. Whenever we talk about it, we laugh. It's annoying for Angie, of course. But it does seem somehow appropriate that nature should have this small form of revenge on a big metal object invading its domain.

August 24, 2002

There is mist on the Spring Branch every morning. If you stop on the bridge, you can see the wood ducks taking off, moving slowly, like shadows, trailing their feet to make *V*s in the water. I know it is a mistake to attribute human qualities to wild animals, but I wonder if they do it on purpose, dangle their feet a few minutes longer than necessary, just to enjoy the cool softness of the water and to make a pattern in it, leave a mark, if only for an instant, on that glassy surface. "I was here. We were here." I stand on the little bridge and watch them, and I want to reply, "I know. I saw."

August 25, 2002

The reason springs are so fascinating is that they come from hidden places and they seem to flow endlessly. At least, they never seem to ebb. They are mysterious, and yet they are constant, dependable, the way we want God to be.

A spring is a geological event. No one arranges for it to happen; it just happens and keeps on happening for years, for centuries, no one can predict how long. While seeming to defy gravity, a spring must obey certain scientific laws, although even geologists have trouble explaining how it all works. Or at least, they have trouble putting it into words.

At certain unobserved and unrecorded moments, Big Spring pushed huge blocks of dolomite off a cliff and then proceeded to bubble and gleam and dance around them, eventually, we assume, wearing them away to shiny little pebbles. We cannot imagine the length of time that must have taken. A person could not stand watching long enough to see any change, and so the spring seems to be eternal.

When I look at the spring, I try to give it meaning. Important words come to mind, although they seem to be clichés. The word purity applies. We love springs, because they are pure. We try to bottle that and sell it. "Pure mountain spring water" is available in the refrigerators at gas stations and convenience stores. But if you want to know what it means, come and stand here and be quiet.

Power is a quality of springs. We know that, because we have tried to use it. Most of the springs in the Ozarks have mills and mill wheels associated with them. But there is no mill at Big Spring. Who knows why? Maybe a sense of awe got in the way of it. But that seems unlikely. I suppose it was just an accident of history.

Sometimes, people go to springs for healing. Eureka Springs across the state line in Arkansas became famous for its "cures." To my knowledge, no one claimed to be cured of anything at Big Spring, except perhaps of cynicism or the blues. When I go there, I experience a change of mood. But that is not the reason for its existence. It just exists.

August 26, 2002

Leo Anderson lost an eye building the stone cabins in the state park. He was a St. Louis stonecutter, who came to Van Buren in 1932 because of the Depression. Instead of going on relief after losing his job, he decided to start a fishing camp on the Current River near Big Spring. The CCC hired him as a "local employed man" (LEM). In 1979, he told an interviewer:

> I got the sum of forty-five a month and board out of the deal, and went home every night. They let me go down the path home and then back up the next morning. I was in charge of a crew that was getting stone out [of the quarry] for those stone cabins, and I got hit in the eye with a piece of stone. I have gotten hit thousands of times on other jobs, but it just didn't cause any damage, but this one eventually led to the loss of my eye.

He expressed no bitterness. I wonder if he ever received any compensation. Probably not. Not monetary compensation. I wonder if he felt compensated when he realized that the cabins were beautiful and would last. Losing an eye is losing an eye, and dying is dying. Sometimes people say, usually about a war, "At least he didn't die in vain." Maybe Leo Anderson gave up his eye for something. For the rustic English Tudor-style cabins at Big Spring. It may not seem like much, I mean in comparison, for instance, to Van Gogh's ear. He gave up his ear as an expression of unbearable emotion and the emotion translated into art. Which is now worth millions. Leo did not have unbearable emotions, or at least, if he did, he did not say so. He came to work every morning in the mountains and then climbed down at night and went home, probably feeling lucky to have a job and a place to go at the end of the day. He was just trying to make a living during the Depression and in the process he lost an eye. But he ended up making something beautiful.

If you ever wonder why God bothered to make the world at all, just talk to a man who has built something—anything—with his own hands. Even if he lost an eye doing it, even if the thing he made was imperfect. I am not saying that someone who builds a doghouse or a model airplane understands the nature of God. I do believe they have had a glimpse of heaven.

August 27, 2002

In some ways, it was all a big show. In May 1930, the Van Buren Light and Power Company ran power lines out to the park to light up the campground and illuminate Big Spring with a five-hundred-watt floodlight with "color effects." The state Game and Fish Commission planned a grand opening for the season with a brass band and distinguished speakers. The brass band never showed up and some of the speakers failed to appear, although the state attorney general waxed eloquent on the value of the Ozarks as a tourist attraction, but the floodlights worked perfectly. Over two thousand people watched and most of them seemed to think the spring looked even more beautiful in artificial light than it did during the day.

August 28, 2002

They altered it. There was an enormous natural spring, but people felt the need to make it prettier. Doc Price said to me, "You have to realize that what you're looking at is a man-made landscape." In 1930, the spring came thundering up out of the ground, just as it had for thousands of years, but it ran off into several rough channels like the spread fingers of a man's work-worn hand. The CCC came in and changed that, with shovels and 'dozers, reshaping the ground and guiding the overflow of the spring into one wide groove, called the Spring Branch. "They must have worked like galley slaves," he said. "It was all hand labor and they moved thousands of tons of earth." They created the deep clear pool in which the spring waters surged and boiled and the wide slow channel that carried the clear green water to the fast-flowing Current River.

They also kept the river from covering up the spring. In 1933, a momentous flood threatened to push the river back into an old abandoned channel. An editorialist for the *St. Louis Globe* wrote:

> [The] Current River, now in flood, is said to be threatening to cut a new channel to the face of the bluff and thereby submerge the outlet permanently—thereby transforming a gushing spring into an underwater, and therefore, bubbling one, which makes all the difference in the world in spring character and beauty, even though it changes the flow of water not at all. . . .
>
> So if this gusher is really threatened, if the current wrath of the Current River promises less bark than bite, if there is possibility of this sparkling gift of nature being smothered, something really should be done about it. The Current River should be made to follow the course it has followed, even if we have to stake her in the man-driven piles. As much as we love the Current River, we love Big Spring more.

It was a matter of love. But it was much more complicated than that. The editorial writer expressed a love of nature, but weighted that love with human values. He did not approve of simply letting nature take its course, but reserved the right to evaluate nature's course in human terms. He loved nature when it was beautiful, but not when it was capricious or threatening. If natural processes took a turn of which he did not approve, he felt justified in reversing or controlling those processes to achieve the desired effect—the effect desired by humans, responding to a picturesque scene and, no doubt, mindful of the tourist trade. He did not approve of nature if it spoiled the view.

The federal government agreed with him. In 1934 the CCC built five large dikes to prevent the Current River from flowing through that old channel and inundating the spring.

These dikes, made of vertical timbers and rocks, were big enough for cars to drive over and quite ingenious in their construction. J. S. Hazelton, the construction engineer, described them:

> The dikes consist of two rows of piling, ten feet center to center, and tied together with heavy planks. The cribbing thus formed is stabilized by rock weighted mattress work hurdles. Pile clusters tied together with heavy cable are interspersed in the area between the dikes.
>
> At the point where the dikes are tied into the high bank or hillside, an area extending forty feet each way from the center of the dike is built with an apron of rip rap on each side of the work to prevent scour at this point.

One of the CCC men, Floyd Downey, remembered driving posts into the old riverbed "like telephone poles with a pile driver." He went on to describe the construction: ". . . and then we took guy wire which is like your strands going down from telephone poles and we wrapped it around [the posts] in such manner that . . . brush and dirt and silt coming down would collect and make a natural dike." In this case, good old American ingenuity benefited from the availability of cheap labor.

There is no doubt that the CCC work at Big Spring represents the best efforts of the architects, planners, engineers, and enrollees who took part in it. Through their toil, the National Park Service achieved a realization of its vision of a picturesque tourist park that centered on a natural wonder. The question in my mind is, what are the limits of that vision?

Traditionally, the NPS treated wild places like set pieces, enhancing real nature with stage props, such as cut and dressed stone, half-buried to resemble natural outcrops. This was flattery by imitation. Harmless enough, but implying that the real thing failed to measure up to artificial standards.

Real springs could be unruly, bubbling up willy-nilly and flowing away in unpredictable rivulets, mixing with the soil and creating a muddy mess. For instance, according to Linda Flint McClelland:

> CCC work at Yosemite included rehabilitating springs and making them safe sources of drinking water. Landscape architects saw this as an opportunity to develop beautiful rock gardens, following the precedent established at Apollinaris Spring at

> Yellowstone. In the mid-1930s, the Cascades Camp transformed several of Yosemite's springs from unsightly and muddy spots into appealing places of tranquil beauty.
>
> At Iron Spring, the upper spring was boxed and covered with soil, and water was piped to the lower spring which had been dug out and lined with rock.

The CCC at Big Spring followed these precedents, well meant but grounded in a nineteenth-century quest for picturesque landscapes. This painterly view of nature may have been better than the purely utilitarian idea that nature exists for man's economic benefit. But is there another possible view? Does nature have to be pretty if it is not useful? Can it just be? Can people find a way to see nature as something truly separate from themselves? As something deeply nonconforming and fundamentally wild? And then, can they see themselves as part of that?

If you love a landscape or a spring, can you leave it alone? Or do you have to try to change it (or her or him)? Do you have to make improvements? And if the loved one changes in ways you never anticipated, can you accept that? Or do you have to try and turn the tide?

SCHEVENINGEN, THE NETHERLANDS

In February 2002, before I went to Big Spring, I flew to the Netherlands to give a paper at a history conference. I remember a crowded commuter train, a gray landscape, the North Sea. It was windy, very windy, a force-ten gale, and very beautiful. A nice man at the bed and breakfast explained to me that I had picked a bad time. Today, it is extreme, he said. I wanted to walk on the beach, but there was a forty-mile-an-hour wind, blowing sand into my teeth. You picked a bad day to go to the seaside. The man extended his arms at his sides, laughing. The next morning, the wind was less violent, but still gusty. I stayed in the dining room for a long time, eating a boiled egg, cold meat, and bread, and looking out the window. Out on the beach, a middle-aged couple walked briskly in perfect unison as though they had done it a thousand times before. There was a slender girl in a shiny black coat; the wind bent her body forward into a graceful C. Her hair streamed out in front of her and it was jet black.

I thought of a brush, dipped in ink, forming a letter on a stark white page. The next day was rainy and calm. I watched a woman scrubbing the inside of a curved glass window in her apartment. The sea had turned a dark, metallic gray.

August 29, 2002

I settled into the Partney House about four miles up the road (Route Z) from the dining lodge at Big Spring. It is a big old L-shaped farmhouse that has been divided into two separate two-story apartments. There are lots of doors. I can enter through the old central hallway (in the interior corner of the ell) or through either of the two kitchen doors, front and back, or through the side porch. But I keep most of the doors dead-bolted and enter through the old hallway.

An L-shaped porch shelters both entrances, mine and the one that opens into Terry's apartment. He is a water quality researcher who goes to work early and comes home late. Sometimes I see him at the community center in his karate clothes. He lets me use his telephone, as mine is not yet connected. Both apartments must have stairways. Mine is in the main hallway, to the right of the door. The hallway goes straight through to the rear of the house and is lighted by two tall windows. On the left is a sort of pillared opening to the living room and the screened porch. To the right is a short passageway to the kitchen.

Upstairs, at either end of a hallway, are two good-sized bedrooms. One was very dirty and I had to spend a long time dusting, vacuuming, and cleaning out cobwebs and dead wasps. There were live ones, too, mostly outside the windows. The other bedroom is large and comfortable with two closets. I put my clothes away neatly, folded my towels, and made up the bed with a deep green comforter. The bathroom, which I scrubbed, is adequate, but still doesn't look very clean.

In the early evening, before the sun goes down, I sit on the screened porch and look out on a farmer's cut hay fields, full of deer. I work for a while at the desk in the living room and then I listen to music.

It is very dark at night, no streetlights and no pole lights. The darkness is unbroken, but there are sounds in it. Sometimes eerie sounds.

Renata Culpepper, the archaeological technician, said that flocks of blue herons, when they are agitated, gibber like monkeys.

Every morning at nine o'clock, five hummingbirds come to the feeder outside the kitchen door.

Ryan Stone

Ryan Stone grew up in Licking, Missouri, and is the author of the short story collection *Best Road Yet* (Press 53, 2010). His stories have appeared widely in publications such as *The Madison Review, The South Carolina Review, Big Muddy: A Journal of the Mississippi River Valley, Natural Bridge,* and *Elder Mountain: A Journal of Ozark Studies.* He teaches writing and literature for Danville Area Community College in Illinois.

The Hunters

There's a gas station on the highway with a sign:

> WELCOME HUNTERS—Everything You Need—Ammo, Tags, License, Beer, Ice.

The list is short, but accurate. Bill pulls the Chevy over, inspects his partner's sleeping eyes. The eyes dart about beneath the lids, as if he's searching for someone in a crowded room. Gravel catches in the Chevy's tires, spins and smacks against the underbelly of the pickup. Bill thinks of paint jobs.

They make this trip every year; every year the trees are fewer, the grass browner. In the little, over-run town coffee shop a woman whose name changes each year serves them undercooked eggs and grisly bacon. Bill stuffs his mouth full of eggs, spits them out as he eats and his friend, his partner, Len, gets a fully disgusted look in his eye. Usually, in the coffee shop, the conversations around them are so loud, so improper, there is no reason to keep up; conversations about good deals on haying equipment, the price of beef cattle and how tasty the coffee is. In the last few years, the coffee shop has gotten annoying, perverse almost with men in tight jeans and baseball caps grabbing at the waitresses' punctuated asses. Bill, although he's grabbed his share, finds the whole mess trivial and has begun, over the past two years, to believe the coffee shop is more of a ritual than any necessity. Thus, the gas station.

They've never stopped here before. The station has four hoses situated on a single island. There are only two pumps, so it's first come first serve yourself or fight it out. Bill imagines the place in the seventies and men in Studebakers and worn down Cadillacs beating each other with the window squeegees. Plummeting for that last drop. The Chevy gargles to a halt, strained under the weight of a two-hundred-mile consistent road trip. Bill throws open the door.

"Hey," he nudges Len, "want something to eat?"

Len shrugs, his eyes are blurry. A girl walks out of the station. Her legs are long, her blond hair separates and lifts in individual strands in the November wind.

"Why don't you gas up the truck?" Bill asks.

"Why don't you go fuck yourself?"

Len is not in a good mood. Len's wife, a buxom dancer and part-time prostitute, is leaving him for her bouncer at the club. Bill turns back, sees the girl with the flying hair; she's fumbling for her keys in a brown leather purse. "Damnit," he hears her shout and she spins, quite elegantly, on one heel of her cowboy boots and hurries back into the store. He can see her through the plate-glass window conversing with the clerk who is shaking his head. The flying hair lady is nothing like Len's wife. She is too skinny and framed. Len's wife is everywhere. Her body falls out in places most people's doesn't and her hair, although it is never combed, is short on her head, red and polished looking from the gallon of hair spray Len claims she uses per month.

"Bill," Len says, "sorry."

"Yeah. Get the truck gassed up, would you? I'm going to get some of those peanut butter crackers."

"You know that's not real peanut butter?"

"Good enough."

"See if you can score some dope," Len whispers and crawls out of the truck, fumbles with the gas hose. Since the miserable wife experience, Len has been getting high to control his pain and anger. He says, without weed, he would kill the bouncer and Mattie and drive his Thunderbird that he keeps in the garage covered up with a tarp over a cliff. Bill hasn't smoked since his college stint. He knew a guy who grew it in his windowsill underneath the porcelain sill in the concrete blocks. When the monitors would check his room, he'd simply slide the plate in place and tell them to come on in and have a look around, have a beer. They were less strict about beer back then, Bill thinks and then thinks he should get some beer.

The blonde is still digging in her purse when Bill enters and the door slaps against a small bell strung from the ceiling. It makes a happy jingle and the clerk looks up, his face distorted as if it's painful to work there. It probably is, Bill thinks and searches the racks for the peanut butter and cheese crackers.

They don't have name brand. Only something generic that looks like the peanut butter is crusty and crumbling, but his stomach tells him to buy it anyway. He picks up a six pack of beer, cheap, and the crackers, a bottle of water, some beef jerky and a Coke.

"I just had the shittin' things in my purse," the blonde says.

"I didn't seem 'em, Brenda," the clerk shoots back. "Hell, there's a bunch of places they could be in that damn thing." He's leaning over the counter trying to peer into her purse. From Bill's angle it appears as if he's trying to stare down her sweater. Her jeans, he notices, are tight, rounded around her body perfectly, but he shakes it off thinking of his own life, his wife, his son and all their problems. There's plenty of room for inept marriages. All of his friends are in one, including himself. Len's married to a hooker; there's Pete, who has two kids with one woman, three with another and one on the way with a seventeen-year-old. Pete's forty. A few others have apparently normal lives, but behind the shadows of the shrubbery in front of their suburban strongholds there are dark forces at work. Like Larry who has two mistresses and only one dog. The guy has more women than animals. Or, Jones who doesn't have a woman, but lives with one and everyone thinks, or knows, he's gay and trying to hide it. Sometimes, Bill thinks his life is like a Springer rerun. He wonders how he and

Len can watch the show so much and laugh at the midget strippers and the men marrying barnyard animals.

"Ah, shit," Brenda exclaims. "Give me the damn phone and I'll call Travis. He can come and get me and when I find the stupid, fuckin' keys I'll get the car." She's huffing a bit and Bill approaches the counter.

"How's the take?" he asks the clerk, glancing briefly at Brenda who blows her hair out of her face with a puff of sarcastic wind.

"Fair. Down from last year I heard."

It's the same line they always say in the coffee shop. Every year the numbers of deer taken falls, but everyone seems to get a deer. Bill stopped believing them, but he reads the papers and according to them it's down as well. He spreads his hands on the counter, searching for Len outside through the dusted window. Len is sitting in the truck.

"Gas too. Number . . ." he strains out. "The blue Chevy." It's the only car at the pumps.

Brenda is on the phone, tapping her overly fake, red nails against the receiver. They make a splitting little noise that cuts through the silent station, breaks over the compressor noise of the beer coolers.

"Marty," she says suddenly, "is Travis there?" She looks at the Marlboro clock above the counter. "When will he be back?" Tap, tap, tap on the receiver. Bill wonders what it sounds like on the other end of the line, if it sounds like thunder. "Shit, Marty, can you come and get me. I'm out at Penny's on the highway. Yes. Lost my keys." She pauses and her eyes narrow. "How the hell am I suppose to know! I had 'em, lost 'em, can't find the damn, fuckin' things and I'm out here on the highway with no way home. Yes I looked in my purse, all over the goddamn store." More tapping, faster. "Shit, Marty." She hangs up the phone with a bang followed by a short tone ring.

"Twenty-two fifty-six," the clerk says to Bill, turns to Brenda. "Well?"

"That son-of-a-bitch is out at Clancy's shootin' pool, rubbin' up against that bitch whatshername no doubt. He won't be back till late tonight."

The clerk shakes his head, gives Bill his change. Bill rolls the money over in his hand, he has smooth-edged nickels and rough dimes and quarters. A few pennies with their sharp, intense smell. He knows if he sticks them in his mouth they will ferment his breath with a tangy scent. His mother told him sucking on pennies would turn his mouth green and eat out his stomach, but under his bed, late at night, he'd flip open his change jar and have a snack.

Brenda is out the door and walking toward her car. Her hair is again in disarrangement. Bill leaves as well, the tingle of the tiny bell runs up his spine, gives him goose bumps. Len is back in the truck, his head tilted back and his Adam's apple rising, lowering, rising, lowering. He swallows and the apple buckles. Bill hurries into the truck.

"See that girl," he says. Len sits up.

"I saw her a long time ago, man. Look at that hair."

"We're going to offer her a ride. She's stranded out here and her boyfriend won't come get her. She's lost her keys."

"Some guys are pricks. Some women are bitches," Len says.

Bill pulls the Chevy up close to Brenda. I've got to be cordial so she doesn't freak, he thinks.

"Ma'am," he feels strange calling her ma'am. She's at least ten years younger than he is, "this may seem a bit forward, but would you like a ride? In to town I mean?"

She turns. Her eyes are green and she's been crying. She kicks the gravel at her feet and it sprays up on the Chevy's door.

"I'm not stupid. I'm not getting in with two guys I don't have fuckin' clue who they are."

"I'm only offering," Bill says. He's sweating. He can feel it on the back of his neck. It's been years since he's spoken to a woman besides his wife. He can't even remember the name of the girl he dated before he got married. He feels very lost as if there is only one surrounding around him, trees or sand or water, and he can't find his way out.

"You're a damn fool if you think I'm getting in there. My boyfriend will be here in a little bit and he'll kick both your asses."

"Is he the one at Clancy's?" Bill asks. Len looks over at him and grins.

"Yeah," and she cries a bit, her nails near her eyes. Bill hopes she won't scratch herself with those nails. They look lethal.

Bill opens the door, "Come on," he says, "we'll cart you back to town and you can get a ride there."

"I just lost my keys," she says. "They're probably in the station. I should go look for them some more instead of just panicking the way I always do."

"It'll be alright. We'll give you a ride."

"No, it's okay."

And Bill's out, he's grabbing at her arms and slinging her towards the door. He's forcing her into the cab and Len's shouting, but Bill can't hear him. Brenda's arms fling and her nails reach out and slice into Bill's forearm. The blood rolls up through the cut and begins to caravan down through his arm hair. Brenda is in the truck, Bill is slamming the door, squealing the tires.

"Hey!" he hears the clerk's diminishing shout through Len's open window.

Len's voice cracks over the Chevy's deteriorating engine. His arms are waving around and he's shouting "Kidnapping, kidnapping." Brenda sits between them, her face down, her hair covering it and the sides of her forehead. She sobs in intermittent gasps.

"What the hell's amatter with you?" Len shouts.

Bill focuses on the road, his eyes and shoulders feel relaxed for the first time. The passing headlights do not bother him and he doesn't have to squint. The exhaust pulses upward from behind the tailgate like a random, overactive cloud. It's frozen in the wind created by the Chevy. Bill doesn't have a plan and he's hoping the girl won't scratch him again. The cut is wider than he thought and blood drips down on his pant leg, stains and spreads out like a fungus. Still the Chevy lurches forward and a scattered snow begins to fall. It's a wet snow, crusts the hood of the pickup, glazes the windshield until it's like looking through broken glass. Bill hits the wiper switch and nothing happens. The blades stick where they are, stubborn and cold. Len swears and Brenda sobs.

Soon, the windshield is so covered Bill can't see. He leans forward, trying to see under the advancing ice held back by the weak fan motor blowing heated air up through the defrost vent. Len has flipped on the radio. George Strait sings "Ocean Front Property."

"I can't see anything," Bill says. He pulls the Chevy off the road and leans back. His spine feels as if it's been whacked with a two by four. "Look what you did to me," he shows Brenda the cut.

"Fuck you," she says.

Bill laughs, out loud, hearty and warm; a laugh reserved for Santa Claus. He opens the Chevy's door. "Lean up," he says. When they do, he reaches behind the seat, finds the lever covered in grease and lifts the seat forward. Somewhere he has a windshield scraper. It's old, half broken, but it will have to work. He finds it. The scraper is covered in grease and dust. Bill laments his construction job. All I do, he thinks as he attacks the frozen windshield, is grease equipment all day, and all I get in my truck, my clothes, my hair is grease, grease, grease. The ice is thicker than he thought and the scraper isn't doing much good. Maybe someone will come along, but then he remembers the girl and how that would look and he has visions of police stations and gruff, local policemen in cowboy hats. He'd been arrested once on a night not much different from this one. He and Len were drunk, swerving down 23 Street when the flashing lights came on. They shot through him like a well-placed arrow and he pulled over, took a test, failed and spent a night in the tank. He didn't lose his license. They weren't as strict back then and he could only imagine how harsh they were for kidnapping. But, it isn't kidnapping. They are only taking her into town and then if she wants to have a drink or get some coffee or something that would be fine. If not, they'd drop her off at a pay phone and give her some change, maybe buy her a sandwich at that godforsaken coffee shop or something and be on their way. The Chevy shook a bit and Bill bore down on the ice. It was chipping a bit faster now. Over his ice scraper squeaking, he can hear voices. When he slows his scraping, he can hear them.

"I don't know," Len's saying. "He's not usually like this. I promise you won't get hurt. I promise he's not crazy." Why would he need to promise? Doesn't she know she's okay; she's warm and they're taking her back to town to have a drink or coffee or something. How can she not know? "He's not crazy," Len says and Bill can see him wagging his head through the ice. The droplets of rain appear in the Chevy's headlights like misguided bugs. They fall and splatter and freeze on the hood. Len's head looks like it's in different sections, he's broken by a line in the ice Bill has made with his scraper. Bill can't believe how sturdy the ice is and notices his extremities getting colder, his nose aching a bit on the tip and his ears stinging. He wonders about the temperature.

"He grabbed, goddamnit. Threw me." Her voice is low, like she wants the engine to cover it, but there's enough in it to carry.

"I know," Len says. He's grinning again, but not his full grin. It's his sympathetic grin. The same one he gave his wife when she told him she was a stripper. Bill can see it, cracked and frayed, beyond his scraper and he finishes the hole he's been working on. It's a small hole, just big enough to see the road, or what's left of the road not covered by ice. He slips as he climbs back in the truck, falls into Brenda's lap and she gives a huff.

"Get the hell off a me!"

"Sorry," he says, turns to Len. "Hey, crack out that beer. I could use one." Len hesitates, sits still. "The beer, Lenny, get the beer." Bill points at the brown sack at Len's feet. His friend reaches down, his hand noticeably shaking, and lifts the six pack from the floorboards. It's already warmer than it should be due to the heater. "Damn," Bill says opening a can, "we should've put it in the back." He offers a can to Len, who accepts, and one to Brenda, who, somewhat to his surprise, accepts as well. They drive slow, weaving around patches of black ice marking the road like tar pits, sipping silently at the wide mouth cans; occasionally, Brenda makes a chug sound when she swallows.

The beer is smooth and calms Bill's nerves a bit. He thinks about his wife, about their car and their mortgage and how he can pay off the house in a few more years. He'll quit his job, he thinks, when he gets back. Get a better job and pay the house off five years early and never swim in grease again. He'll buy a new pickup, a gleaming red Chevy that has no defects and the damn wipers work. Maybe Len will go fishing with him on a cloudy weekend when the fish will surely bite simply because they are supposed to. The cut on his arm is scarring and the blood has stiffened in his arm hairs. They crinkle as he turns the steering wheel to avoid an icy spot. He could throw a Super Bowl party this year. A big one, with chips and salsa and a hoagie as long as his dining room table. He could invite all of his friends and they could sit down and watch the Super Bowl like everyone else. Then he remembers he doesn't care much for football.

The night gets deeper. Brenda has finished her beer and hands the can to Len, who stuffs it back into the paper bag. Good ole Len, always the conserver, always the neat one. Bill wishes they had some weed.

"Do you know where we could score some grass?" he asks.

"Jesus," Brenda says. Bill looks at her. Her lips are chapped.

"There's some Carmex in the glove compartment," he offers. "Unused. I've never touched it." Len opens the rusty-hinged door. It squawks as he does and Brenda fishes around for the little white and yellow container. She finds it, twists its top off and spreads the Carmex over her lips. They glisten in the dashboard light. Len offers her another beer. "Another for me," Bill says.

"You can let me off up here. I have friends here," Brenda says. There are faint houselights in the distance, off the road and stuffed back in some trees.

"They got any grass?" Bill asks.

She stares at him. Her eyes, he notices, are green. "They might."

Bill swings the Chevy into a partially hidden driveway. There's a mailbox that says Wells set on an old wagon wheel. The wheel is covered in ice. He drives as fast on the driveway as he did on the highway, slinging gravel and mud up over the sides of the truck.

"Slow the fuck down will ya?" Len says, but Bill plows on right up to the porch of the house. He throws open the door.

"I'll go," Brenda says. "They don't know you." She climbs out of the truck, struggles up the small embankment in front of the house. There are lights on all over. Windows lit up like passages to other places. Bill expects to see dark figures staring out at him as he sips his beer. He can see Brenda at the door, she's knocking and the hollow clumping sound echoes back to Bill. He thinks he feels it shake his beer can. The door opens, a man stands in the light. Bill can only see his silhouette. He's nodding, a good sign and letting her in, even better. It's only seconds before the man is outside, coming down the embankment, carrying something.

"Hey, man, did she ask you about the grass?" And the first blow hits Bill in the stomach, buckling him like a folding table. His eyes swell in his head as the air pushes out of him. He feels the second blow slam on his back and he can't breathe, can't even see. Mud cakes to the side of his face, is jammed in his nostrils. He feels blood boiling up his throat. The Chevy's door opens and Len is out.

"Get the gun, Clarice," someone calls, "there's two of the sons a bitches."

Bill feels hands pulling on him, lifting him and he hears the truck door open, close and he's in the cab. Len is driving and Bill's head is rocking, bumping gently against the back glass. The Chevy is running full tilt down the driveway and hits the main road, swiveling, spinning. He sees Len grabbing the wheel, jerking at it, right left, right left. Bill looks out and the droplets are spattering on the windshield and they look like tiny mosquitoes and just beyond the headlights there is nothing and the nothing eats the light, comes closer and closer until it's upon him.

Jo Van Arkel

Jo Beth (Walker) Van Arkel was born in Kansas City and within two weeks of her birth shuttled down to the Ozarks to be in the company of all of her relatives, living and dead. Her mother hailed from Hog Eye, otherwise known as Charity, Missouri. Her father was a Berryville, Arkansas, man. She received her MFA in Fiction Writing from the University of Oregon and teaches writing at Drury University. Her stories have appeared in literary magazines including *The Northwest Review, The Literary Review, Sou'wester, Elder Mountain, Big Muddy, Roanoke Review,* and others. She is the author of three books: *The Things I Got Growing Deep Down Inside*, a collection of stories, and *Give Me a Hat to Wear*, a collection of poems, and *In Dog Years, A Small Book of Short Shorts.* She has a new book forthcoming. The short story "Swimming at Flat Bridge, 1963" won the Missouri Writers Biennial Award funded by the National Endowment for the Arts.

Swimming at Flat Bridge, 1963

Mother and Aunt Mel were already tight-lipped because we'd been swimming at Flat Bridge three hours with no sign of the men or even their flat-bottomed river boat. They got tight-lipped when the men went on weekend fishing trips by themselves. It was like they knew those men were having fun without them. Probably whizzing off the side of the boat and cussing and looking out for women sunning themselves on the river banks, and Mother and Aunt Mel didn't like it one bit. Only Aunt Wildeen didn't seem to care. She was the youngest, and she had been sunning herself on the banks of the river by Flat Bridge all afternoon, while a few of the Poindexter boys stole glances at her as they paddled by in their underwear. She did look good in a bathing suit. She had on a two-piecer print of yellow flowers with bottoms that came to just below her belly button. Her blond hair was tied up in a red scarf. She was married to Uncle Benny, my dad's youngest brother.

They'd only been married three months. She was from Chicago, and she always kept her hair done up and painted her toenails and wore lipstick so red it was all I could see on her face when she talked to me. She had never been outside of Chicago until she married Benny, and they moved back home. She called herself "Pioneer Wildeen" and said her friends from high school would never believe she could move this far south. She typed letters and mailed them off and got letters back from places like Milwaukee and Toledo. I watched her type once when I was over at their house to bring Uncle Benny my dad's monkey wrench so Benny could work on his bathroom pipes. She typed a whole page in about a minute.

Her name before she got married was Wildeen Wilde. I remember that because I read it on the invitation, and because at the party after the wedding my Uncle Benny, who was already drunk before he even stepped up to the altar, took my daddy by the lapels and danced around the room with him saying, "I married a Wilde woman!"

I was in the wedding. I threw flower petals on the floor just before Wildeen marched down the aisle in her wedding dress. I was thirteen, and it was the first time I'd ever worn a long dress, and it wasn't bad except for the girdle and nylons, and the lace on my slip which made me break out in a rash.

For some reason Aunt Wildeen liked me from the first time she met me. Uncle Benny had brought Wildeen over for dinner to meet Daddy, and when Benny said, "Oh yeah, and this is Esther," Wildeen came straight over to me and shook my hand.

"You're tall for your age," she said to me.

I nodded and let go of her hand.

"Your hair's too short and could use a perm," she said. She studied my face. "You've got good bone structure though. You'll always be pretty 'cause you've got good bone structure."

Benny thumped me on the head as he walked into the family room where the ball game was going on the TV. "We call her Mudface, for short," he said, and he laughed.

"You will always be Esther to me," said Wildeen. She said the words as if she'd just heard them in some movie and had been waiting for the right moment to use them herself. I liked it though. I liked being included in her drama.

I looked at my mother, who was standing nearby. She had a smile on, but it was one of those that didn't show any of her teeth. "Would you like something to drink?" she said to Wildeen. "Iced tea? Lemonade?"

"I'll have whatever the boys are drinking," Wildeen said. And she went straight into the family room, sat down in Daddy's big chair by the TV and said, "Who's playing?"

Aunt Wildeen was Catholic. A priest did their wedding. All through the ceremony the priest and Wildeen and Benny crossed themselves and knelt and said things in Latin. I'd never seen a priest up close before. This one had a fleshy neck that spilled over his collar, and one side of his face was covered with tiny red webs. Daddy said they were capillaries and later at the party while the priest was drinking champagne, I heard him tell someone that years ago he'd been hit in the face with a golf club.

Wildeen's parents didn't come to the wedding because Benny wasn't Catholic even though he promised the priest he would raise his kids Catholic and go through the classes to convert. A few Wilde cousins showed up for the reception though and stole six cases of champagne. I watched one of them named Rudy carry a case out to his trunk and place it next to two other cases. He saw me standing nearby and said, "It's for the honeymoon, kid. We're taking it over to the motel where Wildeen and Buddy are staying to surprise them."

"His name is Benny," I said.

"Oh. Right." He took a crumpled dollar out of his pocket and gave it to me. Then he lit a cigarette, climbed into his Impala, and rolled down the window. "You Catholic?" he said to me, blowing smoke from his mouth and nose.

"No," I said.

He nodded, still looking at me. "I've gone out with girls who weren't Catholic," he said, like he was trying to tell me that there was still hope. He smoked on his cigarette a bit more and stared at his dashboard. Then finally he said, "Well, gotta run." He started the car, and before he drove off he flicked his half-smoked cigarette out the window.

I wiped the butt off on the hem of my dress and finished it. I'd been smoking for a year, in the field behind my house. I hadn't told anybody. It takes a lot of practice to look right smoking, and I wasn't very good at it yet, because cigarettes were hard to come by. I usually had to steal them from my dad or from Aunt Mel when she left her purse open on our kitchen counter and she and Mother were out back clipping fresh flowers or something. On this particular night though, I didn't even hide but stood out in the parking lot in my long pink dress, smoking and hoping someone would catch me, pulling at my girdle which was starting to itch and wondering, since I'd just learned in last year's gym class the facts of life, if Wildeen and Benny had ever done it before or if this night would be their first time.

Aunt Wildeen had that effect upon people. She made people think about physical things. So my mother and Aunt Mel got thin-lipped around her, and Benny was always grabbing her by the hips, and even my dad who never listened to women talk because he said he didn't like the high-pitched sound of their voices—even Dad would smile and watch her lips move as she was speaking. And now, at the river, while crawdads skittered around on the rocks and dragonflies, locked together in twos and threes, lighted on people's wet heads, the Poindexter boys kept swimming past Wildeen and craning their necks like a bunch of hungry turtles.

"Ess," my mother yelled at me from the bank. I was standing in river water up to the top of my thighs, the water swirling about me, cold and brown from the mud I'd stirred up with my tennis shoes. I didn't especially like swimming, but the sun was too hot for just sitting on the rocks of the banks. I couldn't just lie there motionless, minute after minute like Wildeen did. "Esther!" my mother said again.

"What is it?" I answered, without turning back to look at her.

"Don't let Philip go down the river so far! He's heading for the drop off. Mel says he's going to drown."

"I can swim," Philip yelled. He was chucking stones at a log on the far bank, trying to hit a row of turtles sunning themselves, but so far he hadn't come within ten feet.

"No you can't," said Aunt Mel.

Philip was my ten-year-old cousin, Aunt Mel's only son. I hated him. He liked to pull the legs off of june bugs and pinched hard enough to make blue marks on my arms and was always reaching for my bra strap to snap it when I wasn't looking. His dad kept Philip's hair cut in a tight crewcut, and he had one of those hard boy faces. I had to sit next to him on the hot ride down to the river. I nearly always got carsick and I thought if I did this time, I'd be sure and throw up on Philip since he had been sitting next to me farting and laughing the whole trip.

"Philip," Aunt Mel kept saying, "if you pass gas one more time, I'll slap your face."

I kept wishing she would. Please, oh, please, I'd think. Slap his face. But she never would.

If he was drowning, he wouldn't have let me save him anyway. So, while I waded slowly in the direction of where Philip was swimming. I stayed just far enough away that I wouldn't get there in time.

The Poindexter boys were horsing around on Paralysis Rock. Paralysis Rock was a big clump of rocks if you want to be particular. They jutted out over the river and formed a kind of diving platform, but the water was too shallow to go head first so a person had to half jump, with his knees tucked up under his chin and let his rear end hit the bottom first.

The Poindexters had a family plot right next to ours in the church cemetery. In fact, they had the oldest family plot in the church yard, at least that's as far as I could tell from reading all the headstones on Decoration Day while Mother and Aunt Mel placed wreaths and cried over the headstones of Granny and Granpa and Uncle Short and the twins, baby brothers to Mother and Aunt Mel who died at six months of age, one within a day of the other. Besides the twins' grave (it had a single headstone as they were buried together, arm in arm from what Mother tells me when I can get her to talk about it), the oldest Poindexter headstone was my favorite because there was a picture on it of the occupant, Harris Poindexter. His face, somehow transferred to porcelain and embedded in the stone, looked not much older than mine and he had this shocked expression, hair half standing up, eyebrows raised, mouth open . . . like dying had caught him off guard. His gravestone had some dates I can't remember and the words . . . "died too young." And whenever I stood in front of his gravestone I got a creepy feeling all the way down to the heels of my feet that Harris Poindexter was looking back at me. And the way his face looked, something about his eyebrows and his open mouth, made me feel like I owed him an answer to some question I just missed hearing.

I noticed now that all of the boys on the rock had that same kind of look about them, thick dark hair, thick eyebrows that always seemed half raised, except for one that the boys called DeWayne, who had sandy-colored hair and eyes so close together as a baby and it looked like someone had squeezed his head together as a baby and it never popped back out.

Mother didn't care much for the Poindexter boys. Anyone who would swim in his underwear for the whole wide world to see and with ladies present was no better than an animal. She always called them "Those Poindexter Boys."

"Ess," she had said, as we were unloading towels and blankets and the picnic baskets with strawberry soda pops and sandwiches already gummy from the heat, "don't go near those Poindexter boys." She used her low "you know what I mean" voice. The way she looked at me then, with a woman-to-woman look, made me wonder if by swimming in their thin underwear those Poindexter boys set sperm loose in the murky river water. I'd learned about sperm in gym class too. Mrs. Lee, my leathery gym teacher, had warned us in her high-pitched voice that "sperm could swim upstream in even the swiftest of currents so determined is it to reach its destination!"

Mother didn't warn me about looking at those Poindexter boys though. Mother and Aunt Mel were lying on their stomachs with their faces away from the river and separated from Wildeen by about ten feet. They were propped up on their elbows talking about someone and paying no attention to me. So I waded thigh-high in the water and pretended to study the river bottom for crawdads and watched closely as the Poindexters pushed and shoved one another on Paralysis Rock, the thin skin of their underwear clinging to them and showing the hint of something pink bouncing around just beneath the surface.

DeWayne was wearing boxers and was just about to be shoved over the edge of the rocks to where I might get a good enough view of something to report back to my friend Debra Jean, who took gym class with me and had once said she saw a flasher standing in a second-story window of the public library (he had the shade drawn down to about his waist and was tapping at the window as she walked by on the sidewalk below so as to get her attention, but she said it was dark and she hardly saw anything at all) when all of a sudden someone came up behind me and shoved me under the water. I thought it was Philip, the little creep, so before I even came up for a breath, I grabbed his feet and yanked as hard as I could so that he came down in one loud splash, and it was only after I saw the yellow flowered bathing suit that I realized it wasn't Philip at all but Wildeen. I stood up in the water right then and pushed the hair back out of my face and reached for her arm, saying before she even came up out of the water, "I'm sorry, Aunt Wildeen. I thought it was Philip," because I figured she'd be mad at me for getting her hair wet, since most women once they get older don't like to get their hair wet when they are swimming, so they're always doing side strokes, even with their bathing caps on, the way Mother and Aunt Mel do, but when Wildeen came up sputtering and tugging here and there at her suit she was laughing so hard she could barely catch her breath.

"I saw you," she said in her loud voice like she didn't care who heard us, and she didn't, I knew that. "I saw you trying to look up those boys' shorts," she said still laughing.

"I was looking for crawdads," I said just as loud. I could feel my face getting hot, and I wasn't sure if it was from being in the sun and water for three hours or from being mad at getting caught and having to lie about it.

Wildeen pulled the wet red scarf from her pony tail and bent over throwing her hair out ahead of her. Even wet her hair was blond and wavy. She twisted her hair up into a tight rope and wound her red scarf around it again. As she lifted her head to look at me I could see short curls springing up like thin copper wires all over her head where her hair refused to be held in place.

"Well, you won't find any crawdads up there," she said, waving her hand in the direction of the Poindexter boys. "But," then she winked at me, "you might find something else that bites!" She laughed again, and I could feel my face getting hotter. Wildeen said, "Come on," and she swam off in the direction of the drop off.

I looked back at Mother and Aunt Mel. They had their heads down now so it looked like they were sleeping. Like I said, I didn't care for swimming much, and didn't like to get my hair wet because it made my cheekbones look bigger, and it emphasized my pointy chin. But when I saw Wildeen down by the drop off, waving at me, I just dove in and swam straight for her and when I came up out of the water she was still laughing. "You're the funniest looking swimmer I've ever seen," she said. And I thought of my pointy chin and big cheekbones and how dumb I must have looked. But instead of getting out of the water and going to sit on a towel, I laughed too.

I turned my back on everyone else, on Mother and Aunt Mel and the Poindexter boys and Philip and laughed as loud as I could. And that's when I understood why Mother and Aunt Mel didn't like Wildeen and why Benny was so crazy about her.

Wildeen dropped back in the water and began backstroking up the current. I was swatting dragonflies away from my shoulders and the hairs on my back stood up as the hot sun dried the water off my back. And that's when Aunt Mel screamed.

It was an awful scream, not real loud but wavering like the last sound of someone being strangled before their air passage is closed off completely.

"Oh, God," she said. "Philip!" She ran down to the river's edge. "Esther! Where's Philip?"

Mother was off her towel, too. I turned around to the log where the turtles had been sunning. There were only two left, and I watched as one slid into the water and swam further downstream.

Aunt Mel started into the water, her arms waving about and her crying out, "Philip! Baby!"

Wildeen was standing in the water now. She yelled to Mother to keep Mel out of the water. She'd muddy it up to where we couldn't see. And I remembered hearing Benny brag about how Wildeen had taken lifesaving classes at the Y in Chicago and how as part of her test she had to jump in the deep water with all her clothes and keep her head above water for nearly twenty minutes.

"Where'd you last see him?" Wildeen said to me.

At first I couldn't even answer. I couldn't even remember. But Wildeen yelled at me. "*Where'd you last see him?*"

"At the edge of the drop off," I said, pointing. "He was by that tree, throwing rocks at the turtles."

She swam in that direction, then stood up, and moving slowly, hunched over, she swept her arms through the muddy water. "Get some help," she said to me. "Get those boys."

I turned in the direction of Paralysis Rock. I could see the boys just beyond the bluff and yelled at them. But they didn't hear over the sound of the river and their own horsing around. A few years back a four-year-old girl had drowned in the river. Down by Eddyville. She floated eight miles and then got caught up under the bridge. Daddy was in on that search. And I remembered him telling Mother about how when they found the girl, the searchers were pulling the body along the river by its feet, and he said it was awful the way they let her head bounce against the rocks. But then when the reporters got there, the searchers were real careful with how they handled the body.

I yelled again, this time so loud it made my ears ring. And DeWayne, the one with the close eyes, came to the edge of the rock. "My cousin—we lost him. I think he's drowning somewhere," I said.

DeWayne said something to the other boys, and they all jumped off the rock together, and I pointed them in the direction of Wildeen, and they thrashed and splashed their way over to her.

She yelled at them, just like she yelled at Aunt Mel. To keep back and not thrash around. She told them to form a line and walk forward waving their arms like this, she said, and she showed them. Once they got to the drop off, they'd try diving. And they did just what she said and everyone got real quiet so that the only sound was the water rushing around us and Aunt Mel whimpering on the shore.

I started thinking about how it would change everybody's life, with Philip drowning. Aunt Mel would never get over it, and I was starting to feel sorry about the whole mess, when Philip walked out of the woods down near the log where I last saw him, the little creep.

"What's going on?" he said.

"Philip!" Aunt Mel wailed. She ran across the shore and threw her arms around him. Then she stood back and slapped his face.

"Ow!" Philip said.

"Don't ever do that again," she said. And she started hitting him again. She kept hitting him and hitting him until he ran from her and even then she chased after him waving her arms to try and hit him some more.

"I just had to pee!" Philip kept saying.

"I thought you were dead! Do you realize that, young man?" she wailed. And Mother was chasing after Mel saying, "It's alright. Everything's alright!"

Philip ran for the station wagon, jumped in and locked all the doors before Aunt Mel could reach him and hit him again.

The Poindexter boys were laughing. DeWayne looked right at me and winked.

I could hear Aunt Mel yelling at Philip to unlock the doors and him saying through the rolled-up windows, "Not until you promise to stop hitting me!"

I looked at Wildeen then. She was standing in the water, watching Aunt Mel and Philip and Mother, not smiling or frowning or anything. Just watching. And I wondered what she was thinking. Something in the way she was standing told me that one way or another, with Benny or without, Wildeen wasn't going to be around here for much longer.

"Esther!" Mother yelled. "Get your things. We're leaving. The boys can just hitchhike home, for all I care."

She was gathering up the towels as she spoke, shaking the rocks from them.

But I pretended not to hear, and dove into the water, swimming toward Wildeen and the edge of the drop-off.

James Whitehead

In 1965, James T. Whitehead (1936–2003) and his friend, William Harrison, founded the nationally prestigious Creative Writing Program at the University of Arkansas, Fayetteville. He taught in that program for the next thirty-four years, from 1965 to 1999. He was recipient of a Guggenheim Fellowship in fiction and a Robert Frost Fellowship in poetry. In 1981, Whitehead presented Jimmy Carter with a poem to honor his presidency and welcome him back to Plains, Georgia. Whitehead's sports novel, *Joiner* (1971), was listed among the *New York Times'* Noteworthy Books of the Year. While winning acclaim as a novelist, Whitehead published widely as a poet; his many, well-received collections include *Domains* (1967), *Local Men* (1979), the chapbook, *Actual Size* (1985), and *Near at Hand* (1993).

The Opinion of an Interesting Old Man

It's plain damned hard to lose yourself these days . . .
or at least you can't the clean way you once could . . .
gone for a week without boiled water and food,
then turning up in town misunderstood

with the whole place mad because they'd planned to say
nice things when sure you wouldn't come their way

again. It's a crying shame the way they're rude
enough to hunt you down within a single day

and just before you get that taste of fear
and just before you feel you're about to pray.
You hear them thrashing through the brush, when you're nude
with love of being lost. They think you're crude

if you plead you'd like to stay. They always intrude
like parents who are appalled by curious play,
and they trade with the oldest lie: "It's for your good,
dear friend. We've come to help you out," they say.

And out you go. Be sure they knew you would.
Be sure they'd rather have you alive than dead.

Just North of Sikeston

One night just north of Sikeston
I had a vision, or at least an insight,
Driving at fifty where before the worst
Was eyestrain. (It was within the legal limit.)

The season was spring and every truck and car
Had perfect manners, held
To their side and blinked their headlights
To keep from going blind—
A lovely thing when you think what could easily happen
On an eighteen-foot road with a lip
If people get a little out of line.
That brought the horrors, the vision,

  or what you will . . .
You see, I realized some mean to die—
Some, too much aware
Of spring and how the earth
Begins to hate them less, will fling themselves
And families across the median.
With the weather getting better, these winter men
Will cram one lane with life
To quiet the ugly wife
And free themselves and children from the long ways
I want to ride with mine for years. Dear God,
I thought, please let him kill in some other state
Tonight, as he seems to . . .
Or, better, let him die
Alone in a ploughed field,
His throat slit by his own hand—
Or in a big motel,
His pistol in his mouth—
Don't let him crush his family, or mine,
Or any other man's. Save, if you can,
A dozen lives too subtle to abide
A fury of metal. Let
No man gone out of round tear living years
On a wheel insanely rolling bloody from
The berm. It's love that dims
Our lights. It's praise that we take care to ease
Ourselves from every curve.

Miller Williams

Miller Williams is the author, editor, or translator of thirty-four books, including fourteen volumes of poetry, *Patterns of Poetry: An Encyclopedia of Forms*, and *Making a Poem: Some Thoughts about Poetry and the People Who Write it.* Among his many honors are the Amy Lowell Traveling Scholarship in Poetry from Harvard University, the Poets' Prize, the Prix de Rome for Literature, and the Academy Award for Literature, the latter two both from the American Academy of Arts and Letters. Reading "Of History and Hope," he was inaugural poet for Bill Clinton's second swearing-in as president. He is now emeritus professor at the University of Arkansas in Fayetteville, and is the father of three-time Grammy Award–winning singer and songwriter Lucinda Williams.

An Unrhymed Sonnet

What is existence? What does it mean to be?
How did existence come to be from nothing?
Is nothing lying still at the core of being?
Why is there life? If life began with God,
did God have a beginning? If God was always,
how did God and always come to be?
If neither began, if they run all the way back,
they run back all the way to what, to when?

If time is a long illusion, what is always?
What hangs itself around the universe?
If this one universe is all there is,
all the more the question wants an answer.

Excuse me. I shouldn't ask these questions here.
Please—just go ahead and cut my hair.

Separatio in Loco

He lives all alone now, in the home they bought,
and finally seems to be managing, more or less.
Not the way he was, of course, with her,
who lives alone now, too, at the same address.

Daniel Woodrell

Daniel Woodrell is the author of eight novels and one collection of short stories. His books are published in more than fifteen languages around the world. Two of his novels have been developed into films, *Ride With the Devil,* and *Winter's Bone,* which won the 2010 Sundance Best Film Award and was nominated for four Academy Awards in 2011. He has received the PEN West Award for the Novel for *Tomato Red,* the Clifton Fadiman Medal for *The Death of Sweet Mister,* the Quill Award from the Writers Hall of Fame of America, the Prix Du Meilleur Polar Award, the Missouri Library Association Literary Award, and others. *Library Journal* named *The Outlaw Album* one of the best short story collections in 2011. He was born in the Missouri Ozarks where he lives with his wife, Katie Estill.

Black Step

The cow trembled in the sideways tree, the broken left foreleg canted in a separate direction from the other legs, snapped sharply to the right and dangling. There'd been moans since the storm in the night pushed on and away and the wind calmed. The cow heard my feet rustle pebbles on the cliff and its tired neck raised the head to look up at me. The cow had wide screaming eyes that were saying things that living things say to me in that language better than words. That language that travels. I've seen it everywhere.

The sideways tree was a lonely old sycamore halfway down the cliff that grew straight out from the face for about ten feet, then curled upwards for another thirty. Far below, the river flowed clean and dense in the morning shadow cast by the bluff, the rocks in its bed singing of centuries spent singing in the rushing, the things that wash by, bump going past, leave marks or bones. And the cow repeated everything again with those shrill eyes pointed my way, pleading as it had since the forest started rattling and lightning shanks stomped down yellow from the sky and the wind huffed 'til thoughts scattered and bad instincts took charge, and the cow plunged through the barbed wire seeking a way out of the suddenly terrifying pasture but found only a way down, and the sideways tree snagged it so it had a long hurt night held aloft to hear the rocks far, far below, and know horror.

I felt responsible for the cows.

I turned and walked across the broad sopping pasture toward Ma's house, tall supple grass flicking droplets to my knees. The sky had been washed baby blue and blank and the other cows were munching away at the greenery, rubbing their hides on small trees. Ma's house is a square two-story built plain long ago and still sturdy. It's painted an invented shade of white about halfway around the house to where the paint ran out, just past the south corner and beyond sight from the road, some certain mix of various whites you have to fetch from town. The rest of the house has been colored with the paler paints leftover in the shed, so it's one color house seen driving by, several others standing in the yard, colors that don't rhyme in the eye but the old wood is well coated. A ladder yet leans there, and a couple of brushes on the bottom rung have stiffened atop a paint can lid.

She's asleep, Ma, snoring in her room, letting the creep of cancer slip her mind a spell, and I go tip-toe through the kitchen to the gun cupboard in the hall. The rifle I want is standing in the back now, behind a cracked oil lantern and a pile of yesteryear phone books, not handy like I kept it. It's an old bruiser, a bolt-action aught-six that has been whipped on by wintry thickets slapping and raw sporting weather since two grandpa's ago, yet it still has a glow to it, a veteran allure. I trust this one most.

The cow screams at me again with those eyes. Screams what you think it would. The sideways tree is too far down the cliff for me to clamber there, even if I was willing. In the valley and downriver a short ways there's a twist of smoke coming from a new house I kept forgetting was there now. A strange but handsome riverside house made of fresh shining wood, with steep roofs on the buildings, and bluish tile, where outsiders have come to live. I stand on the cliff so a stray round won't pop into a tile.

This target seemed so close, so easy, so harmless, not like those when I'd been elsewhere.

I said, "Should've stopped at the checkpoint, Hadji."

The dead cow slumped more loosely over the sideways tree. The eyes finally hushed. One leg strode hard for a few seconds, trying to climb the cliff now it was shot, climb the cliff in death, then abruptly stilled. Those airy sounds flapped from jowls and butt as the meat settled.

A man came out of the house below and stared at me, a silver-haired man in a black tee shirt, until I flapped a hand his way that meant never mind, it's okay, and he nodded. He went about his business, stacking firewood in the yard, a dog trailing him, a cat trailing the dog, a woman standing on the porch. Together it all makes one of those pictures of perfect life that might splay across your mind when you are far off and think of home, somebody else's home, the kind that looks like that and raises your spirits.

In Ward 53, where they fretted about me so, they told me maybe I should paint, take up painting landscapes or portraits, something soothing, but whenever I try the picture explodes on me, the light of day shatters, the humans don't look too human and strange patterns span the sky. Sometimes the sky is all cherry blossoms, one big blush of pink and white, and there's bones sticking up from the mud below with little volunteer vines growing around them, linking them together, like the scattered bones don't truly belong to death but might hop up reunited by vines and dance a loose clattering jig once more. Hopeful, I guess, deep down, which is why they want me to paint.

I have a dozen dead items painted that way.

I know the departed cow in the sideways tree will be next.

Before I went into the desert I'd had a decent job at Spangler Feeds, hefting sacks, stacking salt blocks, sweeping grain dust and such, and they would've held it for me, but the whole feed mill burned down to a knee-high mess of ash and nails while I was away, and the Spanglers decided not to rebuild, just not worth it, so they moved to Florida instead and fish for big ones at sea a lot. They sent a postcard. Where Ma worked didn't help with insurance, so now I watch cows for her while I can and we'll contribute the dough to cancer treatment.

Ma's a Boshell. I'm a Girard because Ma got to feeling guilty after Dad was gone and had my papers fixed so I was legally his even if they'd never married. Dad, Dad, my sorrowful Dad, was a man given to long blue spells pierced by moments of excited yearning, a handsome doomed man I like more and more as the days roll past and I imagine him with his dark curls and thin whiskers and how we resemble.

I carried the rifle with me and marched across the field counting cows. I had got to know them by their color schemes and shapes, and two or three were the kind of cows that had personalities, too, goofy traits or bad tempers that made them stand out among the herd. Only the one had bolted. I walked under the shade trees and around the wallow of red mud and dull water counting twice, then I went to the house to fetch my painting stuff, which they'd been very glad to give me back at Ward 53.

I set the easel above the cow, considered colors I might use, colors that'd catch the feeling of this killed cow, the tragedy of last night that was already nearly forgot, while the cliff and tree and bullet hole'd tell the facts of the story. The color of the actual cow meant nothing now, I'd fit some to her, colors that suited would come about somehow as my brush moved, and the tree would get rendered the same. I sensed blue for the cow and bronze for the tree and blue again for the killing ground that waited below the tense yellow cliff. The sky grew plum and gray and rippled like a window curtain. As I made the picture the scene in my head took over and the cliff turned up flat on me, so the plum-gray sky was standing sentry over to the right, and the cow in the sideways tree hung above level ground but below the branch, disobeying gravity now that it'd died.

The bullet hole was a pink question mark.

Ma had walked the pasture counting heads while I was lost deep inside that scene with the cow, and crept along behind me. I was adding chrome boulders to the stream and when I caught a creeping sound behind I fast as a flinch reached for the rifle, but the rifle wasn't there, and I sprang for the dirt with one hand shielding my face while the other aimed the paint brush. The brush swept back and forth, wanting to spray a wide field of fire, a death blossom, get 'em all, and I felt wiggly in my head as a few drops dove loose to dribble down me.

Ma said, "That cow's money lost now."

They tell me Dad committed suicide for reasons he dreamed up. His mind was too active. He had a round mind and it roamed. He could imagine any kind of hurt. He could imagine the many miseries of this world flying over from everywhere to roost between his ears, but he couldn't imagine how to get away. Ma loved him past his end and has never kissed another man. She loved his mind, his round, roaming mind that made her feel a glowing inside her skin between those spells of blight. He waited all of a calm spring night for some fresh serious pain to come into his heart and kill him. Twelve coiled hours hunched at the kitchen table, frozen peas dumped on the table top, a shotgun leaning against the back of his chair. He arranged rank after rank of cold green peas, took aim and flicked each toward the kitchen sink and kept a secret score. Then he gathered the peas from the sink and floor, rearranged them across the table top, and flicked them all again. Once the peas were ruined he switched to flicking corn kernels, raisins, whatever, until the score was lost in his head and the floor slippery. He drank enough coffee his brain shook in its bowl, then drank whiskey to get that shaky brain calm. At some point inside that addled calmness the heavy curtains parted and he thought he spied a good way out, an answer to it all, stepped to the back stoop and sat and erased his problems in this world, maybe not the next. He died gushing blood on the second step of the back stoop, the step we keep painted black.

I don't truly remember, but Ma has told me about it, made it meaningful to me, saying I followed him onto the stoop, my rusty diaper drooping, and the ejected shell bounced off my belly, and Dad tried to say one last word to me but it drowned in blood that jumped up in his throat, never got said. So now I do sort of recall an ejected shell bouncing from my baby-belly, blood flying, that one last word drowning in red.

He's buried out back, Buddy Girard, and Ma prays at his grave.

Ma? Ma? She's not all there, parts have fallen away and dashed, dashed against her days, parts that fell the day she was pulled from school at sixteen and sent to work at the shoe factory, parts that fell the day the shoe factory closed, the day Marcella died in her crib, the day she was told she had cancer, the day Dad died on that one black step. She has always carried on, though, Ma, hefting the parts of herself that remained, dragging them onward, and remaining more decent than she had to be, which makes me try and stay alive for her.

Ma wants to be buried on the farm. She'd been happy here when she was too young to know better and during the first year with Dad. Her grave will be near the rest, but not quite with them, several paces to the west of the others, under the dirt with Buddy. I've squared the plot with railroad ties and we've planted perennials along the border, purple phlox and daisies and such that wave spirited colors when a breeze passes. The graves overlook the river and are well shaded in summer until about noon, then the good light reaches and grows things there. A spot has been picked for me, also, to the sundown side, and I've found my marker, a reddish river stone with battered edges and a kind of cracked silent dignity. It's too big to throw or kick away. The stone will remain unchanged, no name or date, and someday vines and flowers will cover the stone in tangled green and sweetness. Ma wants a regular wooden cross about three feet tall, painted white, same as Dad had before a high wind flung his away.

You have to know where to stand to stand over his grave.

I like graves that disappear.

Mary is the woman who has chosen me to be the man she needs. She has rooted inside my life and claimed me, claimed me to be her man of tomorrow and the days after, claimed me for loving, too, I guess. She lives with her momma four miles away, near where Chime Creek joins the Twin Forks, in a trailer with her kids, two of them, Joe and Nora, neither old enough for school but both already hunkered down into a fretful shyness, a reluctance to be noticed or speak up. Mary likes to visit me after dark, once the bars have got boring, raise dust driving her heavy rattling car into Ma's yard and park under the spreading oak, radio music kicking holes through the night quiet.

She grunts getting out of the car, slams the door. Most times she'll have a movie in her hand, whatever beer is left tucked under her arm. Her moccasins are silent crossing the dirt.

This time, same as always, I greet her with, "Mary."

"Yup. Once again." She's taller than she wants to be and rolls her shoulders forward to shorten her neck, drops her chin, sags her upper self like a flower that's got a blooming too heavy atop for its stem to carry. She holds the movie toward me, shakes the box. "How 'bout a picture show, Darden?"

"Funny?"

"Could be to you."

Mary wants to kiss, so I do, and she wants some sort of familiar caress, one that suggests we know each other's bodies like favorite getaway places we've come to own, so I put both hands to her butt and pull the cheeks spread a little bit, lift her. Mary has a small beer-pooch underslung from her lower belly, but is elsewhere lean, skinny, even, and I can about feel the bone under her butt with my fingertips. She's got pale hair and a few freckles that seem to be forever fading from her face but never go away.

In the living room she right away wants me to get naked. Ma's bed is downstairs so she can be near the john, and she lays snoring in the dining room, just around the corner. The tv is muted but on, throwing a headache light across the room, throbbing between near-dark to suddenly glaring with many skittish flickers between. I know I'm supposed to want this, what she offers, so I try to recall how it goes when this is something you want, crave, gotta have, can't do without, might kill for, die over, mourn when it's gone.

Somehow my clothes come off, drop to the floor, first frost stripping a tree of its last clinging leaves.

"Such a tight, smooth boy," she says. Mary is pushing nine years older, and unlike most women would do she apparently enjoys reminding me I'm way younger. It somehow stokes her needs and juices her good to say it aloud. Whenever she says it she sighs soft and looks like a crouched cat studying songbirds in a low bush. "Lucky ol' me. Lucky, lucky."

All Mary does is scoot from her moccasins and jeans and blue undies. She keeps her shirt on and buttoned, the tails hanging over that pooch. Her lips get around on me some, visiting here and there, then I bend her over the couch, knees to the carpet, and slam her the doggy-way she wants it most times. Slap her ass as she has taught me while I slam, slam and slap, and she snickers, snickers, moans into the cushions. Fresh rug burns get added to the old on my knees and I collapse backwards after, stare at the ceiling, count the cobwebs and get the same tally as the visit before.

She says now I'm home for a while we should get married, and soon, before they send me back, but has only ever one time asked me about over there, how it was, what details I needed to get off my chest, what memories I might want to share with her, and I said, It's all real sandy. Sand blows into everything. Makes soup even turn crunchy.

That's it?

I think I miss the crunching.

"Put this in," she says before my breathing is even righted, and tosses the movie my way. She raises herself to sit on the couch, then uses her blue undies to mop herself dry, catch my come seeping, and stuffs them dampened into her purse. "It's got that guy in it I like."

Somewhere in the flick I fell out of interest. It wasn't funny, and the guy she liked so dodged bullets slower than pigeons and cracked wise at death, which never happened to him or his, and I yawned and went away. On the porch I stared up at the big oak in the yard. Tree frogs honked their raspy honks in unison, and fat brown bugs battered the porch light behind me. Mary's car was under the spread limbs, and I saw that the windows had fogged. I crossed the dirt yard, opened the back door, and there slept Joe and Nora, undressed for bed but without a blanket to cover them. I pointed a finger and wrote Mary's name in the fog above them, then rubbed their used wet breaths onto my face. They'd been there since she left the trailer and hit the first bar, and were probably asleep by the second roadhouse or the third. I picked both up at once, an arm under each, and neither child woke as I carried them inside. Mary looked over from her movie as I laid the kids on the empty end of the couch. She was smiling with her chin down and her eyes wide, and said, "See? I told you you loved them kids."

In the story that happened to me so often, asleep or wide awake, I had got down on my hands and knees to collect red and white parts of Lt. Voorhees, from when his brain housing unit came apart in his quarters, skull chunks denting the ceiling, teeth and ears splatted to the walls, brains a clotting spray, a story that happens to me whenever it wants to, and I can't shunt it aside or stuff it in a box, but can only accept the sunken feelings it deals me time and again. A few times Dad showed up to help me collect the cracked bone and stringy glop, clumped hair, kneeling beside me in a foreign place, calling me "Son" while we raised a wet pile. Some days I start hearing the final words Lt. Voorhees said before closing his door that night spoken over and over, at different volumes in my head, all day long, low to loud, Hope I dream about daylight again.

Hope I DREAM about daylight AGAIN.

HOPE I dream about DAYLIGHT again.

McArdle and Fuller fell by toward the next sundown, or the one after, drawn by boredom and word of my return, wanting to remember high school, with a box of beer and bowls of smoke to make it seem those years ago days might happen again tomorrow if only we got wasted enough. I left the house with them in McArdle's truck and we drove to the river, built a jolly campfire on a gravel beach. Their memories are cleaner than mine, the silly details yet shine for them, are easily found and spoken as jokes or boasts. My head cramps trying to only call up the faces from the hallways. I should be glad for this visit, I know, so I hunt dry wood up the slope, stack it on the fire to grow the flames and say I am, I am glad to see you two, your faces make me feel home.

So-and-so got married, so-and-so moved away, so-and-so fell in the lake or was pushed, drunk as a skunk whichever. It takes only five minutes together before they lean close and ask the standard ghoul-questions I expect from civilians, and I answer, Oh, you damned straight I did.

Then, Maybe more'n used to ride our school bus.

Then, Like tomatoes being busted open with hammers.

Then, Sometimes all you can do is shovel red sand into a body bag and send that home with a name on it.

The empties clatter into the fire, smokes mingle, dusk settles, there is laughter. I recall times together like this, drinking the day away in canoes on the river, chucking dry-ice bombs into blue holes and cheering the boom and spray, and as dark fell driving into town with more cold beer to circle the Sonic, round and round at half a mile an hour, biceps on display out the windows, hoping some town girls would of a sudden realize we were cute, kind of sexy, even, and want to go for a ride in the country, then switching to whiskey when none did.

I guess I joined to become more interesting than that.

Fuller had been our alpha, our main instigator, with showboat muscles and a habit of bruising you good in horse-play, then saying it was only a joke, bro, don't be mad. In the firelight I can see he'd like to mess with me some again, as he did back when, give a demeaning Dutch rub, or clamp on a headlock 'til I croaked 'Uncle,' but he's just not sure anymore, not sure I won't go Kill! Kill! Kill! in my head, yank something deadly from my watch pocket, zipcuff him to a sapling and feed his ass to the fire a pound at a time. I can see the itch is in him, and the doubt, so I helped him clear the confusion, saying, "After the desert, bro, the list of things you're totally certain you'd *never ever do* gets a lot shorter."

Ma's breaths scrape together traveling her throat and have short hisses at their tail, plus something come undone in her chest clatters. Her sleep is a busy place and she speaks mushed words into the sheets, her legs walk to yesterday and back across the mattress, her eyelids totter as the eyeballs rush about in darkness wanting to see everything they've ever seen again. The bed she chose for the dining room is small with no headboard, low to ground, a short fall if she rolled loose in her rambling and tumbled.

Another rough day before noon there was this cemetery in the dust, with row after row of markers for the dead, mud colored or white, each big enough to hide behind, and a high dun wall around the whole place. We cleared one row then crept toward the next, each small distance electric with the idea that this gravestone ahead could be the one Ali Baba is hid behind and waiting, finger on the trigger or arm cocked to throw something that explodes. The air smelled of shit roasting in oil and carried that shrill music that made your skin tighten. One row at a time, crawling inch by inch, from marker to marker, the pressure building with each scoot forward, sweat dripping, hands turned white squeezing, and after several rows you heard some guys go empty, moan themselves into the dust, become still where they were, not about to move on. They make it ten, twenty, thirty rows, but can no longer imagine making it through all the rows and go up, rise above themselves like blank thought balloons. Each marker, each row, who knows what's there, anything could be, you might soon become a chunky breeze exploded sideways or get shot through-and-through, and all those possibilities nourished dread. Your own mind can gut you good so easy. With sprung nerves soldiers lay faces to the dust to avoid seeing ahead and had to be booted by sergeants until the balloons above sunk back down into uniforms and words regrouped to break loose in answer.

Mary wanted to be a bride again and announced she soon would be while we all splashed in the river. Joe and Nora hopped on stick legs in the shallows above the one-lane bridge and Ma sat in a folding chair with her feet underwater and a scarf over her fuzz of hair. I had my goggles to hunt treasure spilled from tourist canoes upstream and had found a wristwatch with a rotted band. Mary wore a white t-shirt over her suit, and said, "It's official y'all—me'n Darden are gettin' hitched."

I dove again. People riding inner tubes went by overhead, casting squat shadows that roamed over the bottom rocks and stretched with distance. Legs looked so white and puffed from underneath with bubbles attaching to the flesh like blisters, and voices arrived as deep blurry barks.

Ma said, "When does this happen?"

"While he waits to hear about goin' back," Mary said. The sun was halfway west and shined at a slant that broke around her. Her face was shaded faint but the skin on her neck glowed at the sides. "I'll get it right this time. I've learned some things I couldn't've guessed at before."

Joe and Nora stood still in a trickle of river, bare feet sinking into the gravel bed, staring at me, faces empty, holding themselves in tight. Mary saw and kicked water at them so they'd know it was okay to seem happy just now. They tried.

Mary unloaded a picnic onto a blanket in the shade, beer chilling in the river.

Ma said to me, "You sure this is good news?" Her eyes were mournful and ringed, like those of a hunted thing that has decided to stop running. I would paint her soon. Her chest had been cut away from her first, both sides, but she fell sick in other parts, too, and the sick didn't rest, it prowled her body, salting her with ruin you couldn't see in her face for a good long while. Now the ruin just stares out at me, all the time, from those eyes that know about hope and that body that can't offer any. She leaned my way and whispered, "It's your life, son."

"I just don't care to make big decisions anymore."

"That is one."

"Let's act happy."

"That's another."

I fell on the river and went inside. The water ran chest-deep, and I spread over the rocky bottom and found a big one to cling to. There were all these tiny tatters of different debris rushing past near the bottom and the rushing was all I heard. I clung to the bottom, my feet rising behind and touching air, while my hands held steady on the slickened old stone and kept me from spinning downstream. I held and held to the rock and forgot about breathing, sunk into that choice spot between breathing and not ever breathing, raising up to walk on the bank and picnic or stay under and join that debris already lost to the rushing.

Stink from the cow took over the air. The cow was screaming again, screaming stink, a brown dirge of stink like the dead scream always. Ma and me stood on the cliff with our noses pinched against the loud stink and squinted our eyes, too. Ma's trying to act spry so she can help. She's wearing rubber mud boots and a long dress with no waistline and no pattern in the cloth. A big yellow sun hat shades her face.

Neither of us wants the cow kicked to the river below, to dump such ruin into the clean water, so we decide to haul her up the cliff with three ropes. I've backed the truck near the edge, and Ma swears she can work a clutch and drive just fine, no problem. I tied my ropes to the truck, cinched one around me snug and led the other two down to the sideways tree. There were shrubs to grab at on the cliff face, untrustworthy roots and clumps of stranded weeds, and I tossed my feet at them to slow my falling. The sideways tree was sturdy and the cow oozed. Flying things had got the eyes, the lips and ears, the soft easy meat anything left dead in the open serves up first. I had to sit astride the cow to get the ropes looped around, the first under the front legs, the next under the back, and thickened death-juices leaked from the cow onto my jeans and shirt. I gave Ma a wave and me and the cow scraped the dusty cliff and flew up together, meat and meat under the sky, hooves whirling, boots whirling, one head down, one head raised, one spinning smell.

Ma helps me unlash and says, "You're nuts to go back."

"They cleared me for goin', Ma."

Ma drove and the cow slid across the pasture to the grassless place, and I untied her. My clothes stunk past cleaning, and I flung them off, shirt first, then jeans, and went about in my skivvies and started tossing stuff from the trash heap into the burn circle. The pile grew, and grew tall enough for a ten-foot flame to rise from household trash, old plywood, a tangle of blowdown, hedge trimmings, a busted headboard and stained mattress I couldn't recall. I was near naked in the world and sweating, bending to drop matches, encourage the flames, scorch that stink away. Ma watched me, looking at my tats some, not too impressed by the pictures, I knew, but mostly studying the long ragged divot torn top to bottom on my back and wondering what invention made that wound.

"She found out how much you're worth dead."

"Where?"

"She's been askin' folks all around."

We stood close together fireside, watching the cow burn in the circle as the sun sank. The cow only slightly thinned, but the brain housing unit was soon laid bare and white atop deep glowing coals. Hooves cracked in the heat. Full dark made fire seem the center of all things. A breeze raised little flames that wiggled in the eye sockets and stuck a long tongue of fire lapping from the mouth. Ma'n me stared silently 'til the tree frogs went quiet and owls came out to fly. We left the cow at peace finally in the embers, started toward the house, walking slowly through the spreading weeds of our garden plot where nothing got planted this year.

Steve Yates

Born and reared in Springfield, Missouri, Steve Yates is an MFA graduate from the creative writing program at the University of Arkansas. He is the winner of the 2012 Juniper Prize for Fiction, and in 2013 the University of Massachusetts Press will publish his short story collection, *Some Kinds of Love.* Yates has published short stories in *TriQuarterly, Southwest Review, Turnstile, Western Humanities Review,* and many other journals. In *Best American Short Stories 2010,* one of his fictions was included in the Other Distinguished Stories of 2009, and his fiction has been nominated for the Pushcart Prize. In May 2010, Moon City Press published his novel *Morkan's Quarry* in hardcover. Portions of *Morkan's Quarry* first appeared in *Missouri Review, Ontario Review,* and *South Carolina Review.* Yates is assistant director/marketing director at University Press of Mississippi in Jackson, and lives in Flowood with his wife, Tammy.

The Battle of Springfield
from *Morkan's Quarry*

On the first Wednesday in January 1863, Leighton Morkan was awakened to muster when the stars still burned blue in the winter sky. He rode at a drowsing lope toward the tent city of Federal hospitals and encampments where his Federal Home Guard unit waited. With the sun not yet risen, the myriad dots of canvas appeared gray in the thin dawn light, doves huddled in a fallow field. The frosted ground crackled under his horse's hooves. Leighton had spent a ten-dollar piece from the strong box for the campaign coat he was wearing. Sewn inside the coat was a square embroidered with a girl's name and city—Anna Marie Van Syke, Manhattan—and the message: "AVENGE OUR HOLY UNION." Soon to turn sixteen, he felt like an imposter in it, a Yankee coat, and his father locked in Gratiot prison and lost to him.

As he entered the first lot of tents, a portly man in long johns rushed past banging two skillets together. Leighton reined his horse. Blinking faces appeared at the tent flaps. Cowbells and triangles, bugles, whistles, shouts, men rushed shirtless, pulling up suspenders. They hollered for rifles.

Leighton heard the thunk and concussion of artillery. On the heights just north of Galway, four cannon issued curling puffs of smoke. Thunder followed. Asters of flame and noise boiled and faded deep within the tents. Gray specters scurried around the artillery pieces.

Leighton turned his horse for home, but was met by a cavalcade of Enrolled Militia riding hard into the tents. A burly little Federal officer was running with his sword shining high above his head: "We're the left! Left! Wheel, you bastards!" His face was crimson, legs pumping like pistons. But the horsemen continued their dash into the center of the tents, their faces pale, eyes wide and oblivious, horses lunging almost crushing the little man. The officer swiped his sword in a silver arc. Leighton jerked his leg aside, and the sword plunged between the ribs of his horse. A shudder, then the animal gasped and sunk. Leighton leapt free of the saddle, landed roughly, his knees and palms smarting in the cold. The little officer ran on swordless, screaming and waving his arms at his disappearing cavalry. Leighton stood and blinked. His horse lay grunting, pissing, steam rolling off the aortal spurts that shot from its girth.

The cannon wheeled and began firing across the tents at one of the forts and the roofless Men's Academy. Behind the cannon, in the growing light, Leighton saw horses circling, riders holding hats and rifles high. He saw no flag among them. They cut him off from home. He could chuck his coat and hat, but he still had the blue pantaloons with yellow stripes. Between cannon shots, he heard from the invaders a high trickle of sound. He shook his head, sure his ears were ringing.

Carefully he unhooked his rifle, worried the horse in the last fit of living might wale around and chomp at him. He paused a minute and the horse's white eyes bulged and rolled. He loaded the rifle, cringing at shell concussions. Then he burrowed the rifle in the horse's ear and finished him. Stooping, he tore his pantaloons at the cuff, cupped his hands in the horse's pooled blood. He smeared blood all up and down his calf. It clung warmly to his yellow underleggings. He shouldered his bag and saddle and headed for the hospital, affecting a limp whenever Iowa troops or Guardsmen crossed his path.

At the hospital more than a hundred men in ragged bedclothes and partial uniforms stood outside the compound. Some faces were green, some gray. A tall officer pushed the wounded into formation, grabbed Leighton's arm and swung him to the end of the line. Two corporals issued cavalry pistols and Sharps rifles. The man next to Leighton faltered and grabbed Leighton. He stunk so strongly of quinine, Leighton gulped, his nose twitching. The Federals armed even the surgeons in their browned aprons. They marched the whole lot of them behind the log hexagon of one of the forts, formed them in a battle line, then rushed off shouting at one another and several of the wounded and ill.

Cloaked in ratty yellow, swaddled in bed sheets, blankets tied as capes about their necks, the patients manned what was called Fort Number 4 at the end of a long meadow on the southern edge of town. A dense stand of oak darkened the southernmost end of the meadow. The cannon blasted away. To the east boiled a great melee of gunfire and horsemen. Some of the patients eased themselves to sit cross-legged, or lay down on the frigid dirt and loaded their black revolvers, the muzzles of which wavered like divining rods. The rifles lay in the dirt beside them. One man wandered behind a tree in the enclosure, pulled his pants down and squatted.

Leighton tamped his rifle, and stared at the forest. The log wall sheltered his body to the neck. Hollowed divots allowed soldiers to shoot standing, sitting, or lying flat. Like spots of fog across the hills a trail of wraith-like patients scuttled from the other convalescent hospitals across town. A company of near fifty arrived with bedpans strapped to their heads, crutches stabbing the frozen road, revolvers roped about their necks, bouncing against their bellies, several in wheelchairs, cussing and pointing as the nurses bumped them through the gates, amputees, men with gashes shaved bald on their scalps, a drooling boy missing much of his lower jaw, tongue squirming like a slug in salt.

Two wagons pounded into the fort, and on each of these, revolvers and rifles were mounded along with box after box of cartridges.

The cannon fired and shells yowled like saw blades through the air. The patients ducked at this, but laughed and coughed, smiling when a shell landed far east of the fort.

"Blind Arkies," someone shouted.

They fell quiet. Men dropped their crutches, leaned against the log wall and gaped at the forest. Cresting the stubble of oak, elm, and hickory, the sun's pale light, found among the trees the chests and legs of horses facing the fort. He counted ten. They edged forward. He lost count, dozens, hundreds. Men around him adjusted their bedpans, wiped their mouths with the corners of blankets.

The cannon stopped. A shout sounded from the wood. One thousand cavalry stepped into the sunlight of the meadow. Black pits were the horsemen's eyes, faces as shadowed and malleable as burlap. Cloaks spattered, mottled, bark rather than cloth. Soot streaked hands and foreheads, bare feet red and raw in the stirrups as if the cavalry had burned their way here instead of riding. Rifles, scythes, rakes, hoes, pitchforks, an agrarian nightmare of gigs and shotguns tilted at the ground. Belts bristled with knives, pistol butts. A yellow vapor purled from them, and foam caked the chest of every mount.

Next to Leighton, a man in a cane-bottomed wheelchair set his revolver in his lap and commenced to pray in furious noddings.

The wounded grabbed their rifles, started peeling at the white cartridges, tamping their guns. Leighton felt a tap. The boy with a smashed lower jaw stood holding a cartridge out for him. Leighton took the cartridge, bit the top and handed him the opened package. The boy nodded, patted three revolvers he had loaded himself.

Across the meadow, the cavalry whirled and formed an even line while one rider rode before them. The rider waggled above his head a blackened sword. The rider's lips moved, and he tossed his hair. The cavalry bellowed a raw vowel in answer.

Several of the wounded fired their pistols.

The patient next to Leighton shouted for them to stop. Shambling about, he called for a line of fire. As if healed, the men moved forward with a swift grace, placing the rifle muzzles against the wall, pressing their cheeks to the stocks.

The shouting patient borrowed a crutch and held it high. "Wait on them." The wounded watched him, eyes blinking over the stocks.

In the meadow, the rider circled the sword above his head. The riders' chests rose as if they took one great collective breath, and then from them came the high trickling sound, but now it was a shout, a bouncing horrendous note Leighton imagined only savages could make, the sound of men preparing to leap off a ridge above a valley spiked with pines, a sound as brutal and heedless as the edge of a hatchet.

Horses and riders nodded, surged, and the meadow exploded with hoof and mud, the high yowl lofting above the pounding. Leighton cringed. The patient still held the wavering crutch. The mass of cavalry grew until Leighton could almost discern individual faces, sodden and bewhiskered, eyes black, lips and cheeks blue, pounding, heaving, their steeds gaunt, skeletal miracles of hide and power.

Down came the crutch. Great spikes of flame, the staggered fire of one hundred fifty erupted, a blast as if the patients tore the very cloth of morning to leave nothing but smoke and concussion.

Leighton whooped. Nothing like it. Jesus.

Cavalry tumbled, horses running askew, men thrown and trampled. But still coming. Leighton expected them all to fall, but the wood before him spattered. Bullets thumped into the logs. Something tugged at his coat. He turned expecting the jawless boy holding a cartridge. Nothing. Pistols fired along the length of the wall. One of the riders loomed up, leering, screaming, his face bulging into a fist of holy rage. He lurched over and stabbed a hickory pike into the neck of the man in the wheelchair. The patient gagged and bucked. Pistol fire peppered the rider, who fell. The shaft of the pike remained propped against the wall, its carved point securely sunk through the dead patient's neck.

Blue and silver smoke covered the line of patients. They rose and lurched, black shadows around which smoke and sunlight quivered, the flare of pistols flashing like summer lightning deep in clouds. The shadows shuffled and loaded, bandages and blankets swishing. Metal clanking, men breathing, quick tears of paper, the spat of the powder, all performed without speaking, rote motions in the piles of smoke. Leighton had felt such a moment before when the drill teams on the cliff at the quarry hit exact stride, four teams grunting and shifting, the sledges ringing. The patients stood to the wall, arms drawing the ramrods into the air, sliding them down, steadying pistols, faces becoming gray ovals, indistinct. Their motions were a reverie of union, a purified human effort that vented bursts of fire.

The smoke thinned. The horsemen were gone. All across the meadow, dark lumps squirmed and smoked. Against the woods, the cavalry circled and formed. Through a divot in the wall, Leighton saw a man raise himself to crawl on his elbows, his hands and forearms shattered. His face was white and blue, eyes bulging. The patients watched the forming cavalry. One jerked the pike from the dead patient's neck. He flung the pike over the wall. Another patient wheeled the chair with its corpse back behind the ammunition wagons. In the meadow the wounded horseman quit crawling and collapsed. He lay on his side staring at Leighton and the patients behind the wall.

Any of these men he fired at could be ole Greevins. Or Charley, or Hoyt, or Ferguson. Old friends, drillers, blasters, stone cutters and breakers, men he and his father employed at Morkan Quarry, now cursing the frozen ground of ruined Springfield, enemies.

The cavalry achieved their line. The horses shook their heads. Up went the black sword. Up went the crutch. The cavalry came, men rocking in the saddles, elbows flapping like wings. Leighton beaded. In the nub at the end of his muzzle he caught one single horseman. The circle of the horseman's mouth, the whiskers, the mustache, all became distinct. The iron nubbin of the gunsight erased a portion of his chest then his head as he came riding. Leighton trembled. The rider's shout, that heedless vowel, rose above the hooves. He rode alone, leapt over downed horses and men alone, broke from the thundering pack with just his sword lowered at the wall, and he was screaming. A sword against five weeks' worth of powder and shot.

The crutch wavered an instant, but held. Exhaling slowly, he hooked his finger over the trigger. The man's oval mouth bobbed in his sights, squalling, face red. Down came the crutch. Leighton fired. The man dropped from the horse, which swerved away from his tumbling.

Dismounted the enemy tried again, figures scrabbling like gray lice among the stubble of blackened hearths on the wintered scalp of what once had been his town. Rifles probing as they crept, cracking shots, nearer, nearer, until the patients gathered and discharged fire and smoke, and what had been an onrush of vermin lost heart, faltered, melted away.

Hours of it—cavalry reforming, invalids reloading. At the crest of one charge, Leighton's head was banging, and the hooves and stinking hides of horses sailed above the patients, and suddenly horses and riders staggered inside the fort. Like hornets, the invalids swarmed them. Leighton gripped the gritty hem of a rider's coat and pulled him down only to have the horse nip a chunk from beneath his shoulder blade.

"Damn ye. God damn ye," the Arkansawyer hollered as the invalids finished him with the butts of their rifles.

When the fracas eased, the patient leaned his crutch and his shoulder heavily on the wall, then bound Leighton's wound. Rolling an extra bandage the patient crammed the cloth in Leighton's mouth. Afterwards he helped him reload and heave his rifle back to the top of the shattered logs. Leighton howled and bit the bandage in his teeth.

"One more is all they got. They'll break. I swear it," the patient said.

A burning fury consumed Leighton's mind in which he could picture through red agony every divot of the damned horse's teeth jutting through his flesh, and so he had no conception if the patient with the crutch meant that the horsemen would break, or if he meant the quinine brigade behind the wall had only one more stand left in them. He could fold now, crumple, he was truly wounded. Either way, fold or fight, was death. Men like that dead Arkie behind him did not ride to Springfield to bear prisoners back to some Gratiot like Yankees bore his father, no. They rode for death, for mayhem, for the burning and the blood. He straightened his back, wrapped a filthy, freezing, blue finger round the trigger and faced them.

Sunlight seared the meadow and forest with its winter white. When the smoke dissipated, the meadow, stilled with frost, the brambles, covered in blue crystal, became intensely serene.

They charged the fort again and again. The invalids killed them long into the evening until finally the horsemen shuddered and rode away.

ACKNOWLEDGMENTS

"Four Fine Horses," by C. D. Albin, originally appeared in the journal *Crosstimbers.*

"Photogenic" and "Wounded God," by Walter Bargen, are previously unpublished and come from the manuscript "Whiplash."

"Jethro and Abner: An Arkansaw Counterculture" is taken from Brooks Blevins, *Arkansas/Arkansaw: How Bear Hunters, Hillbillies, and Good Ol' Boys Defined a State* (Fayetteville: University of Arkansas Press, 2009), 154–64.

"River Poetics IV" and "Mrs. Clara Franz: Mother Earth's Daughter," by James Bogan, were published in *Ozark Meandering,* letterset at Timberline Press, 1999, Fulton, Missouri.

"Sacraments" and "Each Black Shell," by Sara Burge, appeared in *Apocalypse Ranch,* published by C&R Press, 2010.

"Farm Road 93," "On the Fifth Day of the Search," and "Going to See the 15th-Century Indian Head Pots at the Hampson Museum, Wilson, Arkansas," by Michael Burns, were published in *The Secret Names* (University of Missouri Press, 1994) and appear here by permission of Michele Lucas and Shannon and Dakotah Burns. "After October Rain" and "Sweet Potatoes" appeared in *Night of the Grizzly* (Moon City Press, 2012) and are reprinted here by permission of Lanette Cadle.

"Mowing," by Marcus Cafagña, previously appeared in *Southern Poetry Review.* "The Old House" previously appeared in *Cave Region Review.*

Bryan Culpepper's cover art appears here by permission of Renata Culpepper.

"The Three Beauties," by Katie Estill, was previously published in *Elder Mountain: A Journal of Ozark Studies*, Volume 1.

Unspoiled Beauty, by Charles J. Farmer, was originally published by the University of Missouri Press (1999). Permission to print the excerpt that appears here was granted by Kathleen Farmer.

"Being a Doaks and All," by Gary Guinn, was first published in the autumn 1997 issue of *The Rockford Review.*

"Father's Day" and "Crossing the Old Farm," by Jim Hamilton, originally appeared in the *Buffalo Reflex*, Buffalo, Missouri. Printed here by permission of Dave Berry, publisher at *Neighbor News*, Bolivar, Missouri.

"Telling Time," by Donald Harington, is previously unpublished. Permission to print here was granted by Kim Harington.

"Tickets to Nowhere," by William Harrison, appeared in *Texas Heat*, published by Texas Review Press (2005).

"Finches or Sparrows," by Andrea Hollander, was originally published in *The Georgia Review* 63:2 (Summer 2009) and is forthcoming in *Landscape with Female Figure* (Autumn House Press, 2013). "Large Boulder Above Honey River" was originally published in *New Letters* 73:4 (Summer 2007) and is forthcoming in *Landscape with Female Figure* (Autumn House Press, 2013). "Ice Storm" was originally published in *Sou'wester* (Winter 2009) and reprinted in *Northern Woodlands* (Winter 2010).

"Listening to Fauré," by Jane Hoogestraat, originally appeared in *Southern Review.* "Bela Fleck and the Flecktones Play the Ozarks" originally appeared in *Gingko Tree Review.*

"The Family, Circa 1919," by Phillip Howerton, was published in *Plainsongs.* "Old Homestead on Federal Land" was published in *Elder Mountain: A Journal of Ozarks Studies.*

"Hawksbill Crag," by Dave Malone, was first published in *Seasons in Love* (Trask Road Press, 2012). "Blackberry Cobbler" was first published as "White" in *Elder Mountain: A Journal of Ozark Studies.*

"Aux Arcs," by Anthony Priest, was first published in *Elder Mountain: A Journal of Ozarks Studies* at Missouri State University in West Plains. "Settling Velocity" first appeared in *Phoebe* at George Mason University.

Faubus: The Life and Times of an American Prodigal (of which "Chapter One" appears here), by Roy Reed, was published by the University of Arkansas Press (1997).

"Geography I," "Called Down," "Caves," and "Border State," by Jan Peterson Roddy, originally appeared in *Elder Mountain: A Journal of Ozarks Studies.* "Silas" and "Collie Holler" are printed here for the first time.

"Fury and Grace," by Pattiann Rogers, was published in *The Grand Array* (Trinity University Press, 2010). "The Background Beyond the Background" appeared in *Song of the World Becoming, New and Collected Poems, 1981–2001* (Milkweed Editions, 2002).

Big Spring Autumn, by Bonnie Stepenoff, was published by Truman State University Press (2008). Permission to reprint this excerpt of the book was granted by Nancy Rediger, editor.

"Swimming at Flat Bridge, 1963," by Jo Beth (Walker) Van Arkel, was first published in *The Place That Holds Our History: The Missouri Writers' Biennial Anthology* (1990). It was reprinted in the author's first book, *The Things I've Got Growing Deep Down Inside* (Aegina Press, 1994).

"The Opinion of an Interesting Old Man" and "Just North of Sikeston," by James Whitehead, appeared in *Domains,* originally published by the Louisiana State University Press (1966). Permission to reprint here was granted by Gen Whitehead Broyles.

"An Unrhymed Sonnet" and "Separatio in Loco," by Miller Williams, were published in *Time and the Tilting Earth* (Louisiana State University Press, 2008).

"Black Step," by Daniel Woodrell, was originally published in *New Letters* and included in his short story collection, *The Outlaw Album.*

"The Battle of Springfield," by Steve Yates, is an excerpt from *Morkan's Quarry* (Moon City Press, 2010), slightly revised to fit this format.